THE SOUL MENDER

THE SOUL MENDER

R.S. Dabney

A Red Pen Warriors Publication

2016 Red Pen Warriors Publishing
Printed in the United States of America

THE SOUL MENDER
© 2016 R.S. Dabney
Cover illustrations by Andy Blalock
All cover art © 2016
All Rights Reserved
ISBN-13: 9780692472019
ISBN-10: 0692472010

For Weebs

Acknowledgments

First, I must thank my amazing husband, Nathanael, for all his support and assistance over the past few years. Writing a book puts an author through many emotional ups and downs, and he never failed to encourage me and lift me up through the whole process. This book wouldn't be here if it weren't for his love, dedication, and belief in me. I am so grateful to have you as my *other half!*

Next, I'd like to thank my mother, Carey, and sister, Alexis, for enthusiastically helping me edit and letting me know how much they believed in my story. Their excitement and support kept me going.

I'd also like to thank my dad, Walt, and my mother again, for telling me throughout my whole life how important it is to do something you love—to not just be a bystander in your own life. Thank you both for letting me know it's okay to follow a dream.

A huge thank you to Bill Poston for making the publication and marketing of this story possible and for believing in me as an author. I can honestly say that I now believe in fairy godfathers! Thank you a million times over.

A special thanks to my dear and talented friend, Andy Blalock, for working tirelessly to create the exact face of The

Soul Mender that I imagined. Thank you to Kinsey East for the exceptional cover layout and design. You really brought this to the next level! And to Kasey Durbin, a profound gratitude for your incredible attention to detail and assistance in making the publication, publicity, and release of this story everything I imagined it to be. You all are amazing!

To The Red Pen Warriors: thank you for giving me confidence, inspiration, invaluable critiques, and most importantly, lasting friendships. You guys have taught me so much and given me more than you can imagine. Janice, Sarah, Julia, Leslie, Diana, Lee, Shirley, Helen, and Mike—y'all rock!

And finally, thanks to you the reader, for picking up this book and completing the final stage of this journey with me. I hope you enjoy reading it as much as I enjoyed putting it to paper.

Prologue

Dark hair swirled around the faces of two figures looking down on the lights of a city far below. They stood motionless on a precipice, unmoved by the wind and pelting rain. Sharp daggers, gilded and set with precious stones, hung from scabbards hidden beneath long coats that billowed with each gust.

"Does she know?" the smaller one asked, heavy-lidded eyes focused on the distant horizon.

"The old woman is afraid. She wants to protect her, but she knows what is at stake," the taller man replied. Golden rays flecked his eyes, mirroring a sun that had yet to show its face.

"The Germans know where she hides," the first said in a heavily accented voice. "She will be dead within a fortnight. She may die before the secret can be passed on."

The tall man's eyes flashed, but his face remained stoic. "The woman is afraid, but she is not a fool. She will alert the girl in some way."

Gazing toward an unknown future, their silent stares vanished into the roaring sky. "It won't be easy this time. The world is gearing up for war, and they know this is their last chance. They'll be desperate," the short man said.

The tall figure nodded and turned, his trench coat fluttering.

"What now, Emir?" the man at the ledge asked.

"We wait," the man called Emir replied, disappearing into the darkness. "We wait until Riley Dale decides whether or not she values her life."

CHAPTER ONE

The bruises grew out of nowhere across her skin, as they so often did. It started with incoherent shouts and screams somewhere in the back of her brain and always ended with black-and-blue or raw red marks somewhere across her body. *Please, not now.*

Riley Dale sat at a table beneath the shade of an apple tree in her backyard, staring down at an unopened textbook and rubbing the sore mark on her arm. It had been a long time since the phantom voices ranted in her head, and now was just about the worst possible moment for them to return. *The voices and the visions.* Her skin tingled as the words of the men on the cliff from last night's dream burned in her ears. *"We wait until Riley Dale decides whether or not she values her life."*

She rubbed her temples, trying to force the voices from her head and focus on what was really important. Forget studying. Forget the voodoo doll someone must have made in her image. Gabe would arrive soon, and she had finally worked up the nerve to be honest with him. She'd rehearsed what to say a thousand different ways but still wanted to vomit each time a car door slammed or voices drifted over the fence. Chewed fingernails tapped the cover of the textbook. She sucked in a rush of breath as the side gate opened and Gabriel Hart stepped in.

"Riley." His muscled frame slid into the seat across the table. "Is everything okay? You sounded worried in your text."

Riley forced a smile, trying to exude confidence like other girls did in these situations. But the shrieking returned, and she cradled her head, fighting tears brought on by the glaring pain.

"What's going on?" He dragged his chair next to hers and rested a hand on her trembling fingers. "What the hell happened?"

The shouts receded, and she lifted her eyes to his. "I didn't bring you here because I'm hurt, Gabe." She straightened and plastered the forced smile onto her face again. "I wanted to tell you something. Something I've wanted to tell you for a long time."

She searched his amber eyes for hope but only found concern. "We've been friends for a really long time," she said. "You've always been there for me, and I thought you just saw me as a sister. But we're about to graduate college, and you haven't left my side. Haven't dated anyone else." She shrugged, losing confidence, wanting him to piece together the narrative so she wouldn't have to say it out loud.

"I just thought—maybe—we both want more." It sounded silly and lame coming out of her mouth. When she said it to her mirror, it was romantic and elegant, and how would anyone say no? Now she sounded like a thirteen-year-old girl asking a boy to hold her hand for the first time.

It felt quiet, although a bird chirped somewhere above and a horn honked down the street. Gabe said nothing. Riley glanced at him from the corner of her eye, but he stared off across the yard, biting his lip. Heavy clouds hung low over the mountains to the west, promising rain, but so far the morning was clear and mild in Boulder. A warm sun rose to the east over Denver, spotlighting the stormy peaks. It could have been a beautiful day.

"I was wrong." She shook her head and glared at the table. "Forget about it."

"It's not that. It's just…" Gabe ran a hand through his wavy blond hair and sighed.

"Just what?" But another wail bounced around her head as pain erupted across her neck. Her hand flew up, and she felt the welt rising in the shape of five, bony fingers across her soft flesh.

"Shit, Riley. It's happening again, isn't it?" He stood up quickly, his tall frame blocking out the morning sun. "What are they saying?"

Riley shook her shoulders, hurt more by his reaction than the feud being fought inside her head. "I can't understand it. The words are jumbled. Just angry yelling."

Gabe was the only one who knew about her problem. *Problem* was their dumbed-down word for *nightmare*, for the terribly frightening thing that didn't happen to normal people. Riley wanted to throw the textbook at the back door and shatter the glass. Everything was crashing down around her. Graduation loomed, and she still didn't have a job. The response was always the same. *"This is Colorado. Everyone with a degree in environmental science wants to work here."*

And now Gabe rejected her to the chorus of insane voices inside her equally insane head.

"What can I do?" He rested a cool hand on her tender neck and brushed a lock of light-brown hair from her face. "How can I help?"

She leaned in for a second, desperate for what that touch might mean. "You can leave." She glowered at the flowering plants in the garden. "No one can help me with this, least of all you."

"I'm sorry." His hand fell away, and he stood up. "I wish I could give you what you want." His shadow hovered over her momentarily before he disappeared back through the wooden gate.

Tears welled in her green eyes, and she glared at her garden. *Why is growing vegetables so much easier than dating?*

The back door slid open, and her roommate and best friend, Abby Weaver, stepped outside. Riley wiped the tears from her face, trying to hide her aggravated skin under a wisp of hair.

"Ready?" Abby asked, running her fingers through her dark hair and shifting a backpack around on her thin frame.

"Let me grab my bag." Riley followed Abby inside, leaving her backyard oasis to flourish in the shadow of the mountains and her pain and embarrassment to float away into the sky.

Chapter Two

Doctor Abraham Reitz ate, slept, and breathed war history. His lectures were more story than history, and he kept his classes attentive to otherwise dry material. He always concluded each semester with the dramatic tale of Hitler's final days and death, one of his favorite historical moments to teach about.

Both of his parents had survived the Holocaust, although under different circumstances. While his Jewish mother had been imprisoned in Dachau, his father, a German physician there, had engaged in monstrous experiments. Dr. Reitz was the product of a violent assault—the offspring of an ill and desperate woman and her attacker.

Emotional accounts of stories passed down to him filled his lectures. His mother had long since died, and he'd never met his father, although technology these days had made it easy for him to find out exactly who the man was and what horrific things he had done.

With ardent blue eyes, Dr. Reitz watched students file into the dim classroom. Those eyes were a hereditary gift from his dear dad, as were his tall, slender frame and dusty blond hair, now more silver than gold. Genetics and a mirror reminded him each morning where he came from, but teaching about the monsters of the world reminded him of who he was not.

Teaching was cathartic for him. He carried his and his mother's pain from so long ago, and telling the story—his story—served as therapy. He stood in front of the class organizing his thoughts, knowing this was the last day for this particular group of students before finals. *And what a peculiar semester it has been.*

Dr. Reitz did not believe in magic or superstition, but he did trust his gut feeling, and since January it had been telling him there was something different happening within this class. He couldn't pinpoint it, but since day one a feeling had grown in him like a seed, expanding each month. He'd always been in tune with the emotional atmosphere around him, sensing when the energy of the room was positive, negative, bored, excited, or even vindictive. Students knew not to cheat in his class or lie about why their papers were turned in late. He always knew. Friends and family often joked that he had a sixth sense, that he possessed some sort of psychic power. He felt fairly certain that he merely paid more attention to life.

But the energy growing this semester was not the same overwhelming emotion he usually detected. It was a pulse—a vibrating supply of power from a great invisible generator. Today, not only could he feel it, he could swear it had become audible. He looked up at the clock. *Time to begin.*

"It's early 1945." His voice rose with urgency. "The German military is on the verge of total collapse. It is clear that the fates of many men will be decided in the streets of Berlin. Hitler knows this as well as anyone, and on the sixteenth of January, he retreats to his Führerbunker for safety."

Dr. Reitz paused, looking around the room to make sure his students were awake. Satisfied with their responsiveness, he continued.

"Skip ahead a few months to the final ten days: the ten days that led to the demise of arguably the vilest man in history. It is now April 19, 1945. German troops have retreated, leaving no front line. The next day our villain celebrates a happy fifty-sixth birthday while the men fighting his war die for nothing across the continent.

"April 21—Red Army tanks reach the outskirts of Berlin, and things look bleak. The Allies are closing in, choking the life force out of the last cancerous stronghold.

"April 22—Hitler has a breakdown. Cries like a baby when orders he issued to one of his officers to rescue Berlin are ignored. Even the highest ranks know the game is over."

Doctor Reitz raised his voice, throwing his hands in the air as his eyes wildly scanned the room. "Hitler proclaims for the first time that the war is lost. He declares that he will remain in hiding until the end and take his life."

The professor left the front of the room and walked up the center aisle, looking left and right at his students. He paused when he reached the sixth row, overcome by the pulsating sensation he'd noticed earlier. His eyes met the gaze of the pretty young brunette in the third seat down, and he stumbled as a wave of energy rolled over his thin frame.

"Professor, are you all right?" a student asked. Two young men got out of their seats to assist.

"I'm all right." He waved them back. "I must have tripped on the carpet. Now, where were we?" *Good God.*

He moved farther up the aisle. Unease edged in from his subconscious, but he fought it. He did not sense evil. Whatever came from Miss Dale was powerful indeed but not malicious. He felt more disturbed by his heightened senses than the power emanating from the girl.

He reached the rear of the room and stopped, his back to the students. *Stay focused, Reitz. This is your last class.*

"April 27—Berlin is completely cut off from the rest of Germany, and Hitler is more alone than ever." The professor turned around, facing the dusty chalkboard at the front.

"April 28—Heinrich Himmler, a military commander, offers to surrender to the Western Allies, who return a sincere *hell no*. Hitler sees this as treason, orders Himmler's arrest, and shoots the poor bastard who brought him the news.

"April 29 is a busy day for our Führer. He marries Eva Braun and learns of the death of his pal, Benito Mussolini. That evening he is informed that the fighting in Berlin will cease within twenty-four hours. The end is inevitable, and death is knocking at his door, but what better day for a wedding, right?"

A few soft laughs resonated in the room. Doctor Reitz reached the front of the class and sat down in his well-worn chair, his eyes on his hardwood desk. The encounter with Miss Dale moments earlier had taken a lot out of him.

"April 30, 1945," he continued with shallow breath. "Hitler and his new wife retreat to his private study. Guards hear a gunshot and enter the room to find their leader dead from a suspected combination of a gunshot wound and cyanide poisoning, and his wife dead from the poison. Their remains are carried into the garden, doused in gasoline, and burned. The Allies never saw the body."

He looked up, his eyes now ablaze with fury. "A coward's death if ever there was! I'd have liked better to tell you about some suffering, but in the end, an end is an end, I suppose.

"Now of course, there are the conspiracy theories that Hitler was still alive, that the rumors surrounding his death were political propaganda. The exact truth may never be known, the exact details never revealed. All of that burned or vanished with the Führer. But the important point is that whether or not the bastard died, his reign of evil did."

A hand went up.

"Yes?"

"Why wouldn't he have tried to escape? I mean, why stay someplace where you know you're going to die?" a girl in the front row asked.

Dr. Reitz sighed. "I cannot attempt to guess what made the man stay any more than I can guess what made the man kill. I'd say fear had a lot to do with it—fear of the unknown in both instances. Killing and death were his methods of solving problems and dealing with life. Even his own, it seems."

A boy in the third row raised his hand. "Do you think that what happened then could happen again with the conflict in the Middle East and Adil El-Hashem? They're calling him the new Hitler and say he's heralding in the next world war."

Another philosophical question. "Sadly, it is human nature to seek power and to inflict pain and destruction to get it.

Whether it happens again with this dictator or another, I don't think the world will be able to avoid similar conflicts of that magnitude. History is littered with horrible, violent crimes against humanity and proves time and again that it will repeat itself. I think while the idea of peace is noble, and some part of each of us yearns for it, it is a concept that was not wired into mankind's DNA."

Another hand went up, and the professor nodded.

"Do you think what happened in Europe during World War II could happen in America?"

Dr. Reitz's mind flashed to his mother's distraught eyes as she lay dying. Even the peace of death couldn't erase the sadness from her face. *The things war does to people.* "I think it would be foolish to say that something would never happen. With the correct mixture of people and power, I can't imagine why it couldn't."

The room quieted as each student soaked up his or her final moments with the professor. The bell rang, breaking the silence, followed by the sounds of shuffling papers and armrests thumping back into place.

"I will see everyone for the final," Doctor Reitz shouted. "Study hard!"

His eyes fell on the mysterious girl in row six, carefully organizing papers into her backpack. *What in God's name is going on with you?*

———

Riley grabbed her things and made for the back of the room. Needing a history credit and hearing how interesting Dr. Reitz's classes were, she had chosen this course and hadn't been disappointed. Riley loved his dramatic ways. He fit the part of eccentric professor, the kind of mentor whose lessons stayed with you forever. And while the class had no connection to her major, it did have a connection to her culture and personal history.

Her grandmother, Esther, was raised in Germany but moved to America following the Second World War after marrying Riley's grandfather. He was an American soldier and she a poor Jewish farm girl, but somehow they fell in love and ended up in Colorado. Riley's mother was born nearly nine months later.

Five years earlier, Riley's grandfather had passed away, leaving Esther to retreat further into the darkness of her past. The old woman had secrets, and Riley sensed the shadow of fear that trailed her. The Holocaust had been hard, and Esther seldom spoke of her former life. There were times Riley felt she was missing out by not getting to know her grandma better. But how could she when the woman was a shield?

It seemed the only thing Esther wasn't secretive about was her love of nature and growing things. Riley spent many days as a child with Esther, digging holes for seeds and watering the emerging greens in the garden. Riley had a knack for making things grow. It was as much a mystery to her as it was to her friends how she managed to keep begonias alive in December and bring the juiciest fruit to maturity well before it was available in local farmers' markets. Her parents joked that she must have an entire green hand instead of just a green thumb, but her grandma insisted it was magic.

Esther had the same gift. It was one thing they had in common, and the only time they both truly seemed at peace.

Riley shook the memories away. Before exiting the classroom, she turned and noticed the professor staring in her direction. She smiled and departed to meet Abby and some other friends for lunch.

Abby was coming from spacecraft design or some other absurd course. Riley's friend had gone the extra step to double major in aerospace engineering and mathematics. Riley greatly preferred the various biology courses of her environmental sciences degree to the physics classes Abby delightedly endured.

"I'm never going to pass this class," Abby groaned, walking up from behind.

"Aren't you making an A right now?" Riley understood that failing to Abby meant making a B, or sometimes even a low A, but she was still irritated by it.

"Maybe. But my final project is a mess, and I don't know how I'm going to sort everything out in a week!" Abby pawed through her bag, her dark skin shining in the sunlight. "Crap, I left my phone in class. I'll meet you at the dining hall. Save me a seat."

Riley watched her friend dart away. Abby's mom had come to America from Namibia, seeking a better life for her new baby. As Abby had ended up both beautiful and brilliant, not to mention Riley's best friend, Riley knew they'd made the right choice.

She turned toward the food court but stopped as a sudden sense of dread crept up her spine. It was a sunny day, and the wind was light. A chill in the air was unlikely.

She spun around and surveyed the area. A couple sat on a bench beneath a towering pine tree, the woman laughing at something her companion had just said. Students hustled to classes or moseyed down the sidewalks, listening to music and typing on their phones. A man in a tan suit, probably a professor, stood outside a building door reading a newspaper. Nothing seemed out of place. No one seemed to be interested in her at all.

"It's just the dream." She wriggled her shoulders to shake off the icy finger that stroked her spine. "I'm still uneasy from the dream."

She turned and walked toward the dining hall, catching a glimpse of the man in the suit lowering his paper and watching her leave. His dark, gold-flecked eyes registered somewhere in her brain, but she shook the negative feelings away. He was probably a professor she'd seen on campus a thousand times before.

CHAPTER THREE

A week later the girls huddled beneath brightly colored umbrellas as falling rain splashed water up onto their rain boots. All around, students were tucked low into their jackets, precious assignments and projects held protectively to their chests, while they sprinted to the shelter of their finals.

"Good luck!" Abby said, pausing on the way to her next exam. "You're going to do awesome. I can't believe you're almost done. I'm so jealous."

"Thanks." Riley squinted through the rain. "I can't believe this is it." *One more!* "I wish you were graduating too. I hate to think about you having to navigate life without me."

Abby smiled, wiping light mist from her face. "I'm hurrying. Hopefully I won't be too far behind." By deciding to double major, Abby had tacked on an extra semester.

"Well, good luck to you too. I'll see you on the other side." Riley turned and joined her fellow students in the hunkered cluster racing toward the crowded doorway. *History of the World Wars. No big deal.* Grades hadn't posted yet, but she felt confident she'd aced just about everything. *And this last one shouldn't be any different.*

Riley entered the classroom, sighing with relief that no one had yet claimed her seat on the right side of the room: sixth row, third chair over—a position she tried for in every class. The first time she'd walked into a room to find that seat occupied, she'd debated asking the person to move but felt ridiculous, so she took the chair directly behind in the seventh row. Hard as she tried to focus, all she could do was stare at the back of that red head in *her* seat, hoping the chair thief would fail the quiz. Riley felt silly afterward, but she made a point of showing up ten minutes earlier from then on and hadn't lost her seat since. There were some things she tended to be a little OCD about, and during finals it was important that everything be in order.

Students filtered in, and the class began to echo with the sound of nervous chatter, flipping note cards, and tapping fingers. Riley smiled at the classmates who occupied the seats around her. One student sitting directly to her right looked like he might vomit. *Poor guy.*

"Is this your last final?" she asked the nervous student, hoping to help him relax. It would be no good to her if he suddenly lost his morning waffles on her lap.

"One more after this," he said. "I need to make an A on this test to pass the class. I shouldn't have skipped so many times." He smiled, apparently proud of his delinquency.

Yep, you're screwed. "You've got this. Just relax."

The boy shrugged and began sifting through his notes, cramming as much last-minute information as possible. Riley peered over his shoulder, reading the dates and facts as he shuffled through them. *I know that. Okay, I know that too. Yep, that's easy.*

She'd arrived even earlier than usual because of the rain, and now she had to wait for what seemed like forever to finish up her college career. *Still fifteen minutes. Is it extra hot in here today?*

Riley scanned the room to see if other students were experiencing the same sudden discomfort. Sweat began beading off her forehead, and moisture pooled in her palms. The lights became glaringly bright, and a sharp pain stabbed somewhere in the front of her brain.

The anxious student beside her looked up, worried. "Hey, are you okay? You look pretty bad."

Riley tried to stand and fell. *What's happening? Did I eat something bad? What have I done today? Breakfast, finals, Abby, Gabe…Gabe. That's not Gabe.*

Her eyes darted left and right, but she was no longer sitting in the classroom. Instead she found herself standing in…*a storm?*

Grains of sand whipped across her face, burning her eyes. Riley took a step forward but found no relief. *Oh, God, it's happening again.* The wind howled as she groped blindly ahead, trying to find something to grab onto. She glanced down and saw in horror that she was completely naked, the sand searing red marks into her soft flesh. Riley tried to cover herself but quickly realized that she needed her hands to shield her eyes.

Squinting into the tempest, she caught a glimpse of the figure she'd originally mistaken for Gabe. He was tall and muscled, with golden curls that flew in the wind like a nest of swarming yellow vipers.

The stranger stood in front of the most bizarre tree Riley had ever seen. Ghostly silver branches twisted and swirled around each other, creating an impossible maze that stretched forever into the sky and in both directions as far as she could see. The crown of the tree glittered with sterling leaves and sapphire fruits that hung still, unaffected by the violent storm.

The man took a step toward the tree, his armor creaking and moaning. A sword, forged of blinding steel that flickered with the flames of a thousand small fires, hung by his side. He clearly didn't know she was there.

"Hello!" She ran toward the light of the blade. "Help me. I need help!" She had to go to the man. There was no one else. If he wanted her dead, she couldn't hope to escape anyway.

The armored man turned, startled. "How did you find me?" His hand flew to the hilt of his sword, and there was a sound of scraping metal as he drew the weapon from its scabbard. "How did you find this place?"

"Please. I'm so scared. My eyes. Please." She cradled her nude body with her arms, tucking her head low into her chest. It was humiliating to stand in front of this man, naked and begging.

"You cannot be here." He took a step toward her, sword pointed at her hunched figure. "I would have seen this coming."

What is he talking about? "I think I'm dreaming!" Riley shouted. "I fell asleep or passed out or something. I was in class and then here. I can't control it. It just happens. Please, I have to get out of here. Wake me up. Do something!" She glanced up and met the piercing stare of the lone warrior. He had Gabe's eyes. She took a step backward, away from the fiery blade pointed at her throat. "Please," she whimpered again, shrinking further into herself.

The man continued to stare, a mixture of determination and confusion etched on his stonelike face. "I will send you back this one time, but you must forget what you have seen and never attempt to return."

"Yes, okay, anything. Just please!"

The howling of the wind grew to a roar, and each blast of sand felt like razors tearing small pieces of flesh from her body. Riley collapsed onto the ground, writhing in pain. The man stepped closer until he stood towering over her crumpled figure. He hoisted his weapon high into the air.

He's going to kill me!

She raised her arms to shield her head and caught a glimpse of the strange tree, still unscarred by the surrounding gale. Firelight from the sword danced off the tree's gilded leaves. It would have been a beautiful sight under different circumstances.

"You are a danger to us all," the man declared. "Your presence here threatens what's left of the balance of humanity." He plunged the sword downward, and Riley's world went still and black.

———

Someone screamed. The harsh noise reverberated through her aching skull. *Make it stop.* It stopped. Light broke through the darkness, and fuzzy shapes moved around the perimeter of her vision. Riley felt her chest rise and fall with labored breaths. Her entire body ached and quivered as if someone had scrubbed her clean with glass shards. She struggled to sit up and felt hands gently push her to the floor.

"Miss Dale?" The voice was soft and gentle. "Can you hear me?"

Riley felt herself nod. Her vision cleared. Faceless forms suddenly had features. She was lying on her back in the History of the World Wars classroom. The voice she'd heard was her professor's.

"Oh, thank God," Dr. Reitz said with a sigh. "Riley, we've called for an ambulance. You're going to be okay."

She winced. "No. I—I'm fine. I just need air."

"But you fainted. You've been out for a good five minutes."

That's all? The vision, if that's what you called it, was coming back to her—the sand, the tree, the strange man with a sword. *"Forget and never attempt to return."* It was an odd request, as she'd never meant to go there in the first place. *But where was there, anyway? And who was he?* This was the first time someone had spoken directly to her in a dream, and it added an entirely new level of terror.

"Please, I don't need an ambulance. I need rest. It's just stress from finals." Riley looked up at Dr. Reitz, feigning confidence.

He studied her for a moment, obviously wanting to argue, but he held back. "I strongly disagree. However, the decision is yours. Please get someone to drive you home, and be ready to take your final tomorrow." He stood and cleared his throat. "Everyone put your things away. We're pressed for time and need to get started."

Riley didn't want to stick around to wait for him to change his mind. "I'll be here tomorrow. Thank you, Dr. Reitz."

She hurried from the room and burst through the doors of the building into open air. Rain pelted her face as she turned it skyward. Cool water soaked through her clothes within minutes, and she groped gratefully at the sodden garments. *At least I have my pants.*

It had been years since these dreams had haunted her. Sure, she had dreamed since then, but not like this—not the dreams where she smelled an assailant's breath or woke up soaking wet, gasping for air. These dreams exhausted her, terrified her, even made her sick. When she was younger, she'd gone to a doctor, who excused them as night terrors triggered by anxiety. He told her she needed to find ways to "create stillness within each day" so her anxieties would not terrorize her at night.

The last nightmare had happened at fourteen. In that instance she'd found herself on an airplane plummeting from the sky, filled with doomed passengers. As the lights flickered, the cabin, reeking of urine, grew smaller with each shriek and helpless sob. Riley awoke from that dream with a black eye, singed hair, and news that a plane heading from Atlanta to Los Angeles had crashed in the desert, leaving no survivors. After that the dreams had ceased. *Until now.* And this time he'd known she was there.

She found a bench and sat, taking deep breaths, trying to calm down. *I had a nightmare, or a daydream. It doesn't mean anything. It can't mean anything. It's one thing for a plane to crash, but a man with a flaming sword and a tree made of precious gems and metals? That's not real. It doesn't exist. I've got too much going on. That's all.*

Still, something was off. *A danger to the balance of humanity? What does that even mean?* Her mind flashed back to the men on the cliff and the bruises on her body. Eight years ago she had dreamed of the chaos on the doomed flight, but she'd woken in her own bed with only traces of the experience on her body. This was different. She was no longer just a bystander but the protagonist of the story—a story she wanted no part of.

CHAPTER FOUR

The hunter sat alone in the dark, smiling. *It's time.* He took a deep breath and exhaled slowly, trying to calm his excitement. The aches and cravings from his body were no longer tolerable. He couldn't sleep, food was tasteless, and he had an unquenchable thirst that could only be satisfied by one thing. And that always meant it was time.

Rising slowly from a chair, he descended to the basement to gather his things. It had been two weeks since the last girl, and this new one was prettier than the others. Tonight would be another perfect execution. The thought energized him.

He'd been at it for months, and authorities still had no leads. *I am untouchable. I am the hunter.* The FBI was involved now, which only made it more exhilarating. *And I'm right under their noses.*

He walked past the large granite slab in the center of his stone basement, stepped over a drain still reddish brown from a previous endeavor, and opened a steel cabinet door in the back corner. Dim light crept unnaturally through the chamber, casting wicked shadows from cages stacked against the walls and hooks hanging from the ceiling. He surveyed the various tools and implements—saws, knives, pipes, screwdrivers, a chainsaw...

He chuckled. *That was a mess.* He eyed the knives. *Which one will make you squeal most?*

He liked it when they really put on a show—the screaming, the pleading, the bargaining. It was especially tantalizing when they swore they wouldn't tell anyone. *Don't they know that only makes it easier for me? Only makes me want it more?*

His gaze settled on a long, sleek Bowie knife. *That one always brings them to their knees.* He grabbed a box of latex gloves from the counter and a roll of wire from the shelf. Plastic wouldn't be necessary. This one was coming home with him.

He silently ascended the stairs and locked the front door behind him. Making sure no neighbors were around, he slid into the silver sports car parked in the driveway.

CHAPTER FIVE

R iley lay in bed, watching the ceiling fan blades circle round and round. With finals over, her family would be in town the next day for graduation. As exciting as it was supposed to be, apprehension clouded all joy. The strange episode during her last final haunted her. She thought about it constantly, trying to make sense of the whole thing.

Abby tried to be sympathetic, suggesting they both go to a psychic to have the dreams interpreted. Riley declined. *Why would I need to go to a fortune-teller when I can see the future on my own?*

She knew the dream was somehow real. Even though it defied all laws of the universe as she understood them, the memory of the man with the sword was still vivid. It was no hallucination. She couldn't forget his face, his words, his eyes.

The blades above spun in rhythmic circles. Maybe if she hypnotized herself, she could relive the experience and find validation. She needed answers. *I'm not crazy, and these aren't night terrors.* She clicked on the TV, hoping to find a mindless program that might trump her problems.

"Breaking developments in Baghdad." A news anchor spoke in the professional, almost robotic voice identified with that line of work. "Adil El-Hashem announced to the world today that his scientists were completing construction of a weapon with such terrifying power, it could end Western civilization. The social media realm is frantic, speculating everything from nuclear bombs to biological threats. The White House has not issued a statement yet, but we expect to hear from the president within the next few hours. What we do know at this time is that tensions with the Middle East only seem to be getting worse."

Riley sighed and flopped back down onto her pillow. El-Hashem was a dictator and murderer of his own people. She recalled news images from her childhood of mass graves filled indiscriminately with men, women, and children. In fits of rage, El-Hashem was known to have his soldiers destroy entire communities simply because an individual storefront or home did not have his banner flying high. Six months ago he'd declared war on the Western world when he'd bombed the Eiffel Tower and Big Ben. His terror came to America five months later when he'd targeted the Statue of Liberty and the Golden Gate Bridge.

Riley stared at the TV. Years of internal chaos following ground wars with the United States had led to this. The American-Iraqi conflict was an ever-boiling pot, and the gas powering it was always set on high. So far the worst that had happened was the pot had boiled over. But someday, if no one figured out how to turn the stove off, the house was going to catch fire and burn the whole world down.

She turned the TV off. Worrying about the end of the world was not going to ease her mind now.

Her cell phone beeped. *Gabe.*

"Need to talk," the text read. "Heard about what happened. Call ASAP."

Riley rolled onto her side, leaving the message unanswered behind her. Gabe could wait. She didn't think she could deal with anything else at the moment.

———

The auditorium blazed with excited chatter and the bright flashes of hundreds of cameras held by an equal number of thrilled parents. Some rejoiced at the money they would save, others that their borderline-failing students could now boast a hard-earned bachelor's degree. Riley waded through the festive crowd toward her family, a diploma tube held aloft in her right hand and the left clutching her graduation cap, its two-toned tassel bouncing with each step.

They were all there, waiting to congratulate her on a job well done: Coulter Dale, her tall, good-humored father. Sylvia, her petite, incisive mother. Kiersten, her beautiful, successful older sister. And Esther Miller, her timid maternal grandmother.

"Yo, Riley!" her dad shouted as she walked up. "You did it, hon. We are so proud of you."

Riley twirled in her black graduation gown and gave a small curtsey. "I did well, no?"

"Congrats, little sis, how does it feel?" Kiersten wrapped Riley in a hug. Her sister was tall and slender, with green eyes that matched Riley's and large blond curls that softened her angular face.

"Actually, really good." Riley squeezed back. "I can't believe I'm finished!"

"And now you get to move back in with Mom and Dad," her mom joked, giving a double thumbs-up.

Riley gave an exasperated smile but secretly felt relieved. She hoped to find out what was happening and how to make it stop while she still had the support of her family. She dreaded the thought of blacking out again alone in an apartment in Denver—or even worse, at a new job where no one knew her. "You don't have to rub it in." She made a pouty face, playing the part.

Riley made her way to her grandmother and gave her a hug. "Thanks for coming, Grandma. I hope it wasn't too long and boring."

Esther held her purse tightly as she always did. "Oh, no, we're all very proud of you, Riley." Her voice carried a slight accent.

"She's not going to steal your purse, Esther," Riley's dad joked. "You can relax."

Esther's thin lips parted in a tiny laugh as she squeezed Riley's hands. "So proud." They locked matching green eyes, and Riley thought she noticed an extra sparkle of fear glinting in their depths.

"I don't know about y'all, but I need to eat, and we need to get moving if we want to beat this crowd to the restaurants." Her father motioned with his hands for them to hurry up. "Think about what you want, graduation girl."

Riley held her grandmother's hand as they walked to the car. Esther's small frame and thin white curls kept pace with her granddaughter. Riley had always heard she looked like Esther but never saw it. Today Riley just saw a frail old woman with a face that had seen too much next to an able young woman who hadn't seen enough. Now it was just the eyes that gave away their relation.

They fell behind the rest of her family in the massive arena parking lot. Esther grasped her hand tighter. The antique ring she always wore pressed into Riley's flesh. It was an age-old ring, a tarnished metal band with the design of a snakelike maze forming trunks that branched out into the spiraled leaves of two elaborate trees. One tree was gold with a delicate, egg-shaped ruby fastened to the center of its trunk. The other was silver, its twisted, hairlike branches decorated with tiny blue sapphires. She had never seen her grandma without it.

The trees. Riley glanced down at her grandmother's ring, recoiling at the image branded into the metal. She had seen this image recently but had not connected it to the heirloom. Sand, wind, and fire flashed across her mind.

"Grandma, where did you get that? You've always worn it, but I've never asked."

Esther glanced at the ring, her eyes growing uneasy. Riley noticed the change and saw the walls fly up.

"It was a gift." Esther smiled as if nothing had happened. "From my grandmother, who received it from her grandmother and so on. It has been in our family for a very long time."

"And the trees?" Riley pointed at the design. "That tree, the silver one—it exists, doesn't it? Where is it?"

Esther cringed. "It is just an image. Just a design like they put on all jewelry."

"But what tree is it based on, Grandma? They aren't just random trees, are they?"

Her grandmother shut down like a scolded child.

"I'm sorry," Riley said. "I've just never asked about it, and I was intrigued."

Esther forced another smile. *Fake again.* Riley decided on a different approach: the truth. "Please, Grandma, I feel like you know something. I've seen it. I know it's real. I've been there. I've had dreams, hallucinations. There are men that want to kill me. Give me something so that I know I'm not crazy. I feel like I'm losing my mind."

Esther paused, her breath quickening. "You've seen it? But how? It's not possible."

"So it is real?" Fear and excitement flooded her system. "I was there, naked. And that tree—I saw that tree. And a man. A man in armor with a sword of fire. He told me to forget what I saw. He told me to never come back."

Esther's free hand flew to her face to stifle the gasp that she was unable to contain. "He's right. You must never go there. Life is too dangerous, Riley, something I fear you will find out soon. Do not be lured down paths from which you cannot return. Your life is precious too. Don't forget that. You don't have to do this. You don't have to do any of this. It does things to you. Things you can't come back from."

Esther's eyes pleaded. She looked on the verge of tears. Riley scanned them, looking for an answer, but only felt more confused.

"Grandma, I don't know what you're talking about. I've just seen things, but I have no clarity. I feel like I should be afraid, but I don't even know what it is I'm supposed to be afraid of. Please, if you know something, tell me."

Silence.

"Hey, are you guys not hungry?" Riley's father shouted from the car. "I'm about to eat your mother if you don't hurry up."

"Yeah, sorry!" Riley yelled back. "We're coming."

"I'm sorry, dear," Esther sighed. "I've already said too much. I don't want this for you."

Riley took a deep breath and exhaled. The conversation had done nothing but confuse her more. *Well, we were right about Grandma's secrets.*

They reached the car, and Riley climbed in, shutting the door and staring out at the mountains rising over Boulder. Normally she loved the Rockies. She'd get lost for hours hiking, fishing in snow-fed lakes, or picnicking in meadows bursting with wildflowers. The peaks were familiar and comforting to her, but today they felt threatening. The jagged edges of the granite summits seemed forbidding instead of welcoming. She was beginning to feel that everything familiar was a façade hiding some dark secret she needed to fear. *Fear what, though?*

"Never attempt to return."

"He's right. You must never go there."

Riley rested her forehead against the window and closed her eyes, willing the darkness to block out the overwhelming sense of helplessness. Since the episode during finals, she'd felt many things—fear, anxiety, stress, depression. But today a new feeling emerged: anger. Anger at being kept in the dark about something that was a danger to her—something that scared others so much they wouldn't even talk about it.

CHAPTER SIX

Jackson Cain scanned the Oval Office, deep in thought, trying to imagine what past presidents in similar situations had been thinking. His fist fell hard on the solid desktop. *How the hell did this happen?*

He'd run for president knowing the country was ready for change. His passion ignited people in ways they hadn't been in years. He was young, charismatic, and good looking. Cain meant business, and his speeches motivated even the most passive listener.

And now this. What kind of weapon could this monster in Baghdad have developed, and does it even exist?

President Cain's hand crashed into the desk again. *With all the technology the United States possesses, why has no one discovered El-Hashem's secret?*

He shook his head, gritting his teeth. It didn't make sense. El-Hashem was either bluffing or receiving outside assistance. They'd know soon.

A knock came on the door, and his chief of staff, Martin Headley, poked his face inside. "Mr. President, Secretary DeWitt is here to see you."

John DeWitt had been the obvious selection for secretary of state. He'd served in the army during Vietnam, held a seat in Congress for multiple terms, and most recently acted as ambassador to China during the previous presidency. John DeWitt had seen it all, and he was respected among different political parties and leaders around the world.

"Let him in."

A stout man with hard features, sharp eyes, and slick black hair entered the room. "Mr. President."

"John." President Cain nodded, and John DeWitt took a seat in one of the armchairs in front of the desk. "What do you have for me?"

DeWitt sighed and sifted through a folder, then handed a single sheet of paper to the president. Cain scanned the document and set it down slowly, his eyes growing wide. "Impossible."

"I'd like to think the same, sir, but my intelligence is accurate. We've sent the document through tests, and each came back confirming authenticity. That signature is real."

"Son of a bitch," the president whispered. "John, I need you to keep this confidential for now while I figure out my approach. I don't want any leaks to the press. No one must find out. *They* can't know we have this information."

"Yes, sir." DeWitt stood. "We were right. Someone big is helping El-Hashem."

President Cain nodded. "God help us."

CHAPTER SEVEN

Cardboard boxes lay scattered and stacked like a Halloween carnival maze across the floor and furniture of Riley's small bedroom. A week had passed since graduation, but she still hadn't finished packing. The mess was agonizing, but she hadn't found a good way to organize the clutter, having already wasted too much time trying to neatly stack and restack boxes instead of just loading stuff up.

Frustrated with her friend's OCD behavior, Abby had finally come to help, which meant throwing everything into whatever box it would fit in. After a few minutes stressing over the fact that the box with pictures also had socks and jewelry in it, Riley resigned herself to Abby's expedited way of packing.

"I don't want to leave," Riley groaned, putting her hands on her head and leaning back against the side of the bed. "What am I supposed to do back in Grand Junction? I'm going to be one of those losers who gets a degree and then has to move home."

"Chill out, Riley." Abby shuffled through school papers, tossing most into the overflowing trashcan. "You'll find something important to do. You always have. Besides, lots of people are moving home. It's not just you."

Riley glared, rolling her eyes. "I know, but that isn't the category I want to be lumped into."

"Be patient and keep looking for jobs in Denver. You never know; by December we may be living together again." Abby set the papers down and turned on Riley's TV.

The newswoman reported, "Remains of a fourth body have been found in western Colorado just outside the town of Delta, near Grand Junction. Police have not yet issued a statement, but an inside source says strong evidence ties this murder to the three earlier in the year. All victims were brunette females. Police are urging everyone in the area, especially young women, to use extreme caution. While the body count is rising, evidence and the killer still elude authorities. We will share information as it comes in, but for now that is all we know of what are being called the Rocky Mountain murders."

The anchor went on to discuss something else, but Abby had already hit the mute button, her eyes wide and her mouth taut as she turned to Riley.

"Of all the places you could be going, Riley Dale, why does it have to be into the heart of this mess? With everything going on, I had forgotten about Colorado's own Jack the Ripper. You must promise me you will not do anything stupid. No wandering off alone, no midnight hikes, no anything. You will stay at home and play board games with your father!"

Riley knew Abby was right. She loved hiking and being alone for hours in the wilderness. It was calming to be disconnected from the phone, the television, and even other people. Riley felt less anxious when the world wasn't moving so quickly, and being alone with the silence of a few trees and an open sky was the closest thing to stillness she had ever encountered. *Now a monster lurks in my happy place.*

"But we love this stuff, Abs!" Riley tried to lighten the mood. "This is like Lifetime and A&E and all our favorite shows up close and personal. Rocky Mountain murders? Come on! How exciting does that sound?"

Abby rolled her eyes and tossed a wadded pair of socks at her friend's head. "Which is exactly why I'm worried about you."

"I'm not going to do anything stupid. I'll just be a little more alert and carry bear spray wherever I go." Riley offered a cheesy grin that Abby returned.

"Whatever." Abby stood and reached for her cell phone. "I'm hungry. Pizza?"

"Absolutely."

This was one of their last nights as roommates, and Riley wanted to make the most of it. Images of the murdered girls flashed across the TV screen as Riley turned it off. The man with the sword and the dark men on the cliff who haunted her dreams suddenly seemed harmless compared to the monster that hunted in her backyard.

———

The next morning Riley awoke from another dream about the sandstorm world, but this time, instead of the man with the sword urging her to go back, it was Esther. Since discovering her grandmother was somehow involved in all of this—whatever it was—she'd been plagued with dream after dream, twisting what had happened with strange new elements. *What do you know, Grandma? What clarity can you provide?*

She would be home soon and could broach the subject, even if it scared her grandmother. *I will not stay confined to my nightmares.*

Riley and Abby spent the next afternoon packing. Riley wasn't leaving until the following day, but there was a graduation party that night, and she didn't want to worry about last-minute details. Not that she really wanted to go to the party. *Way too many people.*

Riley found a box of Abby's things mixed in with hers and stared down at pictures, football-ticket stubs, and other memorabilia—bittersweet memories from an incredible four years. Memories Riley didn't share. She held up a concert ticket and remembered telling Abby she couldn't go with her to that particular event because she had an exam the next day. Actually it was just an open-book quiz, but Riley didn't know the other people going. It just hadn't sounded fun. Now she was sad not to have a box like that. Her four years had been spent doing what? *Studying? Making good grades?* It had seemed ideal then, but now it all felt like a waste. "Abby, I missed out, didn't I?"

"What do you mean?" Abby cocked an eyebrow.

Riley held up the box. "I didn't do any of this."

"But you made awesome grades. And we had a lot of fun doing other things."

"You made better grades and still did all of this. I was such a loser."

"That stuff isn't for everyone, and you are not a loser. You just like to do different things. It's actually really nice having someone in my life as stable as you. You're reliable. That's a good thing."

Riley set the box down and stared at the mess. *Stable. Reliable. That's what I'm supposed to be in ten years, not right now.* "That's a nice way to say I'm boring."

Abby laughed. "That's a nice way to say I love you and you're important to me."

Riley shrugged and sighed at the overstuffed bookshelf she still needed to pack.

"Plus we've got tonight," Abby said. "We'll end it on a good note. Don't worry."

But it wasn't just the move and party making her anxious. "I'm nervous about seeing Gabe." She hadn't seen or spoken to him since his rejection, ignoring his calls and deleting all voicemails without listening to them.

"It'll be fine." Abby tossed a crumpled receipt into the trashcan. "You leave tomorrow. Whatever he says won't matter, because tomorrow you have a whole new life ahead of you. And I'll be there if you need to make a getaway."

"You're right. It will only be awkward if I make it awkward." *But I still kind of hope he doesn't show.*

———

Gabriel Hart was nervous, a feeling he could usually control and push aside. He paced up and down the sidewalk, staring at the cracks below. Back and forth, back and forth. He knew what seeing Riley meant tonight. She would want nothing to do with him, but she needed to know the truth and to hear it from him. He'd been dishonest long enough.

"It isn't your job to tell her. She needs to be kept safe, and you need to help her become strong."

"But she needs to know!"

"It isn't time yet."

That's how the conversation always went.

Gabe stopped pacing, folding strong arms across his chest. Things were different now. Whether or not anyone wanted to accept it, Riley had been brought into this, and sooner or later she would be faced with the truth. *So why not tonight?*

Chapter Eight

I don't want to go. Riley stood in the kitchen, organizing the silverware drawer while Abby finished getting ready for the party. Abby was a genius but somehow always managed to put things in the wrong places. *Short spoons and big spoons go next to each other, not short spoons and forks.* Each item had a home, and Riley needed it to be there.

She leaned against the counter and ran her fingers through the loose brown curls that fell down her back. It was already late, and she was antsy. The growing apprehension of seeing Gabe at the party blurred all hope of a successful evening.

Abby walked out of her room, strutting down the fake catwalk that was their hallway, dressed in a miniskirt and button-down sleeveless shirt. Her dark hair lay in a loose braid to the side, and her brown eyes were outlined with a light dusting of bronze. "We look good."

"Serial-killer bait." Riley tried not to smile. "But I don't think I'm gonna go."

"Shut up!" Abby's purse slapped the side of Riley's arm. "That is so not funny. And you are going. Remember earlier how you were sad about missing out? You have a chance to do something, so take it!"

Riley sighed and stepped out of the kitchen. Her whole life she'd wished for the ability to let go, to not obsess over little things. Even when life was normal, she had a problem relaxing. Now, as life spiraled out of control, her friends and family all probably figured it was more of the same—more of her inability to deal with stress. *I can do this. I can do this.* She opened the front door and followed Abby outside.

"Wow, that's creepy." Abby stopped walking, and Riley bumped into her back.

An old man dressed in tattered rags and threadbare clothing stood on the sidewalk next to the passenger side of Abby's car. A patched-up beanie covered shaggy white hair, and a matching beard hung thickly from a grimy face. His entire outfit was one ugly shade of brown that faded nicely into his skin as if they were cut from the same soiled roll of fabric. He stared at the girls with ocher eyes.

"We should go back inside," Abby whispered, grabbing Riley's wrist and starting back toward the door.

"Wait." Riley braced against her friend. Something about the way the man looked at her held her gaze. His piercing stare cut through to peek at her fragile soul. Riley hugged her stomach, trying to create a protective shield, feeling more naked than she had in front of the silver tree in her vision. The corners of the old man's lips trembled, forming a smile.

"Why is he looking at you like that?" Abby asked. "Do you know him?"

Riley stared at the man but shook her head. She pulled her wrist from Abby's slackened grip and walked toward the destitute figure.

"Riley, what are you doing?" Abby sounded scared.

"Abby, it's okay." Riley didn't know why she thought it was okay, but strangely, this man's presence evoked a sense of peace, not fear. Her anxiety was gone, and she felt calmer than she had in weeks. Stillness spread like the feeling of a warm bath after a day out in the cold.

"Can you spare some change?" he asked, his voice hoarse and trembling, his eyes never leaving Riley's face. "Please, I'm starving."

Abby grabbed Riley's wrist again and started pulling her toward the house. "We don't have change, sorry!"

"Wait," Riley said again, still looking at the man. She reached into her purse and pulled out a crumpled five-dollar bill. "Here."

She extended the bill toward the man, and he reached out to take it, his hand brushing the tips of her fingers. She recoiled as an intense pulse of electricity raced up her arm and exploded in her brain. *What the hell?*

The shock didn't hurt. It was just startling. She regarded the old man, who looked pleased. "Who are you?"

"What did you do to her?" Abby rushed to her side. "Riley, we're going. Now."

"Thank you, child," the old vagrant said, ignoring Abby. "I am someone you don't know, yet you have chosen to show kindness to me. All things will be remembered. I'd like to think you are ready. Ready enough, at least." He winked, turned on the spot, and walked off into the darkness.

"What the hell was that about?" Abby demanded. "Are you some kind of hero now? Did you not catch that some wacko is murdering women who, not to be out of line, exactly match your profile? A little caution, please!"

"He doesn't kill people, Abby," Riley said, not understanding how she knew this but feeling certain. "Besides, the killer is on the western side of the state. Not here. Come on, let's go."

"Ya think?" Irritation covered Abby's face as she stalked to the driver's side of the car, slamming the door behind her.

Riley couldn't get the old man out of her head. *What does he think I'm ready for? Abby's probably right. This guy is a lunatic. But what if he's not?*

Here was a new piece of the puzzle that she had no idea where to place.

———

The car pulled up to a house lit up like an electric power plant that bounced with the rhythm of a Spanish *discoteca*. Music mixed with shouts, cheers, and laughter from a jumble of eclectic voices blared through the windows, welcoming guests and irritating sleepy neighbors.

"Ladies, looking fine as ever." Tariq Zaman walked up, putting an arm around Riley and Abby. "May I escort you in?"

Tariq and Abby had a thing for each other. They weren't exclusive, but Riley had no doubt it would happen soon. *They'd be so good together.*

"Thanks for doing this, Tariq," Riley said. "I'm glad to be able to say good-bye to everyone before heading out." *An e-mail would have been fine too, though.*

"Of course," he said. "Wish you were staying in town with the rest of us. Hopefully I only have one victory lap to make."

He grinned, a wide goofy smile that complimented his messy black hair. Tariq had another semester before graduation, and Riley had her suspicions he'd dragged out his education to spend more time with Abby.

"I haven't seen him yet," he said before she could ask.

"Oh." Riley composed herself. "I don't care. It's fine if he's here. I'm not worried."

Tariq laughed and gave a hoot of disbelief. "Riley Dale not worried about something? Nice try."

They walked inside and Riley was immediately snatched away from her two companions by a group of girls from her classes. "I'll catch up with you guys later." She watched as Abby and Tariq strolled away arm in arm, laughing.

"How are you feeling?" asked Natasha, a girl from Riley's world war history class and witness to the blackout episode.

"I'm good." Riley tried to sound upbeat. "Just stress, I think. No big deal. My pride is just hurt a little bit."

"Don't worry about it," Natasha responded. "It happens to everyone. At least we're done!"

Does it? Riley appreciated the girl's kindness, even though she was pretty sure Natasha had never blacked out and found herself naked in front of a strange man with a sword of fire.

"So what are your plans, Riley?" asked a girl named Brittany, with a hint of sarcasm.

Ugh, not Brittany. "Not sure yet," Riley said with as much confidence as possible. "Hopefully something will turn up soon." *No drama on my last night out, please!*

"Wow. Well, good luck in Grand Junction," Brittany said with fake sympathy. "I got into law school at UCLA. My family is very proud. Gabe was impressed. He said he's always wanted to visit the West Coast."

"Yeah, cool." Riley tried to sound uninterested. "Good luck with that." She didn't like the thought of Gabe visiting girls in California—especially girls she didn't particularly like.

Riley stood awkwardly for a moment before the tension became too much. "Well, on that note, I'm off to find a drink. See you guys later!"

She wandered through the house, making small talk and hugging old friends. Then she made her way outside and looked up into the sky. It stretched forever, the stars twinkling like moonlight dancing on an alpine lake. Pausing, she recalled the peace brought on by the old man's touch. *I may not have a job, but in reality that means I can go anywhere, do anything.* It was a riveting thought. *The sky is the limit.* And this one seemed to have none.

"Riley?" A voice interrupted her thoughts.

She turned and her stomach twisted. Gabe looked like Apollo—like he'd fit better in a Renaissance painting than in modern-day America.

"Hey, Gabe." She tried to appear like everything was fine. "How's your night going?"

"Not bad." He was standing next to her now, also gazing skyward. "Pretty incredible, isn't it?"

"It's beautiful."

They stood, silent in the moment, the din of the party sealed inside the house. *Stillness.*

"I know what I do is sometimes confusing." He tapped his fingers on the porch railing. "But our friendship means more to me than you could ever imagine."

"You're right, Gabe. I am confused."

He fell silent again. "It's not that I don't care about you. I will always be here if you need anything. And I mean anything."

Riley said nothing.

"And there's something else I have to talk to you about." Gabe cleared his throat, rattling the keys in his pocket.

He's nervous? Good.

"I want to help you," he said. "I have to help you. And I need you to hear me out. Something is going to happen to you very soon, something overwhelming and terrifying, and you will need me."

She eyed him doubtfully. "Gabe, listen…"

For an instant Riley could see Gabe's startled face, but then it vanished. Overwhelming pain filled her head. Stars that had been so pleasing earlier suddenly burned her eyes, as if a welder had set up his workshop in the sky. Screams filled the air.

When her eyes regained focus, she found herself floating above a dense forest. An old man she didn't recognize staggered through the thickening darkness, his breaths falling heavily. As his gnarled hands reached for the prickly needles of an enormous spruce, he collapsed to his knees, dragging himself below the evergreen boughs to hide from his pursuers. Riley heard the baying of hounds and for a few moments was there beside him under the tree, feeling his foggy breath rattling with cold fear while he stared out at the impenetrable darkness. She recoiled as a bloody, toothy snout penetrated his hiding place and rough hands dragged him out. She heard him utter the name Michael, but the rest was in German.

Then he was gone. Now she sat blanketed in shadow in the corner of what appeared to be a small log cabin. Three men stood over a body on the dirt floor. *A woman?* Riley strained her eyes for a better view. Something told her these men were dangerous and would not give her a second chance like the man with the sword had. The woman attempted to sit, giving Riley a glimpse of an old, determined face that might once have resembled her own. Esther lay sprawled on the dirt floor, as heavy boots paced back and forth near her head. Deep gashes covered her face and neck, and her arms and legs were twisted and bound.

I've got to help her! Riley looked for anything she could use as a weapon but saw nothing. The men carried rifles and side arms, stranding her in the protective shadows. Her best hope was for this to be a dream or that she was indeed crazy, or that in a few moments she would wake in her bed with a bad hangover and a fuzzy memory.

One of the men shouted, and Riley pressed farther into the darkness, shoving up against the hard wall, willing it to expand.

"Wo ist sie?" he demanded, heavy boots pacing the floor.

German?

"Ich sehe dich in der Hölle!" shouted the old woman who appeared to be her grandmother.

Why is she in Germany?

The boots stopped. "Dann sterbt ihr zusammen," he whispered, a menacing calm in his voice. The body on the floor tensed, and although Riley couldn't understand what was said, she knew it wasn't good. The man glared at Esther, raised his rifle, and pulled the trigger.

Riley's scream competed with the reverberating sounds of the gunshot. She'd given her position away. The men spun toward where she crouched.

Riley closed her eyes, waiting for the worst, but it didn't come. Instead a face appeared in the darkness, faint at first. It grew larger and more discernable. It was her face, but different—harder and angrier. It hovered for a split second and then vanished.

Riley opened her eyes and found herself next to a frightened-looking Gabe. She cradled her aching head in her hands, wiping the sweat from her brow.

"What the hell just happened, Riley?" he asked, obviously unnerved. "You were screaming. Where were you?"

"I don't know." She sounded equally terrified. "Maybe someone put something in my drink?" She didn't want to tell him what she'd just seen. *He'd think I'm crazy. And I'm beginning to agree.*

"I'm taking you home right now." Gabe put a strong arm around her and steered her into the house.

"Yeah, okay," she said in a daze. "Let's go find Abby." *What just happened? What is wrong with me? Where is Grandma?*

She wanted to cry. She wished Gabe's protectiveness and concern would envelop her completely, blocking out the nightmarish scenes.

He eyed her warily, seeming to understand he wasn't hearing the whole truth. Riley shook all the way home, where Gabe and Abby had to carry her weak body into the house.

"Gabe, what do I need to do?" Abby asked.

"She just needs to get some sleep. I'll stay with her and come get you if something changes."

Riley's bed was already packed, so she took the couch and Gabe lay on the floor in a space he managed to create in the mass of boxes. Riley stared up at the dark ceiling. Gabe's breathing was labored, and she wondered if he was having a hard time finding sleep as well. Streetlights shone through the cracked window blinds, and she thought of the mysterious old man who was out there somewhere. Things were piling up, and quickly now. Any ideas that this was all coincidental were long gone. She hated what was happening. It didn't matter if it was real, a dream, or a fast descent into madness—she needed it to stop.

It had to stop.

Chapter Nine

A phone rang. Riley willed it to be silent. Her mind spun out of control. *From what? Oh, right.*

"Riley, it's your dad."

She pulled the pillow off her head and stared as Gabe handed her the blaring phone. Her hands shook as she reached for it. *Please don't let it be what I think.* "Dad?"

"Riley." His voice was strained. "Hey, hon, I've got some really bad news. I'm so sorry to have to tell you this, but your grandmother had a heart attack last night."

"Is she okay?" It was a stupid question.

He hesitated, and she inhaled sharply. "She passed away, Riley. It happened suddenly. They don't think she experienced any pain."

As if that makes it any better. Riley shuddered, too shocked to say anything. Her vision from the night before had been so real that she almost knew this was coming. *But if Grandma died from a heart attack, why the German men in the cabin?*

She tried to put her issues aside. "Is Mom okay?"

"She will be," he said. "She'll be happier when you get here."

"I'll be there as soon as I can."

Riley hung up the phone and lay back on the couch, numbness and shock creeping through her worn body. *So I'm a psychic now too?*

"What happened?" Gabe leaned into her. "Is everything all right?"

"My grandma had a heart attack last night. She's dead."

"Esther?" he asked, his tone rising. "You're kidding, right?"

"Why would I joke about that?"

"I'm sorry. That's not what I meant. It's just…" He trailed off, eyes revealing that his mind was somewhere else.

"It's just what?" Riley didn't know what to believe or whom to trust anymore.

"Nothing." His hand rested on his forehead as his eyes raced back and forth, giving away the anxiety he tried so hard to hide. "I'm sorry to hear that. If there's anything I can do for you or your family, let me know."

Riley narrowed her eyes and stared at him, hoping his true intent would emerge under close scrutiny.

"Gabe, you were about to tell me something last night before the…episode." She shifted in her seat, tucking untidy hair behind her ears. "What was it?"

He stood and walked toward the window, opening the blinds to stare at the street and the spot where the old man had stood the night before. "I have to go, Riley. I'm sorry again." He walked over to where she sat, rested a hand on her shoulder, and offered a pained stare. "Take care of yourself, will ya?"

"Damn it, Gabe, I need answers." She rose, slamming the pillow down on the couch. Tears filled her eyes. "Please. I'm begging you. Someone knows something. I feel like I'm losing my mind."

"Be strong." He looked at her, his expression heavy, as if he shared the same overwhelming feelings she was experiencing. His golden eyes were full of sorrow, and his back slumped with an unseen burden. "You're going to be okay."

Riley stared, bewildered and hurt. "Am I?"

He paused at the front door. She could hear his deep, strained breathing, as if he wanted to turn around and come back to her. But he didn't. The door slammed as he left, and the room closed in, forcing the last remaining air from her lungs. *Grandma is dead?*

Devastated, Riley couldn't fight back her fear or anger. She knew what she had seen, and it was no heart attack. And with Esther gone, her only source for answers had vanished. *And what about Gabe? On what planet is it being a good friend to leave someone like this?*

A new and terrible idea crept into her mind. *What if I had something to do with her death? What if I don't just see what's happening or going to happen, but I cause it to happen?* That kind of power was terrifying. *And impossible.*

"How are you feeling?" Abby's voice broke the early-morning silence.

Riley looked at her vacantly. "My grandma died last night."

"Oh my God, Riley, I'm so sorry." Abby wrapped her arms around her friend. "Are you okay?"

"Actually, no. Do you remember what happened to me at the party?"

"Yeah, you were plastered."

"I wasn't drunk."

"What are you talking about? You were hammered."

"Abby, I only had a couple drinks."

"You passed out. We practically had to carry you home."

"Stop!" Riley was irritated with this pointless dialogue. "Drunk or not, when I blacked out, I had a really crazy dream." She paused, wondering what Abby would have to say about this vision. "I saw someone murder my grandma."

"Esther was murdered?" Abby's mouth dropped open.

"No. I don't know. They said she had a heart attack."

"Jesus, don't scare me like that!" She relaxed back into the couch. "What do you mean you don't know? I'm not sure where you're going with this."

"I'm not either, but isn't it a little weird, a little too coincidental, that I have some crazy vision of my grandma dying the same night she passes away?"

"I guess. It is a little weird that something like this has happened to you before. What if you have a tumor or something?" Her face contorted into a worried frown.

Riley stared back, unconvinced. Abby tried again. "Or maybe you've got one of those genetic sixth senses."

"Maybe I'm just losing my mind."

The silence hung heavy for a few moments. *Abby must think I'm nuts.*

Abby stood and changed the subject. "Let's get you packed and on the road. I know your family needs you."

"I'm sorry. I don't know what's happening to me. These past few weeks have been so hard."

"I know." She smiled, trying to settle the situation. "And just know that I'm here for you if you need anything. I'm going to miss you."

"I'll miss you too. I'm really lucky to have you as a friend." *Although you should probably keep your distance, because I might be dangerous.*

Riley scanned the mess of boxes hopelessly, wishing she could burn them all and disappear to a place where she couldn't hurt anybody.

Chapter Ten

Gabe swung his truck into the driveway of the large house tucked into the foothills on the outskirts of town. It was a long driveway, bordered on both sides by rows of crowning cottonwood trees that formed an archway the entire length to the sprawling front lawn. Puffy white seeds blanketed the road shoulders, giving the effect that a light dusting of snow had fallen the previous summer night. Dappled sunlight filtered through the windshield as he drove through the shaded tunnel toward the monolith rising from the landscape ahead. He'd been there on many occasions, even lived there, but never with the burden he carried now. Gabe was angry, but he was also... *afraid?*

He turned off the engine, stepped from the truck, and gazed up at the massive home rising toward the sun. Tall pillars held up an expansive tiled roof that stretched ostentatiously across the property. It belonged in Beverly Hills, not the outskirts of Grand Junction, but for the number of people that came and went, and the business going on behind closed doors, the grandiose house was necessary. *Business.* He grunted. *That's what I'm here for this time.*

"Gabriel."

His attention shifted to the great wooden front door and the somber old man standing in its arched frame. The door, a gift from a monastery in Tibet, was Gabe's favorite part of the elegant home. It was impressive because it was old and historic, unlike the rest of the house, which was impressive because of its overwhelming size. The door had been poor but precious, keeping out the winter winds and protecting the monks from raiders at the top of the world. Now it adorned a house that, in Gabe's opinion, stood for something entirely different.

"I thought I'd see you here. Please come in," the old man said.

Gabe nodded and followed him inside. Matching white columns lined the yawning entrance hall, and a deep burgundy carpet accented the sprawling staircase leading to the upper chambers like an extended red tongue. Hammered gold and painted murals gilded the vaulted ceilings. Aromas of honeysuckle and roses filled each breath with air that seemed light and sweet, giving all those who breathed it a cleansing, euphoric feeling. Hundreds of windows opened to the outside world, causing light to bounce around the walls as if suddenly filled with life.

When it was first built many years before, Gabe had actually loved the place. Its beauty and architecture rivaled the villas of Italy and the palaces of France. Recently, though, it had become ominous, even hostile. Gabe shook the thought away.

The old man led Gabe through the house and onto a balcony overlooking the home's perfectly manicured lawn and gardens. Gabe grasped the railing and stared out at the mesa looming above. Below, the voices of a hundred songbirds rose from their perches among brightly colored flowers.

Gabe's eyes followed the pattern in the tiled walkway that led through a maze of blooming lilies and bright yellow snapdragons to the cerulean waters of a Greek-inspired swimming pool he'd spent many days in. Statues of women and children lined the waterway, while a large stone fountain depicting two familiar figures, a sorrowful-looking man and woman, stood exclusively in the center. Gabe eyed the woman sadly.

"Gabriel, be seated." The old man sat in one of the wicker chairs and directed Gabe's attention eastward. "They truly are beautiful, aren't they? I think mountains are my favorite part of nature. They are ever reaching skyward, never ceasing to test their potential. No trees, no birds, nothing but the clouds can challenge their upward reach. They have no heartbeat, and yet ever do they grow."

He smiled, his gray eyes twinkling as a light breeze tousled his snowy hair and beard. "They give hope to each of us that we may one day also reach into the sky and look down on all things beautiful." He paused, watching Gabe's eyes return to the woman in the pool. "The view from a mountaintop, Gabriel, after a long, hard climb, is the most spectacular of all views. The harder the climb, the more rewarding the sight."

It was silent. The warm wind blew through Gabe's hair, and he stared at the highest point of the mesa, sheathed in a ring of angry storm clouds. "I didn't come here to talk about mountains." He turned around.

"Ah, but aren't all challenges and problems we face mountains in and of themselves?"

"You know why I'm here."

"And you know my answer."

"You can always change your mind."

The old man sighed, his weary eyes probing Gabe's. "I am not in control of what happens next. I have done what I need to do to protect what needs protecting."

"But everything you are doing conflicts." Gabe's voice rose as his fingers stroked idly through his hair. "By protecting one, you hinder the other. To do my job, the job you asked me to do, I have to be in conflict with another, who is also doing what you have asked him to do."

A brightly colored parrot landed on the railing behind them, letting out an inharmonic caw and turning beady eyes on Gabe. The old man stretched out his hand, and the bird ruffled green and blue feathers, waddling sideways up his arm to perch like a pirate's pet on his shoulder.

"Free will can be a very scary thing," the man said. "The choices of so very few in this case, as it has always been, will determine the fates of us all. This particular quest, if you want to call it that, is out of my hands. She is not in this position because of me, Gabriel. You know that. We each must do what we think is right and hope that everyone else does the same. Someday that will happen. There will be a day when everyone gets it right, and what a magnificent day that will be."

"She's terrified, you know. She didn't say it, but she didn't have to. She thinks she's crazy." Gabe kneeled before the man. He knew he wasn't supposed to get this involved. He'd fought back his emotions for years, but he couldn't fight any longer. "We can help her. Change your mind. I'm begging you."

The old man grabbed Gabe's hands and held them gently. "Be careful, Gabriel. Your emotions lead you down a very dangerous road. I won't take sides. I never have. This is her path, her destiny. She must decide what to do with it."

"Then you've abandoned her?"

The old man's lips parted to release a small laugh. "I sent her you. I hardly think that is abandonment."

Anger coursed through Gabe. *It is not my place to be angry.* But he couldn't help it. "You actually think she would do it, don't you? You really think she has it in her to betray everyone? Because I've spent years with her now, and I know she couldn't. I know she wouldn't."

A new sadness flashed across the man's face, revealing a drawn, wrinkled side to the previously joyous visage. "Everyone has it in them, Gabriel. I have seen her, and she is a good person, of that you are correct. But we all have a dark side, and it is too unpredictable to trust. I'm hoping she can fix that. By not trusting her, I am helping her succeed."

Gabe felt increasingly helpless thinking about Riley and the man he would be pitted against if he tried to save her. "I've known him for my entire life. You've put us in an impossible situation. You've made us enemies."

"You'd kill him for her, then?"

"I'd kill anyone who tried to hurt her."

"And he would do the same to anyone who tried to harm what he protects."

"Then you've doomed one of us. You've set us up to destroy each other."

The parrot gave Gabe a final seething look and a high-pitched caw and flew off to join the others bathing in the waters below. The old man brushed his shoulder where the bird had sat and rested his chin in his hand.

"I needed two very capable people to watch over things that they would kill or die to protect. You will both do that, and therefore I have chosen correctly. I do hope, however, that that is not your fate, nor his."

Gabe stared at his trembling hands. He'd had this same assignment over and over, and he'd never gotten attached like this. Something in Riley had changed that. This wasn't a job to him anymore. It was a mission he could not fail.

"If that is your final word, then I must respect it," Gabe declared, looking up. "I will keep her alive, and she will end this. We won't let you down."

"You never do, Gabriel, and you never will."

But you will lose my brother, or you will lose me. He stared back at the clouds and felt the rage of the storm rising within him as well.

Chapter Eleven

Riley lowered the window and felt the warm June breeze whip her face as she drove along the interstate. *Today is going to be a long day.* She groaned, looking at her tired reflection in the rearview mirror. *I look like hell.*

She reached over and turned on the CD player her dad had installed after she'd informed him many times that artists didn't sell albums on tapes anymore. She smiled. Even the CD player was obsolete. She was as behind the times as her parents. "Country Roads" by John Denver emanated through the speakers. It seemed appropriate and calmed her nerves.

Riley hadn't been home since Christmas. She'd had school, friends, and a life that kept her occupied in Boulder. *Today, not only am I going home mourning the loss of my grandma, I'm also mourning life as it's been.* But after everything, it seemed like the right place to be.

The good-bye with Abby was hurried, and Gabe's abrupt departure didn't make any sense. *How could he possibly know something? How could he possibly be involved in any of this? Maybe he's having visions too. Maybe it's happening to both of us. I'll ask him about it once everything settles down at home.*

She shuddered, remembering the last time she'd made a similar comment. Esther was no longer around to answer those questions. Waiting for answers was risky.

Riley's eyes drew to the left, where a row of cottonwood trees stretched upward to the white mansion high on the mesa. *Gabe's house.* The mansion sparkled like a great opal in a sea of drab sand, and she wondered what Gabe was hiding up there, along with his other secrets.

She'd never been there, even though she'd known him since childhood. It always felt strange not knowing that part of his life, but he was insistent upon it. His parents had died when he was very young, and he'd been raised by an eccentric uncle whom Gabe said was painfully shy and preferred not to have visitors.

In high school, kids talked about sneaking up to the house and seeing the crazy old man flying on a broomstick or riding an elephant. Riley didn't put much stock in the bizarre stories. The descriptions of the gardens, however, tugged at her to peek into the forbidden realm of Gabriel Hart and his crazy uncle. The flowers, the fruits, the birds, the water features—they all sounded so magnificent. She'd never gone, though, no matter how tempted. She respected that he didn't want people up there. Gabe assured her the things she grew were much more beautiful and impressive anyway. Now, though, as the house looked down upon her with its marble columns and massive façade, she doubted her trees were even half as worthy as the spectacular things that lurked behind the walls.

She glanced back up at the rearview mirror, studying the troubled eyes staring back over the dark circles that accented them.

Life had been bearable up until last night. When she'd thought she was just going crazy, she could handle it—when it was just her that was affected. But the connection between her vision, Esther's death, and her role in it could not be ignored. *Karma. What have I done to deserve this?*

She agreed with the silence. She'd done nothing that warranted this nightmare.

———

Home sweet home. Riley turned into the driveway of the two-story house she'd grown up in, situated on ten acres a few miles west of Grand Junction. Sandstone cliffs and rolling desert hills dotted with sagebrush and junipers dominated the view. It was a harsh landscape, but Riley thought it was heaven on earth. The Colorado River stretched to the horizon, and the Colorado Plateau rose in the background.

Kiersten was already at home, her new Lexus parked next to the garage. Riley admired her older sister, who'd graduated top of her class at Stanford and landed a job making more money in the first year than Riley could hope for in a five-year period with her degree.

"Riley!" her mother called, running toward the car.

"Mom! How are you?"

"Oh, Riley, I'm fine," she sighed. "Your grandma had a good life. I think she was ready to go."

Who is ever ready to go? They walked together in silence up to the house. While Esther was old and had been lonely since their grandfather passed, Riley knew she hadn't been ready to go. She'd seen her tortured on a dirt floor. It was not a peaceful death, not something she had welcomed with open arms.

"Riley!" Kiersten ran from the house and wrapped her sister in a hug. "I'm so glad you're here."

As they entered the porch, Riley's father, silver-dusted hair flying in all directions and cooking spoon in hand, enveloped her in a hug. "All my girls are now safely home. Let's go inside. I've made lunch."

Riley's nose welcomed the warm, rich aroma of chicken and dumplings cooking in a Dutch oven on the stove. It was such a delicious and comforting smell that for a moment her senses enjoyed the mouth-watering assault, and she forgot about her worries and troubles of late. The familiarity of her family's smiling faces and the smell of home-cooked food all made her feel safer than she had in weeks. She wanted to grab everyone in the room and never let go.

"Your grandmother sure loved you, Riley." Her mom offered an encouraging smile.

I can't believe my last interaction with her was so confrontational. "When's the funeral?"

"Day after tomorrow," her dad replied. "We're meeting with someone from the funeral home this afternoon to finalize the remaining details."

"Is Uncle Kevin coming?"

Her mother tensed at the mention of her younger brother, and Riley immediately felt bad for bringing up her estranged uncle.

"We haven't been able to get a hold of him yet." Her dad ladled soup into bowls and placed them on the table. "We've left messages, but you know, it's been such a long time. We haven't had a good number or address in years."

Riley nodded and glanced away. Kevin Miller was the black sheep of the family, always with money or drug problems and only coming around when he needed more of either. He had dropped out of college and moved to Las Vegas to "live the dream," and things had gone downhill from there—gambling, prostitutes, excessive drinking, and then the drugs.

The last time Riley saw him was about four years ago on Christmas Eve when she was in her first year of college and had come home for winter break. It was an impossible evening to forget. The whole family was at Esther's. Riley and Kiersten had been sitting at the counter frosting cookies while her parents and Esther sat in chairs around the tree, wrapping presents. "God Rest Ye Merry, Gentlemen" had just come on the radio, and her father began singing in his deep, melodic voice. Everyone else joined in, and it was one of those perfect family Christmas moments that to Riley was pure magic but to any fly on the wall would have been a gag moment in a made-for-TV movie.

And then there had been a knock on the door. It was Kevin—Kevin and a woman none of them knew, whom he introduced as Delilah. Esther's face lit up. It was her first Christmas without her husband, but her prodigal son had come back for his first Christmas in years. Everything had gone okay the rest of the evening until Riley's mother had walked in on her brother and Delilah in the bathroom snorting cocaine. When confronted, he'd thrown a shampoo bottle and struck his sister in the head. Riley's dad rushed in, tackled Kevin, and hit him across the face. Esther screamed while Kiersten called 911. The night that had been so full of magic broke two hearts—her mother's and Esther's. Esther paid Kevin's bail, and they hadn't heard from him since.

Riley changed the subject. "I'm glad we're all here. Grandma would be happy seeing us all together."

"She is happy, Riley." Her dad beamed. "She's proud of you girls and is probably smiling down on us right now, wishing she could eat some chicken and dumplings." He looked toward the ceiling. "Sorry, Esther." He winked. "Now, who's hungry?"

The rest of the afternoon passed quickly, with Kiersten filling everyone in on her latest accomplishments and Riley's mother telling stories of growing up with Esther. The funeral home director showed up around three to work on arrangements, prompting Riley to get some fresh air. *I need stillness.*

The warm, dry air felt good in her lungs, and the prospect of solidarity and peace lifted her spirits. She trekked off toward the hills, and for a moment being back didn't seem like such a bad thing after all. She could come out every day and be alone with only hawks, junipers, and sighing wind to keep her company. A small mouse scurried across her path, leaving a trail of hurried footprints in the dirt as it disappeared beneath a pile of rocks. *Stillness.*

Riley hiked for nearly an hour before resting. There was an area by the river, not too far now, where she used to go when she wanted to be alone. She found her way to the dirt road leading to her secret spot and was surprised to see a vehicle speeding down the lane. *Nobody ever comes down this way.*

Riley ducked behind a cluster of willows and watched as a sporty silver car blew past, flinging up a scarlet tail of dust in its wake. The driver was dark haired and very attractive, probably only a few years older than Riley. She had a quick glance at him and then he was gone, disappearing around a corner in the distance. *Perfect timing! I wouldn't have minded spending the afternoon with that guy.*

She watched the dust settle where the car had vanished. The sunlight falling through the trees made each red speck its own small fire. *BMW—impressive.*

She walked on, wondering about the strange man alone in his expensive car down an unused back road. *He's probably a junkie—one of the rich guys in town who has a secret life in the backcountry of Colorado.*

Riley found the path and quickened her pace, eager to take off her shoes and cool down before the hike home. A breeze blew across the brown water, disturbing the cottonwood leaves and sending a shiver up her spine. She wriggled her shoulders, trying to get rid of the uneasy feeling as she unlaced her boots and slipped her feet into the chill water. She closed her eyes, soaking in the calming moment. A minnow nibbled at her toes, and she peered out, watching the small fish dart away to the floating reeds on her left.

Her heart crashed into her stomach. Mixed into the tangle of salt cedar and broken cattails where the creature disappeared, a dark mass of hair crept over the water's surface. Riley's spine prickled again, and she waded over to the tangled mess, her breath catching as a pale forehead and frightened blue eyes met hers.

———

Riley had never seen a body before, not even at a funeral, so when she stumbled upon the naked, mangled form before her, the world turned inside out, and time froze in a screaming nightmare. It was a young woman about her own age. Riley's mind wavered on the edge of consciousness as she grabbed a tree to steady herself, purging everything she had ever consumed in her life into the river.

"Oh, shit," she swore aloud, along with many other horrible but strangely comforting words. "Jesus."

The girl looked to be in her mid-twenties, and she had probably been very attractive in life before the butcher had done all he could to change that. Purple and black bruising formed a spotted band around her thin neck, and stab wounds shone sticky and red across her entire body. Dried blood coated her legs in a trail leading up toward her lower orifices. Vacant, lifeless eyes stared up at nothing, while peeling, wormlike lips hung limply from her face, preserving their final scream. Her long brown hair floated peacefully in the slow current of the river's edge, and a stronger sensation than sickness overcame Riley—fear.

Looking up and down the riverbank, she saw no one. The sounds of chirping birds made her want to scream and run for cover in the darkness of the trees. They seemed to be singing, "She's over here! She's over here!" *I have to move!*

Riley knew she couldn't leave without doing something. She thought back to programs she'd seen on TV, but it was one thing to watch detectives try to solve a cold case from the comfort of your recliner and another to be staring directly at a corpse that still had eyes. Her mind became hyperactive, crippling her ability to think. *Stillness. Stillness.*

Riley stood trembling on the bank of the river that had once been a place of comfort. Today it was a nightmare, the worst she'd had yet. Instead of calm, she'd stumbled upon chaos. She gripped the tree tighter, staring at the tumbling brown water and the empty body that drifted back and forth in the shoreline eddies. Her brain filled with a million crawling ants, each working hard to plunge her consciousness into darkness. Mind going blank, world going dark, losing the ability to think altogether, Riley's instinct took over for a split second, and she pulled out her phone to dial 911.

CHAPTER TWELVE

Numbness filled her veins. Riley sat on a cold, hard sofa. Her family sat gathered around, maybe even saying things, but the numbness had taken over not just her body but also her mind. There were other people too. Another family sobbed nearby. Men and women in uniforms bustled around the room. *Police station. They're going to want me to relive what happened.*

She lifted her head and let the unfeeling mental block slide away from her body like frozen molasses. Bright lights illuminated the busy waiting room, bouncing off the brass on the officers' uniforms. Brown couches filled the room and were all occupied. Tan walls grew closer together every second, and Riley worried they'd soon squeeze the air from her lungs.

"Miss Dale," said a husky voice from a tired-looking police officer. "How are you feeling?"

The officer was tall and broad shouldered, with dark, tousled hair and a face in need of a shave. Deep frown lines wrinkled his face, but he did not look unfriendly, just well worn. She felt as exhausted as he looked.

"I'm not really feeling at all." The sound of her hollow voice was startling.

"I understand. We do need to ask you some questions before you can go home, though, so when you are ready, let me know."

"I'm ready."

She followed the officer down an empty hallway filled with the same painful lighting and the same plain walls to a small room containing only a table and a few chairs that matched the hard thing she'd sat in moments before. He took a seat in one, pulling out a small black recording device, and motioned her into the chair's simple twin across the table. A mirror lined one wall. She wondered who was watching on the other side and what they expected to get from her. *Do they think I did this?*

"Miss Dale, I'm Detective James Rutherford. Before I ask you any questions, I need to give you some more information so you know how important anything you can tell me is. The girl you found was named Rachel Stanton, and she was not the first."

He let the silence hang in the air and studied her closely. Deep brown eyes honed in on every move she made—every twitch of her face, every flick of an eye. Riley worried that her mind might fail again. She swallowed hard, nodding, and he continued.

"Four girls have been murdered in the last six months in this part of the state. Rachel is the fifth."

"I've seen the news." Riley stared at her white knuckles.

He leaned forward in his chair, closing the gap between them. Strong hands folded in front of him, and she noticed how dry and calloused they were. He was not a cruel man, she could tell, but he was not soft either. Riley thought of the dead girls. They were lucky to have someone like him on this case. She tried to think back to the afternoon, but her mind, like her body, had purged itself after stumbling upon the murdered woman.

She peered up at him, shaking. "I didn't kill her."

The detective's eyes softened and he sat back. "We know. We checked your alibis, and evidence shows that a man is behind these hideous acts. You're not a suspect. Just a witness. If you have any information that can assist us, you might be able to protect other girls from becoming the next victim. And there will be more. We are dealing with a sick man. A man who can't stop what he is doing."

His words triggered something in the back of her brain. A BMW. An attractive man. A speedy getaway. The dust settled in her mind, and she was once again hidden behind the willows.

"Did you notice his hair color? Was it dark? Light?" The detective's gaze never moved from her face.

"I saw him." Her voice sounded so weak. "I was near the road but still in the trees. He didn't see me. He was driving a silver BMW. I don't know the model or the license plate."

Speaking seemed to bring back some confidence, and she realized she probably held the greatest piece of evidence this detective had to catch the murderer. The image of Rachel Stanton's broken body forced her on. *"There will be more."*

"He had dark hair. He was driving, so it was hard for me to tell anything about his height or weight. But his head was near the roof, so I'm guessing he was tall. He looked to be in his late twenties to early thirties." She blushed and glanced at the closed door. "I thought he was attractive." She felt stupid saying it. "I didn't see much. He was driving too fast."

"Anything else?" Detective Rutherford asked, excitement obvious in his voice.

"That's all. That's all I saw."

"You have been most helpful, Miss Dale." The detective rose from his chair and offered a hand up. "We'll keep in touch. If you remember anything else, please don't hesitate to contact me." His expression grew severe. "You were very lucky today."

Her pink cheeks reddened. She hated feeling like she'd done something wrong, or been useless.

Riley's parents waited in the lobby, anxiety stretched thinly across their worn faces. She walked toward them but was intercepted partway across the room by a dark-haired woman in tears. The woman threw her arms around Riley and squeezed tightly, filling Riley's ear and shoulder with deep, heavy sobs. The woman pulled away, and her pain-filled eyes found Riley's.

"Thank you for finding Rachel," she whispered through her grief. "Thank you for finding our little girl."

Riley stared back, overwhelmed by the woman's pain and wondering if she'd had to look upon her daughter's butchered corpse. She didn't know how to respond, so she hugged the woman back. "I'm so sorry. I'm so sorry for your loss."

The drive home was silent and uncomfortable. Riley didn't want to say anything, and she didn't think her family would know what to say even if she had wanted to talk about it.

She looked out the window of her mom's car and shuddered. Earlier she had wished she'd arrived at the river sooner to spend the afternoon with the mystery man in the BMW. The realization that she was lucky to even be alive was tremendous.

They pulled into the driveway. Riley was surprised at how late it was. Assuring her parents everything was fine, she excused herself to go to bed. She stared at the ceiling, thinking about her life and the out-of-control direction it was spinning in. It kept coming back to this—lying in bed wondering where it all went wrong and how it all tied together. It couldn't possibly be a string of disconnected bad luck. She was jobless. Her grandma was dead. She had seen the murdered body of a girl her age. She had visions that came true.

And worst of all, she had wanted to spend an afternoon skipping rocks with a serial killer.

Chapter Thirteen

R iley awoke the next morning to a shattering clap of thunder cutting through a dark, rainy sky. She had slept better than she'd anticipated, and the dreaded dreams had thankfully stayed away. *There's been too much death.* It wasn't something she'd spent much time worrying about—death—at least not until the last few weeks. It happened to everyone, sometimes after a long and happy life, sometimes abruptly and unfairly. Of course she wanted to go in the first manner, but since there was no real way to control fate, Riley hadn't spent much time stressing about what was in store for her. But now all she could imagine was ending up broken like Rachel, or executed like her grandma. She covered her head with a pillow, trying to keep the thoughts away.

Her room was as messy as her life, but even that wasn't enough to pull Riley out of a growing depression. She used to find joy in cleaning and putting things in order, but now it seemed like a chore to even rise from the bed and put on fresh clothes.

"Riley?" her mom called softly from outside the room. "Can I come in?"

"Yeah, I'm up." She tossed the pillow onto the floor with the rest of the clutter and turned weary eyes toward the door.

Her mom carried a tray with warm oatmeal and steaming hot chocolate. Riley accepted the food and savored a sip of the cocoa. Its warmth spread into her body, clearing some of the despair while offering a moment's reprieve from her collapsing mind. *I can't believe I still have an appetite.*

"Thanks, Mom. Look, I know you guys probably think I need to talk about what happened yesterday, but I'd really like to not go there right now. Can we just focus on Grandma and this family, and not on the rest of it?"

"Whatever you need, hon." Her mom sat down on the bed, eyeing her cautiously. "Speaking of your grandmother…um, well, we came across something unexpected in her will." She looked as confused as she sounded. "She left you her house, Riley."

Riley's jaw dropped. "What?" she asked, spilling hot chocolate on her lap as she sat up.

Her mom shrugged and handed over a plain white envelope. "She understood you, Riley. I know you didn't feel close to her or believe that you had much in common, but she really thought you were special. Mom was full of secrets that she'd never share with any of us. Perhaps she's ready to share them with you."

Maybe this is Grandma's way of answering my questions. The envelope contained two keys and the old ring. Riley held the mysterious little ring in her hand and stared transfixed at the twining trees she recognized so well. Her first reaction was to slip it on, but fear kept it in her palm. She placed the ring on her bedside table and dumped the keys into her hand. One key had a tag reading "house key," while the other was small and bronze with no label.

She returned the keys to the envelope and set it on the table next to the ring. Her head throbbed. She had no energy and was baffled by her grandma's decision to leave her entire house and most valued possession to her. Riley's mind kept wandering back to the recent visions and her last conversation with Esther. *It's all linked.*

"I'll be downstairs if you need something, okay?" Her mom leaned down for a hug and walked toward the door, hesitating in the opening. "I'm really sorry you have to deal with all of this. No one should have to."

Riley nodded. "Thanks, Mom." *If you only knew the half of it.*

The door closed, and Riley's attention returned to the ring. She poked it, then quickly removed her finger as if the object might bite or shock her. Nothing. *Stupid. This is ridiculous.*

Her grandma had worn the ring since Riley could remember. It was harmless. She grabbed it off the table and slid it onto her right ring finger. It fit perfectly, and nothing catastrophic occurred. *Grandma wanted me to have this for a reason. She wanted me to be the one to wear it.*

"I hope this helps me, Grandma," Riley said, looking at the ceiling, imagining the sky beyond. She lay back down and pulled up the covers. The ring felt cool and comforting on her finger. Like the chicken and dumplings—it was familiar, it was family, and it helped still the turmoil in her mind.

Death: the new theme of her life. Riley removed her black dress and slipped into a favorite pair of sweat pants. Esther's service had been beautiful. Favorite hymns were sung; Riley, Kiersten, and their mother read hopeful verses from the Bible; and her father led a moving prayer about life and the wonderful things that come after.

Everyone had been given the opportunity to share stories about the woman they were there to celebrate. It was special to hear about Esther's younger days. Many of her old friends had shown up and told countless tales about Esther's uncanny ability to grow anything, anywhere, anytime; about her love of food and family; and about how she never missed watching the Denver Nuggets play basketball.

Riley shared a story about one of the times she and Kiersten had been playing in the cornfields of their grandparents' neighbor, and he had chased after them with a rake. They had run straight home, jumped the fence, and dived under one of the beds in the house, shaking from head to toe in terror. When the farmer reached the edge of the fence, he asked her grandparents if they had seen two kids run by. They assured him they had not and then came inside to tell the girls everything was okay. It had been frightening, but Esther and her grandfather had laughed for hours about their two little delinquents.

While there had been much joy at the funeral, Riley couldn't shake the overwhelming, suffocating presence of death. It wasn't just the sadness of losing her grandma. It was the idea that she was dead, gone forever—lifeless like the mangled form of Rachel Stanton, both of them completely removed from the world. Riley knew she had a good life, and yet at times, especially recently, it was too much. *How do the people who have it so much worse wake up every day and do it over and over again?*

Even though it was warm outside, she pulled on a sweatshirt, kicked a pair of tennis shoes and a bra out of the way, and headed downstairs. While before she had craved solitude, today she needed company and distraction from her own thoughts.

Kiersten sat in the recliner, typing away on a laptop, designer glasses perched on the tip of her petite nose. She was never far from work. Their mom and dad relaxed on the couch, watching the news and drinking tea.

"We made you a cup." Riley's mother held out a warm mug and motioned to a place on the couch next to her.

Riley accepted the mug and sat. *The news. Probably the worst possible escape.* "Why don't we watch a movie? Something happy? Maybe a cartoon?"

Her dad patted her leg. "We'll turn it off in just a minute. I want to see what's going on with Iraq."

He turned up the volume and Riley sank into the couch. *I should have stayed upstairs.*

"President Cain was in Paris this evening, meeting with other members of the Council for Global Peace," the reporter said. "The doors are sealed, so we have no information yet on what has transpired, but we hope to release new developments as soon as we hear something."

"Sounds like there's nothing new," Riley said. "Guess you'll have to turn it off now."

"On another somber note," the woman began again, "the fifth body found yesterday in Grand Junction, Colorado, has been identified by police as twenty-four-year-old Rachel Stanton. Rachel had been missing since Saturday and was discovered near the Colorado River about ten miles from her home. Reports say that she died from strangulation and multiple stab wounds to the abdomen. This young woman, along with the four previously found, is being linked to the Rocky Mountain Murderer.

"Police do say they are encouraged about finding the killer, as the first real identifying clues have been discovered. They will not release what these clues are, but they seem to be hopeful for the first time since these tragedies began."

The room fell silent. Riley felt all eyes shift uncomfortably in her direction. She looked up and smiled, hoping they would assume she was fine.

Chapter Fourteen

*C*lues? *Not possible.* Anger rose within. The police were telling lies, trying to scare him. *I'm too good to get caught. I'm perfect at what I do.*

He sat in a chair, staring at the screen and the pretty woman who had gone back to talking about the war. *They are just lies. They're backed into a corner and need to tell people something.*

He did like his nickname, though—*the Rocky Mountain Murderer.* Although he thought of himself as the hunter, the other had a nice ring to it as well. He liked that they were talking about him, and not just on local news, but all across the country. *Right now the whole nation fears me more than they do that idiot in Iraq. I could be anyone—a friend, neighbor, colleague, husband…*

The doorbell rang, and he rose to answer it. A young girl, about seventeen or so, with too much makeup and poorly bleached hair, stood holding a box of pizza. Her demeanor changed from bored to intrigued when she saw him. He knew he was attractive. It made the killings almost too easy.

"That'll be $12.75." Her tone was coy and flirtatious.

He flashed a smile. *Stupid girl. The things I could do to you.* "Beautiful night, huh? Let me go grab my wallet."

He caught the girl peering in after him. Probably wishing she was off work and could spend the night wrapped in his arms.

"Here you go." He handed the girl a twenty-dollar bill and winked. "Keep the change."

She took the money, scribbled something on the receipt, and handed him the piece of paper.

"Call me sometime." She bit her lip as she turned to leave. *It's almost too easy.*

"I'm too old for you," he replied with as much false charm as possible. *And I'd slit your throat if you were my type.* "But thanks for the pizza."

He closed the door, grinning. Girls like that made it almost boring, but they still did wonders for his ego. *I'll look into this evidence thing tomorrow. I bet it's nothing, but just in case.* He knew he could flirt his way into answers. Taking a bite of pizza, he flipped through the channels to see who else was making him a priority.

Chapter Fifteen

An old two-story wooden house with dormer windows, wraparound porch, and a peeling coat of brown paint loomed above furrows of newly sewn corn: *Grandma's house.* The yard was xeriscaped with native vegetation—cactus spikes, shrubs, and twisted juniper trees. To one side of the house sat Esther's garden, an oasis in a water-starved landscape. Fruit trees and flowers blossomed in vibrant contrast to the dull sages, earthy sand, and washed-out paint shedding from the house. The home backed up to the foothills, with a great view of the mesa and, in the fall, enough ripe corn to make it look like a ship sailing on a golden sea at sunrise.

These were the cornfields of Riley's childhood, where she'd pretended to be an Indian, a farmer, an explorer, or Hercules. These were the fields of the epic farmer chase. And now these were the fields that held the house and the secrets of Esther.

"Looks like I'll need to help with some painting." Her dad rested a hand on her shoulder. "Still, a pretty incredible piece of real estate for a twenty-two-year-old."

Moving in occupied the day. Riley and her dad shuffled furniture while Kiersten and her mom worked to make the house Riley's. Each passing hour saw more clothes hung in closets, more books lined on shelves, and more posters decorating the walls. Open doors and windows brought fresh air and sunlight inside, quickly resuscitating the old home. At the end of the day, her mom made lemonade in the scrubbed, sparkling kitchen, and they all sat out on the front porch to watch the sunset.

"Thanks for helping me move in." Riley sipped her drink and leaned back against the porch railing.

"Of course," her mother replied. "Do you want someone to stay with you tonight? Or you can always stay at home until you adjust, if you'd like."

She thinks I'll be scared. She's right. "Mom, if I let myself be afraid, I will always be afraid. I'll call Abby and have her come down for the weekend."

"Well, we're leaving a shotgun under your bed anyway," her dad interjected, pointing a stern finger in her direction. "Just in case."

"And every door and window will be dead bolted, locked, and booby-trapped, I promise." Riley grinned.

"You know we worry, Riley. After all that's happened, this world just doesn't seem safe anymore." His voice was strained.

The sun touched down at the top of the hills and burst into a fiery paint splatter. Reds and oranges streaked through the fading blue before being consumed by a deepening darkness. A single star emerged, pulsing in the final moments of pale light before being joined by its infinite brothers and sisters.

"I'm heading back to Denver tonight," Kiersten said as Riley's family stood to leave. "I'll miss you. Come visit soon, okay?"

"I will." She hugged them and watched their car pull away. Letting out a deep breath, she turned to go inside the house. *My house. Time to get used to my house.*

Riley made it through the night, barely. In truth, being alone terrified her. Every time sleep began to descend, she found herself surrounded by images of butchered women, homeless old men, fiery swords, and maniacal laughter. And each time one of those horrors crept in, she'd peer over her covers into the lonely darkness, swearing someone was in there, watching. *I'm calling Abby tomorrow. I can't do this any longer.*

Morning dawned and Riley grabbed for her phone. "Abby!" she exclaimed upon hearing her friend's voice. "You have to come stay with me this weekend. I need my best friend more than ever."

"Riley!" Abby sounded just as animated. "I'll be there. I have some stuff to catch you up on. It's nothing compared to what's been happening to you. Whatever that even means. I can't talk long, but I promise to head down Friday after class."

Knowing that her friend would be visiting soon helped pass the rest of the day and made the week fly. Riley was able to get some sleep and finish unpacking. She kept her mind off things by cleaning, organizing, and reorganizing the house. Every surface was dusted twice, every knickknack moved a half inch to the left, and by Thursday evening the place actually looked like a warm and welcoming home.

"I can do this." She trudged up the stairs to her bedroom. *Abby will be here tomorrow. This place is starting to feel right. I*

*think maybe in some tiny way, the weirdness is beginning to fade.
I mean, nothing has happened in a week.*

Riley got ready for bed and paused before cracking a window. *It's okay. I'm on the second story.*

Warm, fresh air relaxed her. The sound of insects chirping and calling to one another was tranquil. An open window seemed to keep the nightmares at bay. Peaceful thoughts of friends and family, and the warm desert breeze, lulled her into slumber.

———

Riley blinked, rolling over to welcome the day as bright sunlight streamed through the window. The clock read 8:45 a.m.—only twelve more hours until Abby would arrive. After eating breakfast and showering, she snuggled into the brown recliner that had once been her grandfather's favorite sports-watching perch. Her parents had wanted to get rid of the ugly old thing, but Riley couldn't bear to part with it. The fuzzy fabric had worn off in more places than not, and a small cloud of antique dust poofed up every time someone sat down. It was one of those mementos so tied to a person that letting it go was tantamount to a permanent farewell. No one understood that those holes in the fabric and the dust were all she had left of her grandfather.

Riley flipped on the television, but Friday morning programming options geared for five-year-olds ensured the activity didn't last long. She leaned back and surveyed the room.

Everything was in order and then some. *This is going to be the longest day ever!* Her gaze drifted to the ceiling. *Damn.*

She had avoided this moment all week, but she knew it needed to happen, and at least it would occupy some time. Trudging up the stairs to the second floor, Riley eyed the attic door. *There's no reason to be afraid. It's just a creaky old storage room.* But she'd seen enough horror movies to know that bad things happened more often in the attic than they did elsewhere. With her luck she'd probably run into something terrible up there.

Riley turned the knob and pulled open the door leading to the dark room. Hazy light filtered in through a filthy window, and dust motes danced in the muted rays that touched down onto faded floorboards. Boxes stood floor to ceiling along the walls, and forgotten furniture lay scattered where space allowed. Her grandmother's antique sewing machine and grandfather's treasured gun case sat in one of the dark corners.

Riley switched on the light, trying to decide where to begin. She yanked open the grimy window and sighed as a clean breeze broke through the musty wall of mothballs and stale air. Walking to the nearest stack of boxes, Riley pulled the top one off the pile and sat down on the floor to rummage.

There were Barbies, GI Joes, toy cars, and china sets; gold-rimmed books, doll clothes, and small wooden blocks. She thought of her mom as a kid playing with the dolls in the backyard while Uncle Kevin, still young and innocent, ran around reenacting scenes from war stories passed down from his father.

She moved across the room to the gun case and pulled on the locked door. *Maybe this is where the mysterious key belongs.* After examination, however, she could tell the lock was the wrong size. She scanned for any sign of a key but found nothing. *I'll have to search for that later. Never know when an old revolver might come in handy. Dad will feel better knowing I have an arsenal of protection at my disposal.*

Hours passed exploring the remaining boxes, with most of the time spent admiring old photographs. Esther had the same nervous expression in every picture, and Riley couldn't help but feel sorry for her. It was also shocking to see how much Esther had looked like Riley in her younger years. People always remarked about the resemblance, but it had been hard to visualize. Now, looking down at the photos, Riley was staring at a black-and-white version of herself. Some of the pictures made her laugh, some cry, and by midafternoon, exhaustion set in from all of the emotional ups and downs.

"I need a break."

Riley wiped her forehead with grubby hands and stood to go downstairs. As she moved toward the steps, a small, ornately painted gold-and-bronze chest tucked deep under the eaves caught her eye. Senses on alert, she knew without reservation this was the treasure Esther's key opened. *Grandma wanted me and me alone to know what's inside.* Riley retrieved the box from its hiding place, turned off the light, and raced down the stairs to find the key she had stashed in a coffee table drawer next to the recliner.

The key felt cool and delicate in her hand. As she stared at the box, her mind wandered to the ring still adorning her finger. She'd spent weeks being confused, overwhelmed, scared, and angry. Was it all about to become clear? Trembling hands inserted the small key into the opening. The intricate bronze work was a perfect match.

Riley hesitated, remembering the sandstorm and the man with the fiery sword—his warning to never return—the gunshot that ultimately killed Esther. *Is this Pandora's box?* Maybe she didn't want to know what was inside.

But in the end it didn't matter what it was. Esther wouldn't leave anything that would hurt her, or anything she couldn't handle. *Whatever is in this box, whatever instructions she left, I have to follow.*

Her heart pounded as she turned the key in the lock and lifted the lid. *This is it. This will make it all clear. I will know…*

Confusion overtook excitement, which quickly turned to disappointment as she lifted a faded piece of paper off the top. It was a letter addressed to Esther—that much was obvious. But it was written in German. Riley had no way to understand the strange words.

She rifled through the box, pulling out more letters written on the same worn-out paper, all addressed to her grandmother and all signed by the same man, Wilhelm Bieglböck. Near the bottom she came across an unopened envelope addressed to Wilhelm. She unsealed it and pulled out a letter. The scrawl was delicate, the paper a faded pink stationery signed by Esther. This letter, like the ones before, was written in German. Riley slumped, surrounded by inaccessible memories, and stared at the empty box in frustration. *These look like love letters, not answers.*

As she stuffed the papers back into the box, a serrated white edge sticking out of the loose fabric in the lid caught her eye. Two photographs had been shoved into the seam. In the first photo, there was no mistaking her grandmother, whose face mirrored the girl staring down at her. A man, tall and fair, stood next to her holding her hand. He was handsome, though he looked like he'd been through hell. Stringy blond hair hung loosely around a hungry face.

Regardless of his situation, he seemed very happy with the woman next to him. They were smiling, maybe even laughing. Esther did not look afraid but rather alive and in love. Her face was eager for the next big adventure, and Riley knew this picture was what she wanted her to have. No one needed to speak German to know from this photo that Esther had been different.

Maybe her grandmother hadn't left answers, but she had wanted Riley to know she wasn't always afraid—that she had once been free and full of life, and in love with someone else. The photo was dated May 1, 1945, only a month before Esther left for America. Riley pondered the fair-haired lover and why Esther had left him for her grandfather only thirty days later.

The second photo was a black-and-white of a sorrowful brunette holding a stoic infant. The names on the back read "Rina and Abe." The date was identical to the first photograph.

Riley didn't recognize the faces or the names. She laid the second picture back in the box and closed the lid.

The frustration vanished, replaced by a heightened curiosity. Abby had studied German in high school and college, so tonight they were going to learn a lot more about Esther than anyone ever suspected. Riley left the box on the floor by the TV and placed the photo of her grandmother on a table next to a window with a view of the mesa. Esther was so happy, so alive. It would be wrong to shove her back into the darkness of the box. *I wish I'd known this woman. I wish I still had the chance.*

A tear rolled down her cheek. Even at the funeral, she had not really cried, but now she did. Riley missed the woman in the picture—the woman she would never truly get to know.

CHAPTER SIXTEEN

*K**nock, knock, knock.* Riley jumped. She'd been spaced out all afternoon in the recliner, thinking about her grandmother and what possible connection there could be between the photos and her visions.

"Abby!" She threw open the door and flung herself into a hug. "I've missed you. It's lonely without a roommate!"

"I've missed you too!" Abby grinned, squeezing back.

They laughed and went inside to the living room. Abby tossed her overnight bag onto the sofa and collapsed next to it. Riley sank into the nearby chair, hugging her knees tightly to her chest.

"So tell me what's up," Abby said with pitying eyes. "I know you've said you're okay, but let's be serious. Your grandma died, you inherited a big, scary house that you are living in all alone, and you saw a dead girl. You can't be okay. I wouldn't be okay!"

Riley bit her lower lip. "I'm really not doing so well, but I don't have a choice. I'm kind of trying not to think about any of it. Trying to distract myself, you know?"

"Well, if you want to talk, that's what I'm here for," Abby reassured. "But I'm also a very good distractor."

Riley dug into her pocket, pulled out the key, and tossed it to Abby, who caught it with a quizzical look. Removing the ring from her finger, Riley handed that over as well.

"Actually, there is something I need your help with." Riley launched into the story of inheriting the ring and the key, searching through the attic, and discovering the box of letters.

"So the tree on the ring matches the tree you saw in your dream?" Abby's eyes betrayed skepticism.

"Abby, I know you thought I was crazy when I had those episodes at school, but something strange and very real is happening. The tree, the warrior, the storm—it was all real. And when I confronted Grandma about it, she seemed scared. She all but said I was right but that she couldn't tell me anything. And then I watched her die, and sure enough, the next day she was dead. And then there's Gabe. Gabe knows something too but won't tell me."

"I believe you, Riley." Abby nodded. "And I promise I don't know what is happening to you, and if I did, I'd tell you. But how can I help? Where do we go from here? Do you want me to talk to Gabe?"

"No, I've tried that. If he won't tell me, then he won't tell you. Basically, at this point, I need you to be my translator. Grandma left me these clues, so she obviously wants me to know what all of it means."

"I'll do my best."

"We'll get the gist of it. I just feel like it's part of the puzzle, you know? Like this is the next step to sorting out the mess."

Abby gave Riley a look of concern and exasperation. She patted the space on the couch next to her. "What the hell have you gotten yourself into, Riley Dale?"

Riley handed the stack of letters to her friend and plopped down next to her with a smile. "You tell me."

———

Abby Weaver glanced back and forth between her excited friend and the stack of letters, wanting to believe Riley. In her heart she did believe her, but it was too implausible a thing to fully wrap her mind around. Riley had been through a lot, and Abby wished she could do more. If translating these letters would bring relief, then she would do her best.

After all, Riley was her best friend. They'd first met at eight years old, the day Riley saved her life while ice-skating on a frozen lake. Abby had skidded over a thin patch of ice and fallen through into the freezing water. She'd grabbed at the fragile edges of the hole, but each time they crumbled beneath her fingers. Riley was the first person to reach her, and without fear for her own safety, she had pulled Abby from the frigid water. There was a wild spark in Riley's eye that day, and afterward she couldn't remember the incident. Abby did, though, and they had been inseparable ever since. That day, Abby realized there was something different about her friend. She might not always understand what Riley was going through, but if she said it was so, then it must be.

"Let's take a look at these mysterious letters then, shall we?" Abby picked up the top document and scanned the foreign words. "Ready?"

She took a deep breath, shaking. *It's just a piece of paper.*

My Dearest Esther,
The days seem so long, the ones without you unbearable. I
have been in hiding now for three years and realized when I
awoke today that I've forgotten what the warmth of sunlight
on my face feels like. The only beautiful thing from the out-
side world that I have any connection to is you. You radiate
like the sun I so long for. I wonder if I will ever see it again.

I am scared every day for my life. I will not enter one of the
camps with my fellow Germans and fall victim to Satan's Jews. I
will die before I let them take me. Hope that the Allies will come
is fading. Hope in anything is fading. You wrote in your last letter
that you had found Hitler in one of the camps and gained access
to speak to him. He does not deserve the fate you ask of him, but
selfishly, I hope he concedes so that I may once again be free.

You are the one light for all of us in darkness. Please
come soon. I love you.
Wilhelm

Silence filled the room. Abby stared at the letter and reread pas-
sages that didn't make sense. *Fellow Germans in camp? Satan's*
Jews? She observed Riley, who looked equally confused. "Um"
was all she could manage.

"Did he say my grandma had been to see Hitler?" Riley
looked puzzled. "You can't have read that correctly. Esther was
Jewish. There's no way she could see Hitler."

"That's what it says." Abby reread the statement. "'You
wrote in your last letter that you had found Hitler in one of the
camps and gained access to speak to him…'"

"Maybe there's more than one Hitler?" Riley leaned forward, chin resting in her palms.

"I don't think so. Not more than one significant Hitler." Abby looked back at the letter. "And how about the part about not going to the camps with his fellow Germans? It seems a little backward to me."

"Read more." Riley tapped her fingers on the coffee table. "Maybe the others will explain it. Maybe it's code or something?"

Abby picked up another letter from the stack and began to read.

My dearest Esther,

Do you remember the time in Nuremburg before all of this happened, when we spent an entire day by the lake? What I wouldn't give to swim in that water again with you. My thoughts have been on that day of late.

Yesterday the house next to ours was raided and two families were seized. There was a gunshot. Johan was killed. Johan was the butcher in town and a good man. Now his wife and three kids must face the camps alone. I weep for them.

I've thought about what you told me on our last visit, and it seems too fantastic to wrap my head around. I know you would not tell me lies, so I must believe what you say. I cannot accept that I am a killer, though. I cannot accept that some part of me would do the things to others that are being done to us. I sit here in my cage, eating soured food and living in my own waste. How can I be out there doing those things as well?

Please come back to me. I am desperate for your love.
You have all of mine,
Wilhelm

"'Too fantastic to wrap my head around.' Abby, that sounds a lot like how I'm feeling about my situation." Riley hovered over the stack of letters as if she'd suddenly be able to read them.

"Yeah, but it still doesn't clarify anything. In fact, I feel even more confused. He talks about being locked away in hiding for three years and then finding out he's also a killer." Abby paused, trying to make some sense of it. "Maybe he's mentally unstable. Maybe your grandma found out something about him that he didn't know. Like he blacks out and kills people."

"But it sounds like they loved each other," Riley replied. "Esther wouldn't be involved with a crazy person."

"But these are all letters from Wilhelm. Maybe he loved her but it wasn't returned."

Riley shuffled through the pile, pulling out the faded pink letter written to Wilhelm. "Read this one. This is from Esther."

Abby let out another heavy breath and shook her head.

My dearest Wilhelm,
I write to you in haste, hoping you will get this letter and understand why I must do what I am about to do. I have to go back. I cannot stay here any longer. There is a man who will take me to America, a man who loves me and whom I can learn to love in return. Never a love like ours, but

enough to make it through life with some hope. We will never see each other again, my love, and nothing breaks my heart more than that painful truth. Michael says I must go into hiding and that he will ensure my other is protected as well.

I have failed. It will be someone else's duty to fulfill my obligation. While I hate to let everyone down, I know in my heart that I cannot continue. I have, however, succeeded in my endeavors with Hitler and believe the war will be over soon. My greatest hope is that you will have the opportunity to know peace again, the opportunity to breathe free air, and the opportunity to find love and have the family we dreamed of. My departure will keep you safe. I am heartbroken about leaving, but your safety and opportunity to lead a normal, happy life are the most important things to me. I will think of you every day until I leave this world and we can be together once more.

All my love,
Esther

Silence fell on the room again. Abby looked up and saw Riley's wide green eyes searching for an unknown object in the darkness.

"Well, I guess I was wrong," Abby mumbled. "It sounds like she loved him a lot."

Riley nodded, her eyes looking like they might burst from her head. "Abby, she talked about Hitler again and ending the war. Who the hell was my grandmother?"

"Who is Michael?" Abby asked.

Riley ignored the question. "She didn't love my grandfather. She was with him for safety."

Abby was speechless. She wanted to comfort her friend. Reading these letters had not brought answers, only more questions.

"What did she fail at?" Riley continued. "What kind of power did Esther think she had if she was worried about letting everyone down? What the hell does that even mean?"

Abby opened her mouth but could find no words, so she shook her head. "Do you want me to read more?"

"No. I think that's all I can take for now. I need to think. It sounds like crazy talk."

"I feel like this did more harm than good."

"No, this was important. I don't know why yet, but this was supposed to happen. Thanks again for doing this. I know it's got to be totally weird."

Abby smiled, trying to reassure her friend. "It is totally weird, Riley. But I'm glad you're letting me in on it."

Riley reached for the letters Abby had read. She stared at them in silence for what seemed like an hour.

"I think I need a drink." Abby stood and made for the kitchen. "You sure you're okay?"

Riley nodded and continued to stare at the pages she couldn't read, trying to decipher answers Abby knew she'd never find.

CHAPTER SEVENTEEN

D r. Abraham Reitz sat in his book-lined study in his favorite Victorian chair, sipping Scotch and staring at a blank space on the wall. His mind had been troubled of late, ever since the strange encounter in class with Riley Dale, and it only heightened after she fainted during final exams. It was chilling to see a student unconscious on the floor, with no way to help. *But why had that happened? And what was the strange energy emanating from her all semester?*

In addition, the anniversary of his mother's death was approaching. She'd been gone for a long time, but the painful reminder never grew easier to bear. They had been very close. He was all she had, and he'd felt a fierce need to protect her and try to make up for the horrible things that had happened to her. Dr. Reitz glanced at a framed photo on the wall, a faded black-and-white of a sorrowful brunette cradling her baby in gaunt arms—him and his mother right after her liberation from the camp.

Every year around the time of her death, he'd be haunted by nightmares, haunted by the things his wicked father had done to her and her people. His mother never spoke of it, but the burns down her body and the thick, ugly scars on her abdomen, as well as a little Internet research, told him all he needed to know.

My father. His mother wouldn't give up the name either, but he'd figured that out as well, based on where she'd been held and the doctor who'd served the camp at that time.

The doctor. Teeth clenched, he reached into a drawer on the small table next to him and pulled out a faded photograph of an unsmiling, uniformed man. Abraham had his looks but little else. With shaking hands, he stared at the face on the paper. He kept the photo not for love, but to remind himself that men like that existed. *Curse you, Wilhelm Bieglböck. I hope you're rotting in hell with the rest of them.*

Chapter Eighteen

Jackson Cain lay in bed staring across the room at a portrait of George Washington. He used to love that painting. It reminded him of the courage and strength it had taken to form the great nation he now led.

Recently, though, the portrait seemed to mock him, seemed to say, "I can defeat the British army and build my own nation with a bunch of boys in mismatched trousers and piss-poor muskets, but you can't even win a war with the strongest military in the world and the most high-tech equipment known to man." *Fuck you, George.*

The meeting in Paris hadn't gone well. El-Hashem had sent a video of himself beheading one of his own men, whom he'd wrapped in an American flag, his hair bleached and his face painted white. While the video had been troublesome, that hadn't been the really disturbing part of the meeting. It was the decision they had come to, the Council for Global Peace, which kept him up at night now, swearing at George Washington. Even though he knew it was the only option left, he couldn't shake the feeling that it wasn't the right option. *But if there's only one viable course, it has to be right.*

The president lived on a pedestal, both for his country and for the world, and they were all looking to him to fix this, and to fix it in one particular way.

His wife stirred. He'd awakened her again. "You're restless, Jackson."

He smiled. "I'm always restless, sweetheart. It's part of the job."

"Can you talk about it?"

The simple answer was no, he couldn't talk about it. But he needed to.

"We're dropping bombs next week on Iraq. And I mean bombs, plural. We will level Baghdad."

His wife was silent, her expression hidden except for a small tear that formed in the corner of one eye.

He looked away, agreeing with her. It was horrific. But El-Hashem had terrorized the world for too long. He'd killed thousands of his own people and others in attacks around the world. His message to them had been clear. Now it was time he received one of his own.

CHAPTER NINETEEN

The only time Riley had ever seen her grandmother without the ring was at the pool one summer when it had slipped off her finger in the water and gone missing. Esther reacted as if she'd just been diagnosed with cancer or lost a loved one. Riley and Kiersten tried cheering her up, even dove to the bottom to search for it, but the pool was huge, and they couldn't find it. Tears streaming down her face, Esther had perched on the edge of a lawn chair, pale and shaking. The response seemed odd to the little girls. Riley lost stuff all the time and never got that upset about it.

Worried about their grandma, however, Kiersten yelled for a lifeguard. When the staff learned how important the ring was to the old woman, they blew the whistle for everyone to get out, donned goggles, and combed every inch of the bottom of the pool. Several minutes later a lifeguard surfaced, ring raised high above his head, shouting, "I've got it!"

For years after that, Riley was confused by her grandmother's decision to wear the ring to the pool, knowing how easily it could get lost. Only now did she realize that her grandmother didn't dread losing the ring so much as she feared being without it.

Riley had hoped the letters would shed light on the antique band, but not one had made even the slightest mention of it. After Abby left, Riley spent countless hours attempting to solve the meaningless riddle. But the more she recited lines from the letters, and the more she thought back to what had happened, the less any of it made sense. If there was a connection, it was hidden behind more than a language barrier.

And there was the ring, innocently circling her finger as if it played no part in the conundrum. Without knowing why, she understood that was where it needed to stay. *If Esther was more afraid not to wear it than to lose it, then I should be too.*

Riley jumped as a blaring noise from her phone shattered the silence.

"Hello?"

"Miss Dale. It's Detective Rutherford. Listen, I was hoping you could come down to the station this afternoon. We've pulled some guys off the street who match your description, and we wanted to see if you could give us a positive ID on any of them."

No. That's the last thing I want to do. "What time do you need me there?"

"Any time that works for you. I'll be here."

"Okay. Give me an hour."

In all of the excitement, she'd almost forgotten about the murder. Now bile crept up her throat at the notion of seeing the person who'd killed Rachel. *If I can point him out, then other girls will live. I guess I can handle a little discomfort.*

––––––––

The drive to the station went way too quickly. She despised the idea of confronting what she'd tried so hard to forget. *It's about the girls, though. Not you.*

Her mind returned to Esther and the letters. *If she had been so in love with Wilhelm Bieglböck, then why have none of us heard of him? Surely if she'd been in love with this man, she would have told someone. How painful to keep something like that a secret.*

As she pulled into the parking lot, lost in thought, she almost hit a woman walking to her car.

"Jesus! Watch where you're going!" the woman shouted, holding up her fist.

Riley waved apologetically, trying to refocus on the task at hand. *Talk to Rutherford. Get out as soon as possible.*

In haste she flung open the car door, accidentally scratching the silver paint on the vehicle next to hers. "Shit. You've got to be kidding me."

She surveyed the damage. *Of course it's a nice car. Another BMW. Another silver BMW. There seem to be a lot of those around here lately.*

Goose bumps rose on her skin, and despite the June heat, a chilling substance like ice water began pumping through her veins. Riley backed away, her mind flashing between the day out on the back roads and the present. A flash of silver speeding by. *The same silver? Not possible.* She shook the feeling away. *Lots of people have silver BMWs. There has to be more than one in the entire town of Grand Junction.*

Not letting fear undo her, she scribbled her contact information on the back of a crumpled grocery receipt, haunted by the karma she would invoke if she didn't, and made for the station.

Detective Rutherford entered the lobby looking shabbier and more exhausted than during their first meeting. His dark hair was in need of a good wash, and the stubble that had adorned his face had grown into the makings of a small beard. He appeared more mountain man than detective.

"Miss Dale." He led her back through the same sealed doors into the long, bleak hallway where she'd been before. "I'm glad you could make it. I know this isn't easy, but just remember what you are doing for these girls and their families."

They entered a small, dim room illuminated only by a window looking into another brightly lit room full of men. The men were lined up, waiting for Riley to end their freedom. She hated the whole thing.

"It's okay. They can't see you," the detective reassured. "This glass is one way."

She peered down the line of suspects. "Look, Detective. I really can't be certain. I mean, I only saw him for a few seconds and then he was gone."

"Take as much time as you need. Sometimes it can take a while for something to jar your memory. We're in no hurry."

Riley felt hot and sweaty—not like she was about to pass out and have another vision, just extremely uncomfortable.

Scanning the line, she couldn't recollect seeing any of them before. They were all tall with brown hair, but one was too heavy, one too hairy, another had eyes too close together, and one had a facial scar she definitely didn't recognize. They had similar features, but none of them exactly fit the guy she had seen. *He was so attractive. No! He's a monster.* But in reality, that was the problem she was running into staring down the queue of men: none of them was as attractive as the killer.

"He's not here."

"Are you sure? Do you need more time?"

"No, I'm positive. None of these men are the man I saw."

The detective sighed, clearly disappointed. "Well, thanks for coming in. I know this isn't easy. I'll walk you out."

They strode down the hallway in silence, Riley feeling guilty for not being able to help more. The detective paused at an open door and leaned in to speak to the officer inside. Riley stopped to wait.

"I have something I need you to sign, Zach. Can you meet me in my office here in five?"

Riley glanced at the man sitting behind the desk—the incredibly good-looking man with dark hair she'd seen only once before, sitting with the same posture in which he now sat. Pale gray eyes glinted above a dazzling smile.

"Sure thing, James." He grinned. "Whatever you need."

Riley tensed, overcome with a crushing inability to breathe. She swayed, emitting a strangled noise as Detective Rutherford rushed to her side. "Riley, are you okay? Let me get you a chair."

That brought her back. "No!" She took one last fearful glance at the man called Zach and bolted for the door. All she wanted to do was put as much distance between herself and that cubicle as possible. *I must be wrong. I must be wrong. This can't be happening.*

It was one thing to try to spot the beast from behind protective glass. But to walk right up to his cage and unknowingly dangle your finger in it was too much. *I have to tell the detective. But I can't go back. I can't go near that place!*

The only option was to run and hide. It was like the cornfield and the farmer—safety lay in hiding under the bed. She ripped the piece of paper with her contact information from the windshield of the BMW and jumped into her car, barely touching the brakes until she skidded into the driveway of her home. Inside, she locked and dead bolted every door, then stood in the kitchen screaming, allowing the terror to escape from her body. This was a new kind of evil, a wickedness lurking among the good. *And playing like he protects them! A police officer? I could call 911 and end up with him!*

Riley leaned over the kitchen sink and vomited. She'd seen death through death's eyes, and who would ever suspect someone they all trusted? It made her question everything she thought was true. *If someone who is supposed to protect you is really the greatest danger, then what?*

The shaking wouldn't stop. Her breathing was erratic. She thought she might faint. And then a more terrifying thought crossed her mind. *He's seen me. He saw my face. What if he knows why I was there and who I am? He could get my information from the detective. And then what?* But she didn't really need that question answered. He would come for her, and she would be number six.

Her only hope was that the detective didn't share information about his case with everyone. *After all, my safety is important too. He wouldn't jeopardize that, would he?* It was too much to hope for. She had to call Rutherford and hope he believed her.

CHAPTER TWENTY

Zachary Stone removed his gun belt and tossed it onto the couch. He cracked open a beer and stood in the darkness of his home, wondering about the strange girl at the station. He knew what the detective was working on—knew whom he was trying to find. *So what connection does this girl have? Is she the "evidence"?*

Sure, she was his type, and if he ran into her in a dark alley…But for the life of him he couldn't remember ever encountering the terrified girl before. Her unusual reaction to him made him nervous. Typically, women swooned and fell all over themselves in his presence, but the brunette had looked at him like he was the devil. He smiled. *Maybe I am.*

But he still didn't like it. Whatever she knew or thought she knew was too much. The girl obviously hadn't told Rutherford anything, because when Zach saw him, the detective didn't appear to have any knowledge of his extracurricular activities. He wasn't itching yet, wasn't hungry, but this one would have to go.

He wasn't about to be done in by some nosy little bitch.

CHAPTER TWENTY-ONE

Detective Rutherford sat in his office, finishing up some paperwork before going home to his family. It was Friday, and that meant pizza night. He loved pizza night with his wife and two sons. They always ordered a large pepperoni and watched whatever movie the two young boys picked out—often some cartoon James didn't really care about but enjoyed because it made them so happy. Nothing was more precious to him than his family, and he couldn't imagine what he would do if anyone ever hurt them.

"Goddamned son of a bitch," he swore under his breath.

This case was wearing him down. He couldn't understand what the parents of the murdered girls were going through, but he knew he'd be broken if he ever lost one of his sons or his wife. Since the murders began, Rutherford's sole focus was catching the killer, and today he'd expected a breakthrough. The idea that another family might lose their little girl made him sick, sometimes even physically. He'd vomited more in the past few months than ever in his life, and his wife was worried. But whatever the toll on his own body, he couldn't stop—not just wouldn't, but couldn't. If one of his boys disappeared, he'd hope there was someone willing to fight for him, and these parents needed someone to fight for them. His phone rang.

"Detective Rutherford," he answered, and heard only breathing on the other end. "Hello? Can I help you?"

"It's Riley," the voice stammered.

"Riley. Is everything okay? You had me scared earlier and a little confused, to be honest."

"Detective, I'm terrified. I need to tell you something, and more importantly, I need you to believe me."

Ten minutes later, James Rutherford hung up the phone and stared openmouthed at the door to his office. One hand twisted through his disheveled hair while the other pounded the desktop. Riley's story fit. It explained why she'd fled the police station earlier, but the idea that Zachary Stone, a fellow officer, and even a friend, could be capable of something like this was impossible. *Or was it? What do I really know about him?*

Zachary Stone was well liked by everyone, especially the females, for obvious reasons. He was a good officer, someone you'd feel comfortable having your back when shit hit the fan. He came from an upstanding, wealthy family who had done more charity work in the community than probably everyone else combined.

But he drives a silver BMW. And Riley swore up and down that it was him. She had no reservations.

"What the hell do I do?"

Investigating a fellow officer for murder would be daunting and dangerous. But he had a job to do, and he was confident the system would uncover the truth. Rutherford picked up the phone and called the chief.

A gruff voice answered. "Hello?"

"Yeah, Jimmy, we've got a problem. You're gonna want to get down here quick."

Chapter Twenty-Two

R iley awoke in a cold sweat from a nightmare about being chased through the bright hallway of the police station by a faceless man with a bloody knife. When the hallway finally ended, she'd turned in time to watch the blade sink into her chest, and she saw the blood squirt out onto the man, forming a red face on the blank palette that looked a lot like Zachary Stone. And then she woke up, reached for the glass of water on the bedside table, took a sip, and tried to calm her mind. The clock read 1:00 a.m. *It's all in your head. It's not real.* Besides, Detective Rutherford had told her he'd have a patrol unit watching her house until they could apprehend Zachary Stone.

As she rested her head back on the pillow, an all-too-familiar chill began creeping down her spine, as if her brain knew something before the rest of her and was passing a message to her feet in slow motion. It screamed at her to open her eyes, and when she did, she saw the curtains fluttering at the open window, the clock ticking away the hours, and the door still soundly shut, holding back a dim light that crept up the stairs.

Why is there a light?

Eyelids cracked into small slits, she heard rather than saw the door quietly open. The outline of a man was visible, his looming figure backlit. He stood motionless, staring at her through invisible eyes, waiting. Slamming her eyes shut, she hoped he would disappear. *It's part of the nightmare. It's just part of the nightmare.* Her brain whirred into overdrive, attempting to save itself from the inevitable. Riley peered into the darkness once more, but the man's outline remained unchanged. *This cannot be happening.*

Her heart crashed in her chest, up and down, up and down, as if a drummer marched in the room with them. She wanted to rip the thumping traitor from her body and fling it where it couldn't reveal her location. *Like he doesn't know.* Under the blankets, her hand crept up her chest to press on her heart. *Please stop.*

"I know you saw me." The voice was like the knife from her dream, slicing at her life. "I know you see me now." The noise slithered out through the teeth of the motionless shadow beast.

Holy shit. What am I supposed to do? This stuff doesn't happen in real life! Should I pretend I didn't hear? She peered out through partially opened eyes, trying to block out some of the terror. "What do you want?" she squeaked. The voice wasn't hers. It was some defeated animal that bleated through her mouth.

He laughed. It was a quiet laugh that left room for all sorts of horrifying answers. Riley racked her brain for where she had left the pepper spray and cursed herself for not working harder to find the key to the gun safe. The shotgun her dad had left was still in its case in the closet beneath the stairs. She was utterly unarmed and unprepared to take on what was coming.

Her fingers clenched the sheets, white knuckles threatening to pop through her skin. *But I locked all the doors!*

Riley tried to control herself as a small whimper escaped through her mouth, sneaking out with help from all the pressure built up within. She longed to be anywhere, even back in the tempest of sand. There at least she had a chance. Here would lead only to horrible and unthinkable things.

The mattress sagged with the weight of another human form, and Riley thought of the dried blood caked on Rachel's thighs. Her legs crossed protectively, clenching with all the strength they had.

"Please," she whispered, not even sure he heard her.

"What I don't understand," he began, "is how on earth you came to find out my little secret. You see, I'm very good at guarding it. I will do anything to protect myself."

Silence. Riley trembled, clutching her sheets for protection, willing them to be made of steel and spikes. Her eyes adjusted, and she could make out his features. *The blood face.* She didn't need light to know who it was.

"No?" He laughed. "I'll try another approach. Have you ever seen a lion hunt in the wild? Crouching, hidden, stalking its prey, and then in an instant making the kill? It's clean. It's perfection."

He paused again. His brown hair was a disheveled swath on his head, and his dark clothes clung to the shadowy form. "Now, I'm usually the lion. In fact, I am always the lion. So it makes me incredibly angry when someone tries to turn that around on me. You see, I am the hunter, and you are the prey.

In nature, what do you think would happen to the gazelle who tried to turn and face off with the lion?"

More silence, except for Riley's heavy breaths and occasional whimper. *Please let this be quick.*

"I'll answer for you, then." Humor vanished from his voice. "The lion would snap the gazelle's neck and tear out its throat."

He reached down to the floor and shuffled through a black backpack Riley hadn't noticed before. "You should have stayed out of my business instead of trying to be a hero."

She lay frozen with fear as his weight shifted, knowing the backpack contained things that would cause pain. *I'm dead either way. I have to do something.*

The message her brain had been trying to send throughout her body finally reached its destination, and she rolled from the bed and sprinted for the door.

Rough hands grabbed her by the knees, and she crashed onto the floor, hitting her skull on the solid oak dresser on the way down. Her head spun in black circles, and blood trickled down her face into her eyes and mouth. Riley gasped for air that wouldn't come and choked at the taste of sticky red iron coating her tongue. She vomited, out of pain or fear she didn't know, and urine ran down her legs, warming her trembling thighs. *Oh, God, no! This can't be how it ends.* Tears ran down her face, mixing with the blood and snot dripping from her chin.

"The more difficult you make this for me, the more painful I will make it for you." The voice no longer held a hint of humor as he moved toward the door, shutting it and sliding the dresser across it.

He returned to where she lay and pressed a booted foot to her chest, compressing her already-struggling lungs. Even through the darkness, she felt cool eyes bore into hers. "I'm going to rape you, and then I am going to kill you. But you will die slowly. You ruined what I had going, and I don't take too kindly to that."

He sat on her abdomen, leaning toward her ear. She groaned. "They know who I am thanks to you, sweetheart. I don't have to worry about making a mess anymore."

Cold hands tightened around her throat. She struggled under his weight, trying to scream, but only a muffled gurgle surfaced. She thought of her family, how this would break them. She thought of her life and all the things she would never do. She thought of Gabe. *Where are you, Gabe, when I need you most?*

Riley looked into the devil's eyes, hating him for taking everything from her and the people who loved her. He reached into his back pocket and pulled out a rag, stuffing it into her mouth. Bile burned her throat, and she gagged, trying to scream and wiggle and flail her arms, but no noise came out, and she couldn't move.

Zachary Stone pulled out a long knife and turned the blade over in his hands, clearly taking pleasure in watching her eyes grow wide and the tears come faster. She felt the coolness of the blade as he gently rubbed the tip up her bare legs, abdomen, and toward her throat, leaving shallow cuts that glistened with warm red beads. He shivered with satisfaction.

How? It was all so inconceivable. *How did it come to this?*

Every ounce of strength in her body fought to push him off, to scream, to do anything, but it was futile. He was too strong, and now that she was bleeding and possibly concussed, she stood no chance. All her life she'd imagined doing great things, but now it would all end at the hands of a monster. She felt her spirit retreating, trying to escape the sinking ship before it went down with her. *No!*

Her assailant sat up on his heels, turning for an instant to reach into the backpack, and in that moment Riley mustered the last bit of fight she could and threw her body upward. The thrust knocked him off balance, and she moved, trying to ignore the searing pain in her head and the stinging bites along her legs. There was only one way out, and if she thought too long, she might remain to face the beast instead. Without a second thought, Riley yanked open the window and threw her body into the night air.

The force of the ground meeting her side sucked the wind out of her lungs. Pain coursed through an already broken body, and she let out a muffled scream just as a bellow of frustration roared from the floor above. She couldn't move. *I can't just lie here.* But her body would not heed her wishes. *I'm paralyzed. He's going to get me!*

"*Please!*" her mind screamed in frustration and agony, begging her body to move. "*Please!*"

A tingling sensation spread through her, loosening the lock on her nerves and enabling her to rip the gag from her mouth. Fresh air burned her ragged throat, but she sucked at it anyway. As she sat up slowly, her head began to clear. Riley leaned forward on her knees, willing them to hold her, crying out in pain.

The sound of the front door slamming brought her the rest of the way to her feet. Her knees trembled, unsteady from fear and pain. He would be on her in moments. She had no keys—they were in her purse by the front door. There was only one place to go. She ran toward the cornfield as fast as her body would move. *The cornfield. Hardly a place of sanctuary.*

"You're so fucking dead." The voice carried a new kind of hatred.

Heavy, uneven breaths came out forcibly. The dirt furrows made it difficult to run, and without the ripening corn stalks to hide in, her position was obvious. She laughed at the irony of the situation. *I'm being chased through a cornless cornfield by a serial killer. What an unoriginal way to die.*

The sound of heavy footfalls resonated closely behind. She blinked as fresh blood from her head seeped and spilled over her eyelashes, clouding her vision in a red, sticky fog. *It's okay. You're just running from the farmer.* But her grandma and grandpa were not there to protect her this time. Tears streamed down her cheeks as she realized how alone and desperate she was. There was no place to hide in the field, and once she reached the edge, there was no car to escape in. Sharp rocks and broken corn stubble stabbed at the soft arches of her feet, tearing new holes in her perforated body.

And now he was so close she could sense the mortality that hovered over her. *Please, this can't be it. I'm not done. I have so much left to do, so much more to offer. Help me. Not here. Not now.*

She felt something swipe her back and then a chunk of hair tore from her scalp. More blood. *I am going to die here. I have already died here.* Her blood would spill for the last time in this cornfield. She'd always imagined the last battle being a little more epic, but at least she'd die in a place that meant something. *Please just make it all go away. Please take me as far from here as possible.*

A hole appeared in the ground ahead. Riley jumped to avoid it, but her foot snagged the edge and she fell. Hearing the familiar bellow of frustration from above, she braced for the final blow her body would have to endure.

But it never came. Instead the world faded to black, and with it her mind faded into nothingness.

CHAPTER TWENTY-THREE

Death—an unavoidable, yet inconceivable idea at such a young age. Riley didn't know what would happen once she crossed the final threshold. Of course she'd grown up hearing about heaven, and while it sounded wonderful, it also sounded too good to be true.

But what if there isn't a heaven? Is there nothing? Absolute nothing?

That was hard to stomach as well. Riley groaned as pain flooded her body. When she thought of her own death, she always imagined it at the end of a very long and happy life—never a violent finality at such a young age. *I am too young to be dead.*

She blinked, wanting to open her eyes, but it was so bright on the other side of her lids.

Why am I in such a bright place?

A dull crackling bounced around her brain. Pain harassed her body, poking and prodding every open sore and bruise with a sharp jab. *I can't be dead yet. There's no way heaven would feel this bad. Maybe I'm in hell…*

These thoughts continued for what seemed like hours as the bright lights still flickered like flames outside her tender lids. After a while her head began to clear, and she found the strength to let the fires in.

A man stood above her, outlined in the blinding light. She couldn't distinguish anything about him other than a worried expression and a mumbling she didn't understand. She closed her eyes again and took a deep breath. *Time to face whatever happens next.*

"Are you okay?" The voice was clear now, concerned. "Oz, are you all right? You look terrible."

What did he call me? Her eyes focused on the gray circles that were the devil's eyes. His brown hair lay smooth on his head, and he wore a crisp police uniform—so different from moments ago. Confusion, fear, and anger surged within. This nightmare had to end. *I guess he likes to play with his prey.*

Strong arms reached into the hole, and she took the moment to strike, biting down with all her might, trying to draw blood, tear skin, anything to hurt him as much as he'd hurt her. She wouldn't be a victim any longer.

"What is wrong with you?" He yanked his hand away, wiping the small drops of blood onto his dark pants.

"Stay away from me," she growled as she crouched as far from him as possible. "Don't touch me, don't hurt me, don't even say another word to me. Just get the hell away."

His eyes swept over her. "Are you on drugs again? I thought you were past that. You were doing so well."

Riley's eyebrows raised and her jaw dropped, but she couldn't find words.

Keeping a safe distance, Zachary sat back on the edge of the hole. "Well, if I can't help you, at least let me sit here with you until you're able to move again. You had a pretty bad fall. I don't know what you were running from, but maybe I can help."

Is he kidding? She let out a dry, humorless laugh. "Help me? You sick bastard. Why would you help me? Get it over with. Kill me. Or let me go. But don't play games."

"Kill you?" A disbelieving chuckle came from his mouth. "What are you doing to yourself? You said last week you were done. I'm really trying to help, but at some point you have to put in some effort as well."

Rage and incredulity stuck in her throat. She tried to speak, but all that came out were hissing screams. Frustration boiled up from the pit of her stomach and spilled out through her mouth as indistinguishable noises. She threw fistfuls of dirt in the air and at Zachary Stone, screeching in pain and fury each time she moved. Zachary perched on the edge, silently watching the fit unfold. When it appeared she was not in imminent danger, Riley's body relaxed a little, and the questions poured out.

"Why is it daytime? It was the middle of the night. Now it's got to be after noon. Why didn't you hurt me? Why did you just sit there, watching?"

He let out a slow breath. "You just fell moments ago. Maybe five minutes tops. I was coming by to check on you when I saw you running into the field. I followed and tried to grab you so you wouldn't fall, but I didn't make it in time. You hit your head and blacked out."

Riley reached up to the bloody gash on her forehead, wincing as her injured ribs stretched uncomfortably. Her hand came back sticky and shaking and she balled it into a fist.

"You're sick," she seethed, heaving her aching, broken body from the hole onto level ground across from him. *Was it just last night this happened?*

Riley glared at the strange man to let him know she was no longer afraid, even though she felt terrified. *Why is he acting like this? He's crazy.*

"I'm going now—that is, if you've lost interest in murdering me, which apparently you have. I'm going home and I'm going to call the police. And your bullshit story won't throw them off. Detective Rutherford knows you did it. I called him yesterday. You don't stand a chance."

Zachary Stone sat across from her, looking more confused than ever.

Riley stood, brushing the dirt off her clothes. The hurt was agonizing, but nothing seemed to be broken. She could at least hobble home. *God, I'm going to need therapy after this.* With another long glare at her assailant, she turned toward her house.

"Please don't do anything stupid." He remained on the ground, eyeing her warily.

"Okay, weirdo," she laughed, throwing her hands into the air. "You'll be in jail, but okay."

"Oz?" His voice grew soft and sad. "Come see me if you need anything. I only want to help."

"That's not my name!" This time she turned to face him. "But sure, you're a crooked cop. If I need assistance from a *murderer,* I'll mosey on down to the station." Stomping her feet, she fought the urge to run home as she spun back around.

"And Oz," he said again.

Shut up! "Why do you keep calling me that?"

"Your hair looks nice." He ignored her question. "That color looks good on you."

"Go to hell."

She wasn't sure where the confidence came from, but it felt good. Empowering. Riley was still scared to death, but for some reason, in the light of day, the fierce lion had walked out from behind the curtain, transformed into a house cat.

Something was obviously seriously wrong with this guy. *My hair color? Maybe he's some weirdo werewolf character that only comes out with the moon and then is a normal human being by day.*

"Can I walk with you?" Suddenly he was standing next to her, reaching an arm out to help her move.

"Get away from me." She leapt aside and convulsed in pain, moaning and clutching her ribs.

Zachary Stone threw his hands up in surrender and stepped back. "My car is parked in front of your house. I have to go this way."

"Fine. Just stay over there. Stay well away."

He moved off to the right, matching her slow pace.

Riley stared straight ahead, wanting to ignore him but not trusting enough to completely block him out. Her eyes constantly darted around, but he kept his distance and didn't say a word. Moving seemed to loosen her limbs, even though it also made the blood flow again from her lesions.

It quickly became apparent that Zachary Stone's behavior wasn't the only thing that was off. She was still making her way home through a field. However, instead of newly planted corn, she found herself surrounded by...*an orchard?*

Row upon row of fruit-laden trees sprang up from the land that once produced corn. Ripe and rotting apples lay strewn upon the ground and hung heavy from drooping branches. She kicked one and it rolled across the shade, landing in front of Zachary. He stooped to pick it up and took a bite, smiling. Riley glowered, glancing upward toward the mesa and hills. They at least stood unchanged, which offered some comfort.

"Where did you bring me?" she asked, chancing a glance.

He shook his head, shrugged, and continued eating the apple. Riley rolled her eyes, wishing she was brave enough to fling one of the wormy ones at his head. She walked in the direction of home, using the geography to guide her, since the rest of the area was almost unrecognizable.

The sight of Esther's house brought a temporary wave of relief, followed by further confusion. She had been looking forward to a shower, a nap, and a phone call to the police station, but there was one problem. *That's not my house.*

Structurally it appeared the same—two stories with dormer windows and a wraparound porch. But a fresh coat of white paint had replaced the chipped brown coat, causing the house to contrast starkly with the surrounding vegetation. *And the yard...*

Lush ferns fanned out from the trunks of exotic trees. A cobblestone walkway wound past flowers Riley had never seen before, blossoming in colors she didn't even know existed. Pausing next to a pond, she watched a large koi lumber through water hyacinths and lilies. The contrast of the sterile house to the elaborate garden was startling. *Okay, so I am dead, and this is heaven…*

"If only you dedicated the kind of passion to the rest of your life that you do out here, maybe things would be different for you." His voice sounded hesitant.

Riley had forgotten about *him*. She glanced at Zachary Stone, who stood at the edge of the path, watching her walk through the garden.

"Leave," she said through gritted teeth. "Get in your car and leave."

He nodded again and walked past, keeping his hands in his pockets. She watched him step into the patrol vehicle and wave, not taking her eyes from the car until it had turned the corner at the end of the road and disappeared.

Disheartened, she tried to think of what she had done to deserve this and which of Dante's nine circles of hell she was currently residing in. Somehow all of the bad things that had happened must have culminated in what was probably a gruesome and tragic death and caused her to end up here.

Riley opened the front door and gasped. Broken furniture lay scattered across the living room. Dirty dishes and moldy food littered the kitchen, and the house had an overall smell of filth and…*marijuana?* Riley gaped at the downstairs in disbelief and horror. *This is my nightmare.* She walked to a cabinet and opened the door, staring hopelessly at grimy dishes, cups, and utensils stuffed haphazardly into each crevice. Turning toward the furniture, she saw her grandpa's brown recliner upturned and slashed, the stuffing spilling out onto stained carpet. *Who would do this? Maybe I have a roommate. A druggie limbo room-mate.* She laughed and cried, stepping over an empty whiskey bottle as her other foot crunched down on a broken piece of glass.

Riley thought of her family and wished she could go back and warn them that being good wasn't enough. You had to be perfect, or you ended up like this. She'd spent hours cleaning and organizing the house, hours making it perfect. It made sense that her hell looked like this.

She found a phone plugged into the wall at the base of the stairs and called the police station. *Even if I'm dead, I want this guy out of my purgatory.* The phone rang three times before the soft voice of the receptionist answered. "Grand Junction Police Department. How may I direct your call?"

"I need to speak to Detective Rutherford. This is Riley Dale. Tell him it's an emergency, please."

"Miss Dale, have you gotten yourself into trouble again?" the voice asked.

"What? No." *Can't anyone give me a break?* "I just need to talk to him."

"Hold on then." The receptionist sounded bored.

Riley twisted the phone cord in her hand as elevator music hummed mechanically until the detective's deep voice interrupted the monotony.

"Can I help you, Miss Dale?"

"Zachary Stone was in the field behind my house. He tried to kill me last night, but I got away." *Or he let me go?* "He must have known I called you yesterday to report him. He wanted revenge. He tried to kill me just like he killed those other girls!"

Relief swept over her. Maybe if Zachary Stone got put away in this hell, he would be stopped in the real world as well.

"What are you talking about, Miss Dale? I didn't hear from you yesterday. And what girls have been murdered?" He paused. "Are you using again?"

Riley's fingers froze on the cord as her head began to throb. "I was in your office yesterday. You had me try to pick out a murderer for you!" she yelled into the receiver, anger and frustration mounting. "I found a body by the river. It was Rachel. Rachel Stanton. You have to remember her. And there were others. Four others!"

"Rachel Stanton died in a car accident last week. It was a tragedy. I don't know what you're playing at, Riley, but if you're doing drugs again and trying to blame Zach, I don't have any sympathy for you. That man has gone out of his way to help you, and you do nothing but spit in his face. I'd have given up on your sorry ass a hell of a long time ago."

The detective's words slapped her in the face.

"Zach?" She couldn't believe what she was hearing. "As in Zachary Stone?"

"Yes, Riley," he said. "I don't know what you did to him during your time here at the jail—I thought he was above the shit you pull with everyone else—but you had enough of an effect on him that he has bent over backward trying to help you."

"Excuse me?" she shouted into the phone. "That's him, though! He's the killer."

"Enough. I suggest you clean up whatever it is that you're doing and watch what you say. You owe a lot to Zach. Think about it. If it were me, I would have left you to the dogs. People like you deserve to be forgotten. I'd let you rot in a cell if he hadn't come to your rescue every time."

She slammed the phone into the floor and then ripped it from the wall. "Arghhhhhh!" she screamed at the hole in the sheetrock. *This isn't fair. I don't deserve to end up in a place like this. I haven't done anything!*

She limped over to the upturned recliner and righted it as best as she could before collapsing onto the torn fabric. Tears immediately began to flow as the loose cotton clung to her clothes. *It isn't fair. None of it is fair.* She hugged her knees to her chest and sobbed, heavy racking breaths accompanying each tear. When she had wished to be anywhere but the corn-field, she hadn't known this place existed.

Chapter Twenty-Four

Heavy darkness let Riley know that she'd fallen asleep. The only light in the house came from a lone glowing corner on the floor created by the light of the full moon drifting in through the window. She trembled as visions of the previous night flooded back, expecting to see a demon dancing in the shadows or a blade glinting in the light. Nothing made sense anymore.

Riley was afraid of her own home, or what had once been her home. She stood painfully, turned on the hallway light, and crept up the stairs, hair on end. Her room, like the rest of the house, was a disaster. Plates with molding food sat one atop the other on the nightstand, while wrinkled clothes formed a solid layer of fluff on the floor. The last time she saw this room, she'd been pinned to the ground, awaiting certain death. *I will find no peace here, no comfort.* Riley wanted to explode. Her whole life had been ordered, but now she'd been flung into a chaotic hole she couldn't climb out of.

She walked into the closet and cleared a space between piles of broken CDs and wadded papers. Riley unfolded one and saw it was an exam with her name written at the top next to a D-. She crumpled it back up and flung it against the wall. This was a place with no hope, a place to torture people into madness, a place with no refuge and no one to turn to. *Except maybe one.* The one person who scared her most, the one person she could not go to for help, was the only person who offered it, the only person in this crazy world who seemed to care if she was okay. Angry tears spilled from her eyes as her fists clenched.

"Is this what you want?" she screamed at nothing. "Does it make you happy to see me here like this?"

Silence. Riley curled into a tight ball and flashed from angry to defeated to scared. She remembered learning in school that human beings are born with only two fears: the fear of falling and the fear of loud noises. Most people aren't born fearing spiders, snakes, clowns, the boogeyman, *rapists, or murderers.* Those fears are learned, developed as a result of someone's pain and through negative encounters with the world.

Riley had been born afraid of everything, though—afraid of crowds, afraid of strangers, afraid of the dark, afraid of the unknown. Her anxiety had caused problems her whole life in the courage department, but suddenly she realized she'd had no grasp on fear until the previous night. Narrowly avoiding violent rape and murder made the mess in the bedroom seem harmless. It made the parties she'd missed in college appear tame. *What do I really know about fear, and what was just a waste of my energy?*

Clarity finally dawned. She should have seen the signs— the visions, the run-ins with strange people, and the ring. Maybe she wasn't dead after all. Maybe she'd just finally cracked and was lost within her own mind. She wasn't dead. She was crazy. But sadly, this new certainty didn't ease the pain. Being lost within herself was much more terrifying than death.

Chapter Twenty-Five

Riley jolted awake to the sound of a phone ringing nearby. She blinked, almost forgetting where she was until the smell of unwashed clothing wafted into her nostrils. *I should burn this place to the ground.*

"What do you want?"

Riley leapt at the sound of a human voice. A girl said, "Hell no, I'm not coming in. I was there two days ago. I haven't done anything wrong!"

Oh great, this must be my disgusting roommate. Welcome to hell. Riley peeked through the cracked door and saw the side profile of a girl about her age, with a similar height and build. Purple streaks cut through dark hair that covered the side of her face, and tattoos decorated an entire arm in an elaborate sleeve of tangled wildflowers. The girl sat on the bed facing the door, dressed in black leather and combat boots, with an unlit cigarette dangling from her mouth.

"All right, I'll come in just to shut you up, Stone. But I don't need to check in with you all the damn time. You aren't my babysitter. And I don't know why you're sayin' you saw me yesterday, 'cause I was at a friend's house. Maybe you're the one on drugs."

The mystery girl hung up the phone and walked out of the room, mumbling something under her breath. Riley heard footsteps on the stairs and the front door slamming.

Stone? She knows Officer Stone and she's going to see him? Should I try and stop her? No, let her go. It doesn't matter anymore. Riley stood, confused and sore from her five-star stay in the closet, and looked around for something fresh to wear. She found a pair of pants and a purposely slashed T-shirt still on hangers, and prayed they were clean. She grabbed a worn pair of boots and laced up, wincing against the open cuts on her feet inflicted by the cornfield.

Riley walked down the stairs, out onto the front porch, and stretched, feeling hungry for the first time since the nightmare began. *There's no way I'm eating anything inside this house.*

Looking around for a vehicle, she saw nothing. She walked a full circle around the outside of the house but found no bike, no scooter, no wheels of any kind. *Ugh. I guess I'll walk into town then.*

Food is a priority, but so is everything else. I need to get to the police station and talk to Detective Rutherford. She sighed. He had to help. He'd been on her side all along. *Maybe the incident on the phone was a fluke.*

The sun beat down with stifling radiance. Riley's boots crunched on the gravel as she walked down the driveway to the road, staring at the apple trees that should have been corn and wondering what she'd do about money when she got to town. *I'll steal if I have to.* She cringed. This place was already turning her into someone she wasn't. *The criminal they seem to think I am.*

Riley reached the main road and scanned the unfamiliar scene in front of her. Topography indicated she was still in Grand Junction, but by the look of everything else, she couldn't possibly be. The familiar houses of the neighboring farms had been replaced either by rundown trailer homes or multimillion-dollar mini mansions. It was a confusing mixture of poverty and wealth that didn't fit the image of the middleclass neighborhood she had lived in...*what, only a day ago?* The mesa still loomed over the scene below. Riley wondered if it knew something was wrong.

After minutes of trying to process the new world, her eyes finally fell on a familiar sight. The farm directly next to hers—the one that belonged to the farmer who had chased them from the cornfield so many years back—looked completely unchanged. Newly planted corn still spread out from the modest white farmhouse with its unmistakable turquoise shutters and window frames. The large maple tree in the front yard still reached toward the sky with branches that made any child yearn to climb to the top. Nothing, it seemed, had changed about that house from this world to the next.

Riley had never met the man who lived there, but he had been a friend of her grandparents. After the big chase, she had been scared to death of him and refused to meet the man face to face. For all she knew, he was some kind of hideous beast who liked chasing innocent children from his precious fields. *Michael Flynn. That was his name.*

While the familiar house beckoned to her, she decided to head for town, unable to shake the feeling that any place offering comfort here was probably a trap. She kept picturing the candy house from Hansel and Gretel and refused to end up on a platter at someone's dinner table.

Riley walked in the direction she thought led to town, or at least where town used to be. Hunger and thirst hovered like the sun. Injuries throbbed all over her body, and the baffling situation she now found herself in began to take its toll. There was only one place she could go right now. Without money, there would be no food, and she refused to start shoplifting as a means of survival. The police station would be safe. Zachary Stone had offered aid, and she would accept, in a public place full of people who would take him down if he tried anything. There was simply no other option.

The temperature rose with each step, and soon it felt hotter than the days had ever been before she ended up here. Sweltering wind blew dust in the air that stuck to Riley's perspiring body. She gave up trying to wipe it away, preferring the dusty sweat to the muddy streaks it created when disturbed. A car full of young men drove by, honking their horn and making catcalls. Riley looked at the ground and willed them to drive on, praying they wouldn't turn around.

The sound of another horn grabbed her attention, and she peered up through the dust as a man in an old Ford pickup pulled over to the side of the road just ahead.

A tall man in his seventies hopped out of the truck and walked toward her, his face stretched in a friendly smile.

Riley studied him, noting the laugh lines and wrinkles that appeared in places on his face where unhappy people usually have downturned creases. Thin white hair flew around his head, and his weathered face showed evidence of hard work outside.

"Riley Dale," he said, approaching her cautiously. She backed away, and he stopped, not pressing her. "Do you need a ride somewhere?"

"Do I know you?" She wanted to trust the friendly-looking man, but her trust in others had greatly decreased over the last few hours.

"Michael Flynn." He grinned and extended a hand. Riley stared for a moment before accepting the gesture, finding comfort in his golden eyes that reminded her of Gabe. "I think I scared you out of my fields back when you were a kid." He winked, his eyes twinkling with unspoken humor.

How does he remember that? No one else seems to remember anything about me from my past. "Where are we?"

"Grand Junction." His expression faltered ever so slightly.

"Am I dead?"

He threw back his head and laughed. "You really are a strange one, aren't you? If you were dead, how would we be having this conversation?"

She recognized the same look she'd gotten from her grandma and from Gabe—a look suggesting he knew more than he was willing to let on. "The police station. I need to get to the police station. Can you take me there?"

His face darkened for a moment, then flashed back to a cheery demeanor. "Yeah, sure. I'm heading into town to run errands. I'll drop you off on the way."

Riley slowly crawled into his truck, looking around for sharp objects—rope, duct tape, anything that meant he could harm her. She didn't sense any danger or malice in this man, only that he might not be telling the full truth. She sat like a board in the front seat, staring straight ahead.

"Is everything okay?" His fingers drummed the steering wheel.

"It's a long story. I really don't know what's going on."

He shifted gears and pointed toward her hand. "That's a nice ring. I remember when Esther wore it."

Riley yanked the metal object from her finger and rolled the window down.

"I wouldn't do that if I were you," Michael cautioned. "Although I'm sure Esther had the same idea about it at some point."

Riley held it loosely out the window as the wind danced over her fist, trying to claim the ring from her. "It's brought nothing but bad luck since I put it on. It's cursed and I don't want it anymore. No matter how much it meant to Grandma."

Michael sighed. "Cursed, maybe. But you can't break the curse by throwing it away. I've found the best thing to do with bad luck is to keep it right under your nose. That way it can't pop up and surprise you. You never know. Maybe the object that curses you is the only one that can set you free."

More riddles. Riley pulled her hand in and slid the ring back onto her finger. Buildings became more frequent, signaling the approach of town. People milled around outside, ate lunch, dropped off mail—all normal things, but they still felt wrong. Riley peered at Michael Flynn as he stared ahead at the road, a private smile still twitching at the corners of his mouth.

"Hey, you just passed it." Riley sat up and craned her neck back as the sign identifying the Grand Junction Police Department flew past.

Michael Flynn nodded and kept driving.

"Hello! That's where I need to go. Let me out!"

"Riley, I can't take you there. I'm sorry. It isn't a safe place. You're going to have to come with me. I'm going to help you."

Panic and anger at being lied to rose up inside. *I shouldn't have trusted him!* "Let me out!"

"I'll explain everything to you soon, but right now my priority is to get you to safety."

The car rolled to a stop at a red light, and Riley had a split second to make up her mind. "I'm sorry, Mr. Flynn. I want to believe you, but right now I can't."

She flung open the door and sprinted toward the station. Curious bystanders stepped aside as she pushed past, fleeing the shouts from the truck still behind her. Michael Flynn was trapped in his car by others waiting at the light. He wouldn't reach her before she made it to her destination, but she didn't stop running until she'd raced through the automatic front doors and skidded to a halt in the modest lobby. Breathless and panting, she approached the window, where a tough-looking woman sat behind the counter. Her name card read Alvarado.

"Can I help you?" Officer Alvarado asked, barely looking away from her game of solitaire.

"I need to see Officer Stone." Riley clutched at the stitch stabbing in her side. "It's kind of an emergency."

The dark-haired woman continued to stare at her computer screen. "Officer Stone is with someone right now. He'll be busy for a while."

"I'll wait then." *I'm not going anywhere. I don't have anywhere to go.*

The woman indicated a clipboard on the counter. "Sign in. I'll let him know you're here."

Riley scribbled her name and turned to find a seat. The lobby didn't look much different than it had the last time she'd fled this building upon first encountering Zachary Stone: tan walls, uncomfortable chairs, fake plants in the corners, and magazines no one cared about in stacks on coffee tables. She sank into a chair, sucking in a painful breath.

"I think you've made some sort of a mistake."

Riley looked up and realized it was Officer Alvarado who had spoken.

"The paper shows you signed in earlier and are in fact the person with Officer Stone right now."

Frustrated, Riley sighed at the ceiling and inserted as much confidence and sarcasm into her voice as possible. "Not unless there are two Riley Dales."

Officer Alvarado raised an eyebrow, a look of doubt that suddenly switched to apprehension and understanding spread across her face. "Two Riley Dales…" She trailed off. "Excuse me. I'll be back momentarily. Do *not* leave this building."

Riley thought about Michael Flynn's warning of danger, specifically in this place. *Maybe I should have listened.*

A poster on the wall caught her eye. It was a picture of Detective Rutherford smiling in front of a sullen group of handcuffed criminals. His dark hair was held tight in a crisp, wavy style, and the stubble she'd seen on him earlier had been shaved into smooth, perfect skin. It looked like someone had taken the worn detective and turned him into a Ken doll.

The poster stated he was running for mayor. "The law is the way, and justice is the light" was written in bold letters at the top of the page, with the words "I will lead the people to a safer tomorrow" at the bottom. Riley smirked, amused by the plastic detective and his canned statements.

"Will you be voting for me?" a husky voice asked from behind.

She whirled around and found herself face to face with Detective Rutherford himself. He sported perfect hair and a pressed suit, but his forced smile revealed yellowed teeth that didn't match the flawless image he tried to convey. *Is this even the same man?*

"Oh, I'm still registered in Boulder. I won't be voting. Sorry."

"Shame." He shrugged. "The people need someone like me who believes in following the rules. *All* of the rules."

He held onto the last comment and her gaze a bit too long, smirking as if part of some funny joke she was not allowed to hear. "Come with me, Miss Dale. I hear you have an emergency you need handled." He held out a manicured hand.

She glanced at his dark eyes and felt a twinge of fear. "I'd really like to speak with Officer Stone. I've got questions that only he can answer."

"I see." His smile faded into impatience. "Well, anything you might tell him can be told to me, I assure you."

"I called you yesterday asking for help, and you wouldn't give me any. You treated me like I was some lunatic. Why would I trust you?"

"I apologize for that." His phony yellow smile returned. "I'd very much like to hear what you have to say."

Riley clenched her teeth, not heeding her internal struggle. She didn't trust him. In fact, he really creeped her out. But then again, she'd come here to see Zachary...*who tried to kill me the other night.* "Fine. Lead the way."

She followed him down a series of hallways, past the room where they had first spoken on the day Riley found Rachel Stanton's body in the river. They continued beyond the main offices and questioning rooms to a corridor filled with stale air, empty jail cells, and narrowing walls. Her skin crawled at the isolating feeling rising within.

"Where are we going?"

"I want to go someplace where we won't be disturbed. I understand you have important information for me—information that could harm you if it ended up in the wrong hands. I just want to keep you safe."

She looked at him quizzically. "So you believe me about Officer Stone?"

"We have much to discuss, Riley."

She didn't trust him or like the way he kept talking to her, but she was hungry for justice, and he acted like he could help. The hallway ended at a locked door, and the detective produced a ring with more keys than Riley had ever seen.

A flight of steps led down into what appeared to be a basement area containing more cells. Fluorescent lights flickered, making her feel like she was in a horror movie, descending into the bowels of a beast she'd never escape from. The cells down here were different than those above. They had solid doors, no windows, and were mostly dark, save for the sliver of light that crept beneath the doorframe. *Solitary confinement.*

Riley paused at the base of the stairs, not wanting to follow the detective into the dungeon. Everything about this new Rutherford seemed off. Fear and uneasiness replaced the comfort she felt in the other's presence. *And why all the way down here?*

"Almost there," he said. "I have so much to tell you."

Her feet moved freely, desperate for help and answers, but the rest of her followed with resistance. He stopped at door number seven, pulled out his key ring once more, and heaved open the heavy metal door.

"After you." He motioned for her to go first.

The room had a small board of a bed hanging from the ceiling by four heavy chains, and a rusting pot in one corner that must have been the toilet. The light from the hallway illuminated part of the room, but most remained hidden in shadow. Riley wanted nothing to do with the dark, secluded cell. "Are you serious?"

"Like I said, Miss Dale," the calm voice slithered out. "You want assistance, and I don't want to be disturbed."

She turned apprehensively and walked into the small room. The detective followed but did not close the door. "Have a seat." He pointed at the bed.

She crossed her arms and sat, trying not to focus on the pressing darkness.

"You are in danger, Riley," Rutherford warned, a smile still playing on his lips.

"I know that." She quivered, unnerved by his calm demeanor. "I tried to tell you yesterday. Zachary Stone is a bad man—an evil man. He tried to kill me."

The detective smirked, and she shifted uneasily on the cot. Her eyes searched the room, but the large form of the detective blocked the only way out.

"Zachary Stone?" He laughed again. "That's funny. There are many powerful people who are eager to see you, Riley. And I am the one who will bring you to them." He stood in silence, a sour smile plastered to his plastic face. "And it would be best if you kept quiet. While the chances of anyone hearing you in here are slim to none, I prefer to keep this little arrangement between you and me." He left the room, slamming the door behind him. The lock clicked ominously into place.

"Hey!" Riley screamed as his footsteps disappeared into the darkness that swallowed her. "You can't leave me down here! Please, let me out! I'll tell you everything!"

She beat on the door until her fists ached and her knuckles bled. Sitting down on the bed, Riley leaned against one of the cold chains and stared at the ceiling. *How could I be so stupid?*

She wished to reverse time, even just an hour—to be back in the car with Michael Flynn, heading to his promised safety. Even if he was lying, her predicament couldn't be worse than it was now. Her mind wandered to her family, friends, and everything she left behind. *Had life ever made sense?*

One time, when Riley was younger and walking home from school, a lone man pulled up next to her and offered a ride. Even then, at seven years old, she'd had the brains to say no and run away. All her life she'd said no and run away. *Why didn't I do that this time?*

The windowless box provided no clues to the time of day. Riley didn't know how long she sat staring at the emptiness of her prison. It was long enough for her eyes to adjust to the faint line of light creeping in under the door. She could make out the laces on her boots and even the dark blob in the corner that was the toilet.

She went to the wall opposite her cot and traced the crude drawings that had been scratched into the concrete. She could make out a stick figure woman with large, round breasts and a well-endowed stick man next to her. A choked laugh escaped right before the tears came, and she sank to the floor.

Suddenly the hallway filled with noise—echoing footsteps and doors grating open against the floor. She shrank into the wall, wishing for a place to hide, wanting to be as far as possible from whoever stood on the other side. Flooding light stung her eyes as the lock on her cell clicked and the door swung open.

"Riley?" a man's voice whispered.

Zachary Stone appeared from behind the door in full uniform, his gun clutched in one hand, his face strained.

"Oh, thank God." He sounded relieved. "Riley, you've got to get out of here. They're after you. They'll be here soon, and if they catch you, who knows what will happen?"

"Why should I trust you?" she snarled, standing and putting the bed between herself and Zachary. "Why should I trust anyone?"

"Because you don't have an alternative," he said. "I think I understand why you don't trust me. I guess where you come from I am a terrible person. But we aren't in that place, Riley. Surely you've noticed. And in the place we are now, you have no choice but to follow me if you value your life."

If I value my life. Officer Stone's words were absurd, but also the most honest-sounding thing she'd heard in days. *And he's right. My other option is to stay in here.*

She studied his face and saw fear. *Good. We share the same emotion.* "Okay. Get me out of here. But only because I don't have a choice."

They ran down the narrow hallway and up the stairs to the locked door. Zachary Stone unlocked it and went ahead before gesturing for her to follow. They raced past uniformed men who shouted and commanded them to stop, but Riley never glanced back. Zachary tore out the rear entrance, and she followed, ducking as something banged into the wall beside her. She glanced down at the tiny barbs and wire retreating across the floor. *A Taser!* Nearly tripping over a curb stop in the parking lot, Riley sprinted toward a silver car, the silver BMW she'd seen twice before.

"No," she stammered, digging in her heels. "No, I can't get in there."

"Riley, please," he urged.

Loud voices echoed from the building and men spilled out the back door, running at them with Tasers and guns drawn. Glass exploded on surrounding vehicles as bullets rained down, narrowly missing their targets.

"Get in the backseat," he ordered.

Riley yanked the door open and leapt into the car as buckshot peppered the ground near her feet.

"Damn, I look like hell," a girl's voice sneered.

Riley jumped, turning to see her new limbo roommate smirking in the adjacent seat. She had not seen the girl's face earlier and was unprepared for the full-on view. Besides the purple hair, dark makeup, and pierced nose, it was like looking into a mirror—the same green eyes and lips that parted into an identical smile. Where tattoos didn't cover her arms, there were moles exactly where Riley had moles. When she spoke, it sounded like a playback recording of Riley speaking. On the outside they were identical. *Oh my God, I have a twin.*

The girl had a disturbingly dark beauty—a bizarre shadow of herself. Riley gasped, shifting her head back and forth between her identical companion and murdering savior.

"Riley Dale, meet Riley Dale," Officer Stone said as he jumped into the car and sped out of the parking lot and onto the main road. "Are you ready to hear the incredible truth?"

Chapter Twenty-Six

Once, when Riley was in second grade and Kiersten in fifth, Kiersten had convinced her she was adopted—that their parents had found her in a trashcan and brought her home because they felt sorry for her. Riley cried and cried until she got home, and when she told her parents about it, they kindly reassured her she was indeed theirs, and even showed pictures of her mom and her in the hospital the day she was born. Kiersten was scolded, and the concept of Riley coming from another family wasn't brought up again until Riley's birthday a few years back, when Kiersten recounted the tale, and everyone had a good laugh.

Staring at the mirror image next to her, Riley wondered if what Kiersten had said all those years back were true. *She kind of looks like someone abandoned her in a trashcan.*

But Zachary Stone had not said, "Riley meet your twin." He had said, "Riley, meet Riley." It took her a minute to comprehend the implication. She laughed.

"This girl is batshit, Stone. I told you I'm the stable one," said the girl with the purple hair.

"Batshit?" Riley repeated, feeling numb and weary. "I'll tell you all the incredible truth. Either I'm dead and didn't make it into heaven—which I'm still trying to figure out—or I'm having

a very crazy and very long dream. Neither of you is real. This…"
She flailed her arms madly in the air. "None of this is real."

The girl next to her threw her head back and laughed, her bright red lips stretched into a malicious grin. "This is great, Stone! Thanks for including me in your little get-together. I can't wait to mess with this girl."

"Cut it out, Riley," Zachary Stone said from the front seat. "It's going to be hard enough to explain what's going on without you making things worse."

"Excuse me?" Riley said angrily. The tattooed girl howled with laughter again.

"I was talking to the other Riley." Zachary sighed. "If you are willing to listen, I'll explain everything I can. You are very much alive, Riley, and you are not in hell."

She jerked her arm upward as something pierced her soft flesh. The purple-haired girl who couldn't contain her laughter was pinching Riley with long black fingernails.

"What the hell is your problem?" Riley shouted.

"I'm showing you you aren't dead, dumbass. You felt that. You don't feel shit in a dream and probably not if you're dead either."

Riley looked at her. She did have a point. *I hate this girl.* "Okay, I'm listening. But this had better be a good story. It's going to take a lot to convince me."

Zachary Stone took a deep breath. "This is hard. I don't know where to begin or how to make it make sense. Even I don't really understand it." Pleading eyes met Riley's in the rearview mirror.

"I'm listening," she said.

"Now, I don't know all of the details," he warned. "That's actually where we are going—to the capital, to see someone .who knows a lot about this topic. But I'll do my best."

"Wait. We're driving all the way to Washington, DC? Us?" Panic surged at the thought of being stranded with these two for that long.

"DC?" Zach's eyebrow rose. "No. We're going to Los Angeles. The only things you'll find in DC are movie stars and production companies. No help there."

"But—never mind. It's not real anyway." Riley sighed. "Keep going."

Zachary continued, "A long time ago, something happened that caused the world to split. There are a lot of theories as to why this happened, but I won't try to speculate until I can find you the correct answer. Basically, people's souls split in two, and the rest of the world followed. If you had a pure soul in the original world, then your counter soul would be corrupt. They call it a parallel universe—everything in your world is opposite here. Political powerhouses, general sentiments, character traits, really anything human related."

Riley's brow crinkled as she bit her lip. *Unbelievable. My descent into madness continues.* "You're joking, right? This is a great story, guys, and I'm glad you've put so much thought into trying to make me believe I'm crazy, but if you could just let me out so I can go home, that would be great."

"You don't have a home here, Riley," Zachary said.

Feeling helpless, she looked out the window. He was right. She might not believe in these wild stories, but there was no place to go.

"Besides," he continued, "I can't let you leave. If they find you they will kill you, or worse. That's why Rutherford put you in a cell. And that's why I had to break you out. Your world does not know about us, but we know about your world, to an extent. There are rumors. I'm not sure exactly what they want from you, but it won't be good. Occasionally we receive these notices in the mail with a picture of someone, stating that if we come across him or her to inform the government immediately. It's always all over the news when someone makes it over here. There is usually a huge reward, and people are quick to turn you over. And both halves are never seen again."

"So why aren't you taking me in?"

"Because I am the good half of my soul, as it seems you've noticed. I don't want money for destroying another person's life. I never want the responsibility of hurting another person."

Riley's jaw dropped, and this time it was her letting out the uncontrollable laugh.

"You kill people," she said. "You've raped and murdered five women in the last few months, and you tried to do the same to me the other night. That's how I ended up here. I was running from you." She was angry again. Angry and disgusted. "You're a monster. Regardless of who you are here, you can never make up for the things you've done. I don't care if you are the good half of your soul. If hell exists, nothing you do here will ever make up for the things you've done."

She waited for his gaze in the mirror, wanting to shoot daggers, but it never came. He stared straight ahead at the road, a look of sorrow on his face.

"I can't help what I've done in your world, and I can't feel guilty, because I didn't make those decisions. All I have power over are my actions here."

The car was quiet for a moment.

"Look at the girl next to you," he said. "Is she you? Do you take responsibility for the drugs she's taken or the things she's done to get them? You didn't even know she existed. Now that you know, though, are you sorry? Are you sorry for the crimes she committed? Are you responsible?"

"I'm right here!" the other Riley shot back. "I'm not just some worthless piece of shit."

Riley turned and looked at the other Riley, who was now seething in Zachary's direction. She turned away. "No. Because that is not me, and I did not do those things."

"Then don't be so quick to judge me."

"Oh, this is great," the other Riley said with a laugh, apparently having forgotten her anger. "Officer's got teeth."

Riley stared at her in disbelief. *This is nuts. This is not happening.* "Why'd you bring her?" she asked. "I get that the government wants to get rid of me, but what does that have to do with this…" She paused, looking for the right word. "Thing?"

"Just keep insulting yourself," the other Riley said, grinning. "This *thing* is half of you."

Part of Riley felt bad for being rude, but the person next to her was so repulsive. *There is no way you are part of me.*

"That's another piece of the story I haven't gotten to yet," Zachary said. "Have you ever known someone who died in a freak accident?"

"Well, yeah." Riley's mind wandered back in time. "A guy I went to school with got killed by a train when his car stalled on the railroad tracks."

"I'll tell you why that's relevant. We are two parts of one soul," Zachary said. "You and Riley are both just part of an entire being. If that makes sense."

"No," Riley said. "It doesn't, but I'm still listening."

"Basically, you are still connected to the other half of your soul, even though you live in two different worlds. If something really bad were to happen to this Riley, the same thing would happen to you. The split didn't completely divide us."

As the thought sank in, Riley suddenly saw the importance of their third passenger. *If they catch the other Riley, they could get to me. If it's true.*

"When someone dies in one of the worlds, they die in the other as well," he continued. "That freak accident you talked about probably happened because that guy was killed in my world. The body is just a vessel carrying the soul. Having two bodies does not make you two different people. Having half of a soul makes you part of one being. Or at least that's how it was explained to me."

Riley looked at Riley, trying to hear her thoughts, feel what she felt. *If she really is part of me, I should be able to sense a connection.* Nothing. After a few minutes of silence, the other Riley spoke.

"You can call me Oz," she said. "This is getting way too confusing for me with the whole same-name thing. Plus a plain name like Riley fits you better. There's nothing exciting about you."

"Why Oz?" *Where have I heard that recently?*

"Ever heard of L. Frank Baum?" the girl asked.

"Sure. He wrote *The Wizard of Oz.*" *Oh, yeah. That's what Zachary called me in the orchard.*

"Kind of. He stole his story from a girl like you." The girl called Oz twisted a strand of dark hair in her fingers. "Dorothy Gale was a real person who ended up here like you did and found her way back in the end. She must have gone and told her story to this Baum guy and he took it and made some cracked-out version about what our world is like."

"You mean this is Oz?" Riley didn't try to mask her disappointment.

"No, dumbass." The other Riley kicked the passenger seat in front of her. "I said he wrote a story about us, not that any of it was true. We don't have Munchkins and a yellow brick road. He made that shit up."

"So how did you find out about it?" Riley narrowed her eyes at her unstable companion.

"Like we said, every once in a while we get people like you who find their way into our world. One of them told us the story. Let me tell you, I want some of what that guy was on when he wrote it."

Riley shook her head in disgust, hardly hiding her annoyance. "Okay, so why are you called Oz then?"

"Someone once told me I was heartless," she laughed. "I told them that maybe I could go to Oz and the wizard would give me a heart just like the Tin Man. My friend thought it was funny and started calling me Oz."

"And you're proud of that?"

The girl stiffened and turned defiant green eyes on her. "I don't care what people think. I do what I want, and I am who I am. If I want to shoot up, drink, or do what I gotta do to get the shit I need, then it's nobody's business."

Riley's eyes grew wide and her jaw fell open. *Is this girl serious?* She looked toward Zachary's eyes in the mirror, but he stared at the road, a sad look creasing his face. Out the window, the desert rushed past. They were leaving Grand Junction and heading west. Bentonite foothills faded into rolling bluffs dotted with sage and juniper. *I can't believe this girl is supposedly me. We are nothing alike.*

She turned to Oz, who glared back, seeming to dare Riley to challenge what she'd said.

"You're wrong," Riley responded, fire blazing in her eyes. "Apparently it *is* my business. If you die, I die. Remember? I swear if you do any of that while I'm here, I'll…"

"You'll what?" Oz interrupted. "Hurt me? Ha! You can't do shit to me because it will hurt you as well. And you can't leave me because if they get me, they get you."

Riley felt a strong urge to punch her in her smug jaw. *Would I feel it if I broke her nose?* Her mind recalled the random bruises up and down her arms and the voices shouting in her head. *Yes, it would.*

"Face it," Oz mocked, now biting her lower lip. "You're stuck with me for who knows how long, so get used to the idea of sitting back and watching me do my thing."

"You're disgusting." Riley shivered. "And I feel sorry for you."

"And you're an ignorant bitch, and I'm glad I ended up on this end of the deal," Oz spat back.

It was quiet for a long time. Oz put headphones on and blared loud music, making Riley even madder. She felt embarrassed, as if she had behaved badly. All her life she'd done the right thing and hated being in trouble. *All for what? So in another world it could be canceled out by this lowlife?* If what they said was true, every decision she'd made in life hadn't mattered. The better she was, the worse her other half had been. Riley felt bad for accusing Zachary Stone of being an awful person. If this were true, then he was as innocent as she was.

That'll be a hard pill to swallow.

CHAPTER TWENTY-SEVEN

"**I** need to stop for gas." Zachary's voice broke the prolonged silence. "If you need to go to the bathroom or get food, now is your chance."

Food. Riley still hadn't eaten, and her stomach clenched at the sound of the word. They pulled into a service station, and she jumped out of the car—claustrophobic, starving, and needing to be away from that other girl. Hot, suffocating air tasted sweet and fresh compared to the tension inside the vehicle.

Riley glanced around the empty parking lot and then down at herself, suddenly feeling as oily and itchy as she looked. Sliding her tongue across her teeth, she felt the scum that had formed over the past few days without a toothbrush. She cringed, running her hands through greasy, matted hair. *Ew.*

Oz stepped from the car, headphones in, glared at Riley, and lit a cigarette. Zachary headed to the building to pay.

"Wait…" Riley didn't know how to broach the next part of her relationship with the man who'd tried to kill her. "Officer Stone."

He turned. "Please, call me Zach. I'm not your supervisor or a stranger anymore. I know you will probably never be able to call me friend either, so just think of me as someone trying to help."

"Help is something friends do for each other, Zach." Riley smiled, desperately wanting to trust him. Being alone in this place was almost scarier than believing in someone who had once tried to kill you.

"We may be stuck with each other for a while," he said. "Probably best if we can at least find it within ourselves to be kind."

"Agreed." Riley fell into step with him. "I'm not dead yet or locked in a prison cell, so I guess so far you're doing better than everyone else. I'm still confused and don't know what I believe, but I think I trust you. I know I want to."

"I hope so."

They walked into the gas station. Riley glanced longingly down the toiletries aisle at the miniature bottles of shampoo and soap bars. Even just a baby wipe sounded heavenly.

Zach smiled and nudged her. "Don't take this the wrong way, but I'm going to give you some money to get what you need for yourself. Between you and me, you could really use a shower."

"Thanks a lot!" She laughed, covering her filthy hair.

"I'm joking." He grinned as he handed her a wad of bills and went to the register to pay for the gas.

Riley walked down the aisle, grabbing deodorant, mascara, shampoo, and a toothbrush and toothpaste. In the restroom, she washed her hair in the sink, scrubbed the cobwebs from her mouth, and freshened up her face. It was the closest to normal she'd felt in a long time. Her reflection stared back from the mirror. *I look tired. Tired and sad.* Grasping the sides of the sink, she inhaled deeply. *What have I gotten myself into? And how?*

The story she'd just heard couldn't be real. But she'd once told an extraordinary story about her visions and their outcomes that no one believed. If one aspect of her life could be so inexplicable yet true, why couldn't life's facets have thousands of improbable faces? And she was willing to accept the idea that she was in hell or purgatory, or insane. *Was what they said any crazier than the explanations I came up with?*

The answer was no. As much as she wanted a rational explanation, the truth of it was so irrational that only an illogical answer could be correct. *So why not believe them?*

After all, a girl—an exact replica of herself—sat in the backseat saying horrible things. *How do I explain that?* Riley's eyes fell on Esther's ring, focusing on the sapphire-dotted tree. *Could I be in another one of my visions?*

In one dream, the man with the fiery sword sent her back to reality. Gabe woke her from another. *Maybe it's just a matter of time before someone pulls me from this fantasy.*

Riley left the bathroom, resolved to follow whatever plan Zach and Oz had in mind. *What else can I do?* She hated being at someone else's mercy, in someone else's control. Being in control was her thing. Sitting back and allowing events to unfold was not.

She smiled at the young cashier, who gave her a funny look and glanced back at his television. Trying to see what he was watching, she found herself yet again face to face with her own image, this one with the words "one-million-dollar reward" beneath it. *Crap.* She picked up her pace, feet pounding the white laminate floor.

"Stop!" The cashier made it to the door first, one hand turning the lock, the other gripping a shaking pistol aimed at her chest. "I can't let you go." He looked vacantly past her eyes. "I'm sorry."

Riley peered out the window for the car, but it was no longer at the pump. Panic surged as she clasped her hands together. "You have to let me go. Please, they'll kill me!"

"Sorry, lady." He wiped his sweating brow with a free hand. "I need that money."

"But they're going to *kill* me."

"Lie on the floor," he commanded, still shaking. "Put your hands behind your back so I can tie you up."

Riley stared helplessly at the man. "Please."

"Do it!" he screamed. "Or I'll shoot. I'll kill you myself!" Madness clouded his eyes and red hair flew in every direction, giving him the appearance of a demented clown.

She lay on the floor with her face touching the cool, filthy surface and glared down the candy aisle as the cashier tied her hands with unsteady palms. "What kind of person picks money over someone's life?"

"A desperate one. With nothing to lose." He cinched the rope tight around her wrists.

From behind, Riley heard the door rattle and a bell jingling. Craning her head, she saw Zach shaking the door handle and reaching for his gun. *They didn't leave me!*

The gas station attendant looked up, his face turning a shade darker than his hair. "Damn cop is gonna try to take credit for my find. Get behind the counter!"

The tip of his boot nudged her ribs, and Riley wiggled behind the counter to wait, closing her eyes and breathing deeply. She needed Zach to help her escape yet again.

Her captor sidled to the door and unlocked it. "What do you want, officer?" His voice oozed forced pleasantry.

"You've got a prisoner of mine," Zach replied with a firm voice. "If you could please release her back to me, then I will be on my way, and we won't have any trouble."

"You got papers?" the clerk asked as he placed his fists on his hips and leaned against the doorframe.

"I don't need papers," Zach replied. "I'm an officer. I'm taking her in myself."

The clerk laughed. "Nobody transports Demies without a permit. Even I know that. Now get out of my station and quit trying to claim what isn't yours."

"Don't make this difficult." Zach took a step forward, but the man in the doorway didn't move. "Riley, go to the car."

She struggled to stand up behind the counter and turned to face her captor. He took a step back and aimed his gun at her.

"Move and I shoot!" He held his other hand out as a signal for Zach to stay put.

Riley's eyes grew wide. *How many times will I have to face death?*

"You won't shoot anybody." Zach's voice remained calm. Riley was amazed at how relaxed he could be in a situation like this. She was on the verge of breaking down and losing herself to the protection of a numb mind.

"If you shoot," Zach continued, "you won't have anyone to give to them. There won't be any money in it for you. So you can't win. The only way you win is to kill me, and then you'll be enjoying your million from behind bars. So let's go with my first statement. You can't win this one."

Riley looked at Zach for reassurance, and he nodded toward the parking lot. The two men stood with guns pointed at each other, as if in some old Western shootout. She held her breath as she scurried out the door, Zach close on her heels.

"We need to get out of here. Fast." He cut the rope around her wrists as they hurried through the empty parking lot.

"Hey, cop!" a voice shouted.

They turned in unison as the attendant raised his gun, pointing it at Zach's chest. "They'll ignore your death if I've got her to give them."

Rough pavement scraped her hands and knees as Riley was shoved to the ground. Shots rang out overhead as glass from shattered light bulbs and electrical flashes rained down on the dark asphalt.

"Get to the car!" Zach shouted. "Get Oz and get out of here!"

Sighting in on the silver BMW through the shower of sparks, Riley stood and ran, jumping into the driver's seat and cranking the ignition.

"We leaving Stone?" Oz asked from the backseat, reeking of cigarette smoke and too much perfume.

"Shut up!" Riley shouted. "I'm not leaving anyone. I'm trying to save us."

Panic and adrenaline coursed through her body as she swung the car back around toward the front. Zach and the attendant crouched behind opposing ice and Coke machines. Soda cans spilled out from the gaping hole in one and rolled down the parking lot like mice finally set free from a cage. The windows in the building lay scattered across the ground, and a screaming alarm added to the chaos of the scene.

"Get in the car!" Oz shouted at Zach from the backseat. "We don't want to die on your account!"

Riley slammed on the brakes next to the ice machine as Oz flung open the door and Zach dove into the backseat. She hit the gas pedal before he'd even reached to close the door, and it flung shut with the forward momentum. Tires screeched and bullets peppered the side of the car as they sped away.

"What the hell just happened?" Riley yelled, staring wild eyed at the road ahead. "A million dollars? I'm worth a million dollars? Worth enough to kill for? There's got to be more to this story than you're telling me."

"I don't know what they want with you, Riley," Zach said through quick breaths. "The government has always put a heavy price on people from the other world. I told you, we're going to find someone who can give you more answers than I have."

She stared ahead, unblinking. *What I wouldn't give to be in Boulder with my old life.* "What's a Demi?" She remembered what the gas station clerk had called her. "That guy said you can't transport Demies without a permit."

"You're the Demi." Oz lifted her legs up and laid her crossed ankles and dirty boots on Zach's lap. "The other half of me. That's the scientific term for you people."

Riley jerked the steering wheel, swerving as she tried to regain control, having realized too late she was driving off the road.

"Pull over, Riley." Zach moved Oz's legs gently back to the floor and leaned forward. "A lot has just happened, and you need to take a second to breathe. You don't need to be driving right now."

She pulled onto the shoulder, taking deep breaths and trying to focus. *Stillness. Find the stillness.* Riley stepped from the car, unable to shake the fear from her system and trying hard to fight the hyperventilation that wanted to consume her. It seemed every time she let her guard down, something new and terrifying happened.

Zach rested a hand on her shoulder. "Thank you, by the way." He pointed in the direction they'd come from. "For back there. I guess we're even now. I save you, you save me."

"I'm starting to make a habit of getting into trouble." Riley wanted to cry. "And it's just going to get worse from here on out, isn't it?"

He gave her a sympathetic look and sighed. "As more and more people watch the news and learn about you, the hunt will be on. So I'm afraid the answer is yes. There are a lot of greedy people in this world."

"Fantastic." Riley steadied herself against the car, feeling her blood settle down. "I guess our worlds have more in common than we thought."

He walked to the driver's side. "Just don't forget there are still good people out there. In fact, there are as many good people as there are bad. You just have to work harder to find them."

"I really hope to never be in a situation like that again." Riley climbed into the front seat and closed her eyes.

"We're a hot commodity," Oz teased. "But I'm used to this. Pigs are always after me."

"Quit doing drugs and we'll leave you alone, Oz." Zach smiled at her in the rearview mirror. "You make it too easy for us."

Oz leaned in over the console and patted his shoulder. "Aw, but then you'd be out of a job, and we wouldn't want that. You'd be bored without me."

Zach gave a small laugh. It was evident he genuinely cared about Oz, but Riley couldn't fathom why he wasted his time on her.

Riley lay back in the seat and tried to get comfortable. Some part of her still believed she was dreaming or maybe in a coma. Another part of her was still convinced she had died. But as they drove along I-70 through the deserts of southern Utah, an overwhelming feeling of reality hit. *If I'm going to make it home, I'll have to be on the top of my game. And that means trusting no one.*

She had no choice but to continue this mystery journey with Zach and Oz, but for all she knew, the charming man beside her was just going somewhere to turn her in for the cash, or worse. Everything he had done so far was admirable, and she wanted so badly to trust him. *But he could turn his back any second. Some form of Zachary kills people. You want no part of that. Get to this man who knows everything and figure out how to get home.*

Really the only person she felt she could trust was the dope-head version of herself who reeked of tobacco and hummed out of tune to the music grating from her headphones. They had the same interest: to live. Riley knew her survival plan had to include protecting Oz. One thing was certain in all this, no matter how much she hated it: there was no denying that she and Oz shared identical DNA.

They rode in silence. Riley dozed in and out of sleep, plagued by fitful dreams of people trying to capture and kill her. When she finally pulled herself out of the nightmare realm, she looked over at Zach and saw him staring straight ahead at the road. She turned to look out the window at the sunset falling over the barren landscape.

Zach interrupted the silence. "We need a different car. They know what to look for. They probably know which direction we're headed."

Riley nodded. "How do you suggest we get said vehicle? We don't have that much cash, and you can't risk using a card."

"We could steal one," Oz muttered from the backseat. "It would only take me about sixty seconds."

"When you say things like that, it makes it hard for me to believe we're the same person," Riley said with disdain.

Oz snorted and kicked at the front seat like a toddler on an airplane. Riley pretended not to feel it.

"If a car goes missing, they'll be looking for it. We'll be an easy target," Zach said. "Even if I trade mine in, they'll know it's us. You saw the newscast. We're everywhere."

"What about a bus?" Riley suggested. "We can ditch your car somewhere and take public transportation. I know it's risky, but I think it's the best option we've got."

Wheels churned behind Zach's gray eyes. "We'll drive for a few more hours and get on a bus in Vegas. If everything goes smoothly, that should take us to LA."

"Vegas?" Riley had been invited to go there during college but turned it down. Vegas sounded like her idea of hell.

"Why would we want to go to Vegas?" A horrified look crossed Oz's face like she'd just smelled something rotten. "It's like the capital of holier than thou. The capital of no sex, no parties, and no fun whatsoever. It's where you go when you decide that you've given up on all the joys life has to offer." She finished with a dramatic shudder.

Riley turned in her seat, confused. "Then where do people go to do all of that stuff you just listed if not Vegas? I thought that was the whole point of Vegas."

"Salt Lake City," Oz stated, as if this should be obvious. "Where streams run clear with vodka, and white powder falls from the sky like snow. Where rich men come to spend all of their money, and girls like you and me can get a piece of it for a piece of us. Maybe we can go there sometime, and I can teach you the ways of the real Riley Dale."

Riley let out a noise of disgust. The thought of her doing anything more rebellious than playing beer pong on a Monday night was ridiculous.

"I think one of you being wild is enough," Zach joked. "I can't imagine having to keep track of and take care of two of you."

Riley smiled. "Isn't that what you're doing now?"

"Yeah, but you're a hell of a lot easier than that one back there." He winked, and the flutter it caused in her heart made her nauseous. *He's a killer! Sort of.*

"I can solve this problem," Oz said from the back, sounding serious. "I'm not going to the government just because this one's America's most wanted." She nodded in Riley's direction. "In fact, I'm thinking in Vegas I may go my own way. I really don't feel safe with you two. Especially not after that shit at the gas station earlier."

"You aren't going anywhere, Oz," Zach replied firmly. "While you are with me, I swear to protect you. If you leave, they'll find you. Whether or not you're with us, someone will be tracking you too. They're hunting both of you. I suggest you stay with the person carrying the gun."

"You're right." Oz smiled back at him, a little too friendly. "We'll get to LA and rethink everything."

On and on they drove as the world darkened. Riley couldn't help thinking about Gabe and wondering what he was doing, and if he knew she was gone yet. She wanted to think he'd look for her—pointlessly search the entire planet trying to find his lost...*friend.*

"Would you mind driving for a while?" Zach asked, massaging the back of his neck. "I need a break."

"Yeah, sure." Riley rubbed the sleep from her eyes and yawned.

He pulled over, and she stepped from the car, looking at the sky above. Layer upon layer of tiny flickering fireballs hovered millions of miles away yet seemed so reachable. It was as if some giant in the heavens had scattered glitter across a black sheet of paper.

Riley took the wheel and headed west. Oz had fallen asleep, and Zach gazed out the window, lost in his own personal turmoil. Now that her heart wasn't racing and she had her breath, driving offered a sort of therapy. She felt in control of the entire situation, and after spiraling out of it for so long, the simple act of directing a vehicle made her feel powerful.

"I've been wanting to ask," Zach began, "but at the same time I don't want to hear it." He paused, as if searching the road ahead for his thoughts. "You said I raped and murdered in your world..."

Pain creased his face as he tapped his knuckles on the window. Riley wanted to feel sorry for him, but she could only picture the dried blood between Rachel's blackened thighs.

"A few weeks ago, I stumbled across a body near the river. She had been stabbed, strangled, and raped. She was the fifth girl found like that." Riley looked over to see his expression, but it remained fixed in painful concentration.

"The bodies were found with various forms of mutilation. One girl was missing her eyes, another her breasts. One girl's head was found separated from her body."

Riley swallowed. She loathed the man who'd done those things, wanted the worst for him. But it felt wrong for the man next to her to hear this. It must be like finding out you were really Ted Bundy.

"I'm sorry," she whispered.

Zach continued to stare at the road. "And you said I attacked you? Did I..."

"Yes and no. I woke up and you were in my room. You tried to..." This time she couldn't finish the sentence. "But I just got banged up and managed to jump out my window. You chased me, and I thought for sure I was going to die. Then I fell, and you were there. That day you found me in the field—when you said I had run from my house—well, I don't have any idea how it happened, but that's when I ended up here."

Zach rested a trembling hand on Riley's. "I'm so sorry. I know it's a lot for you to understand, but as much as that man is me, he is not at the same time. I am as good as he is bad, and I'm so sorry for what you've gone through. I promise I won't hurt you or anyone else."

Riley finally allowed herself to feel sorry for the broken man beside her. She felt lucky now that the only thing her other half did was drugs and probably prostitution to get them.

Those things seemed harmless compared to the things Zachary Stone had to accept about himself.

"I know it wasn't you." She gave a half smile through the darkness. Even with his features lit up in the greens and blues of the instrument panel like some outer-space alien, nothing about him scared her. "I'm not afraid of you anymore."

He bit the corner of his lip and nodded. "Thanks."

"There's something else I need to tell you," Riley said, as a realization dawned. "I reported you. They know you did all of those things. They'll be coming for you, and if you're caught…"

He looked knowingly at her. "Death row." He shook his head. "Sounds like I deserve it."

"But you'll die too, right?"

"We're all going to die sometime, Riley. And as much as I hate the thought, the other alternative is for the evil me to escape and keep doing what he's doing. I would accept death to save all those innocent people who would die if he—I—weren't caught." He held Riley's anxious gaze. "You did the right thing. And you know that."

"I just can't believe the world is less black and white than we ever imagined. You tried to kill me, but oh wait, turns out you're actually really good as well. And I may have stopped a killer, but I've also condemned an innocent man to death." She turned to look at him. "How does anyone deal with that?"

He let out a slow breath. "It's a strange thing, realizing there's a second story to each book. There really is truth to the statement that even the worst people have good in them, and even the best have a dark side. The hard part is wrapping your mind around them being in two bodies, in two worlds, instead of one."

"Hard is an understatement. It's impossible."

"I just found out my other half is a monster." His face darkened. "Trust me, I'm right there with you."

This all started with my visions. How is it all connected? Riley couldn't stand being stuck in her head. She decided to take his mind from the dark place it lingered. "So how did you and Oz become friends, or whatever you are?"

Zach glanced over his shoulder to the backseat. "I've known Riley, I mean Oz, for a long time. I first met her when she was fifteen and I was a twenty-two-year-old rookie officer. That was the first time I arrested her. She was smoking pot with some other kids. I didn't think much of it at the time, just thought she was being dumb. I mean, we've all been there. But then a year later, I brought her in again."

A vein pulsed in his neck, and Riley thought he might tear up, but he composed himself. "I found her in an alleyway passed out. I had to pull two guys off her and race her to the hospital. Drug overdose. I was scared she wouldn't make it.

"No one came to see her, to check if she was okay. So I watched over her. I was the only one who cared if she lived or died. And in that moment, that week at the hospital, I vowed to protect and help that lost sixteen-year-old girl. I vowed to save her." He sighed. "I don't know how much good I've done, but she's still alive, I guess."

Riley felt sad. Sad and dirty. She was beginning to understand what Zach had just gone through with her account of his other half. *So I've been raped? And overdosed on drugs?* She choked back the bile rising in her throat and bit down on the inside of her cheeks. "And she never changed? Never stopped, even though it almost killed her?"

"Oz came from a really bad family. That girl back there is still just a sad, scared, lost teenager in need of help."

"Yeah, but at some point she has to take responsibility. She can't blame others for her problems forever or she'll always be a victim."

He shrugged. "Since then she's been brought in for prostitution, drug abuse, and hustling cocaine. And she's ended up in the hospital countless times when some of her lesser male clients have taken out their anger on her."

Riley felt her face contort in horror. The worst things that happened to her were bad grades and having to give presentations in speech class. She glanced in the rearview mirror at the sleeping girl, filled with a mixture of revulsion and pity. All Riley had learned tonight was how unfair the world could be. "Why do you do it? Why do you fight for someone who doesn't care?"

"Because *I* care. And because maybe someday she will too."

Riley studied his face, noting the anguish and frustration that ran deep in every line and twitch of his body. *He loves her?*

Zach reached for Riley's hand and squeezed. "We're gonna be okay. I promise. You, Oz, me, the rest of the world. It's always been like this, and somehow we still wake up to another day."

"I'll never wake up like I used to," Riley scoffed. "My life will never be the same. Even if I make it home, how do I go on living like everything is okay? Knowing that my life is tied to someone who doesn't care what happens to hers? Knowing that a man on death row will take the life of his innocent other? Knowing that my kind neighbor is also a rapist or a thief and that my own family has done horrific things somewhere else?"

Zach stared at his hands, and Riley stared at the dotted yellow lines flying past in the illuminated sphere of the headlights.

"Tell me about you." He changed the subject. "I know all about the Riley Dale of my world, but tell me about the other half. The half I knew was in there somewhere."

"There's not much to say." She panicked at the idea of trying to convey intrigue and excitement. She wanted to impress the new Zach. "Compared to what I've learned, my life is simple, boring, and normal."

"Normal is a subjective thing."

She laughed. "Um…I have a good family. I just graduated from college. I love my friends. I don't really do anything bad."

"What did you study in school?"

"Environmental science."

"So you're an animal lover?"

"I love everything that has to do with nature and the outdoors."

He smiled. "What do you do for fun?"

"I don't know."

He shook his head and laughed. "You don't know? Or is it easier for you to talk about morbid, overwhelming things than yourself?"

"I guess so." Riley tried to focus more on the road than on his captivating smile. "I like to hike and camp. You know, really anything outdoors. I'm not so anxious when I'm out there and the world isn't closing in." Her cheeks burned. "I read a lot, and I like to garden."

"So you're an old woman?"

The heat in her face grew. "I guess so."

"We'd get along really well if circumstances were different," he said. "I know of this incredible lake up in the mountains with spectacular views and killer fishing. You'd love it."

Riley's face betrayed horror, and he laughed.

"Okay, too weird?"

"It's a little weird. You know, to be talking about how you tried to kill me and then you offering to take me into the middle of nowhere to go "killer" fishing. It's a little sketchy if you ask me."

"You're right." His hands went up in surrender. "Baby steps."

Riley had an odd feeling. It was strange to talk to a man who'd tried to kill her—to talk about normal things, even. And stranger still, she found the longer she spent with him, the more she enjoyed his company. She even found it comforting.

"So tell me about you, then," she said. "I know the rapist-murderer version, but convince me now that there really is good inside every soul."

"Ouch, that's a hard accusation." He paused. "Let's see. I work at the police department as an officer, which you already know. I wanted to be a cop my entire life. This is going to sound really corny, but I've always wanted to help people.

"In my free time, I like to be outside as well. I love playing baseball and running. I have a handicapped sister who is my life, and every weekend I spend a day hanging out with her and her friends at the house where she lives. I'm not gonna lie. I enjoy a good glass of whiskey every now and then, and I have an extreme weakness for tacos and cotton candy."

She let out a burst of laughter. "You sound normal. Like a real human being. A good human being."

He grinned. "I think that's what I am."

"Do you know how weird this is for me?" Riley released the steering wheel with her right hand and lightly smacked her forehead.

"I can guess."

Tapping her fingers on the console, she wondered if she should broach the next subject. "How long have you been in love with her?" *Too late.*

"What?" He stared at her with innocent eyes. "With who?"

"With Oz. No one does what you do and gets nothing in return unless he's in love."

"It's complicated." He smirked. "That's all there is to it."

"Uh huh." She decided to let it go. *For now.*

His gray eyes twinkled, and Riley noticed his handsome features even more. The beast had transformed before her. She trusted him, believed that he really did have their best interests at heart. This was not the same man who'd tried to hurt her. This was a man who spent time with his helpless sister, a man whose heart ached for a lost and broken girl.

CHAPTER TWENTY-EIGHT

James Rutherford smiled triumphantly at the memo in front of him. *So they're heading west. That can only mean one place. He's taking them to Los Angeles.*

The detective had recovered quickly from the escape and immediately prepared a force to pursue them once any news of the fugitives' whereabouts was noted. Alerts came about two hours after they fled.

James prided himself on always being one step ahead. Through his connections with national higher-ups, he'd acquired an FBI comm unit, which kept him in the loop of the inner workings of the capital. He liked the power that came with confidential information. It was through the use of this device that his secretary heard the message about Zachary Stone and the Dale Demies. Apparently there had been a run-in at a gas station in Utah, and the silver car was spotted shortly after, heading west on I-70.

He twisted the small paper between his fingers. "Maureen," he called out to his secretary.

"Yes?" a plump, timid woman answered, peeking her head around the doorframe.

"Let the boys know it's time to move. They've got a little bit of a head start, but we should catch them if we run with lights on. I think this constitutes an emergency." He winked and ran his fingers through his wavy hair.

"Yes, sir." Maureen backed out of the room. "Right away."

"And Maureen." He grabbed a spare gun—his favorite—from the safe and set it on the desk.

"Yes?"

"Let the president know I'll meet his boys in Vegas. We'll trap the son of a bitch from both sides." *Zachary Stone must be an idiot if he thinks he can outsmart me.*

CHAPTER TWENTY-NINE

"**A**nd do you really think we'll make it all the way to Vegas before someone catches up with us?" Oz spoke up from the backseat. She had been in and out for the last few hours, catching pieces of the conversation from the front but mostly trying to fight off the insatiable cravings inside, intense urges to vomit, and pain all over. "I mean, call me crazy, but there's really only one place that makes sense for us to go, and I think someone will figure that out."

Wiping the ever-running stream of snot dripping from her nose, she clutched her aching stomach. It hadn't even been two days since her last shot, and already she wanted to rip the crawling veins from her body and shove them up someone's ass. *I'm gonna die.*

Oz had experienced this feeling only once before, when her dealer got busted and she wasn't able to get a hit for seventy-two hours. She had been in some pretty bad situations, but nothing felt closer to dying than coming down from heroin. *Maybe a cigarette would help.* Her stomach twisted at the thought, and the back of her throat prepared for an explosion.

"Pull over," she demanded, unable to fight it any longer.

"Is everything okay?" Zach peered over his shoulder.

"Pull over now, damn it. Or I'll puke in the car."

Oz waited until the vehicle was mostly stopped, then flung open the car door and retched all over the ground. She collapsed on the seat for a moment before a second wave hit, and she stumbled out to spew her insides all over a ripe prickly pear.

"What's wrong with you?" Riley asked. "You look terrible."

Oz felt a cool hand rest on her forehead. She wanted to slap it away, but the temperature of it felt good on her burning flesh. "Get me a cigarette from my bag."

"You're burning up," Riley said, ignoring the request. "And really pale."

Oz groaned and wiped the bile dribbling from her chin. "Food poisoning, maybe?"

"Oh yeah? What did you eat?" Zach studied her sallow face with intense eyes.

He knows. She rolled onto her back with closed eyes and pulled her knees into her chest. Zach could be a pain in the ass, but she still hated to let him down. Seeing disappointment on his face was like watching someone kick a puppy. Innocent things shouldn't suffer like that. She hated how he acted like a parent and hated even more that she felt like a child around him.

"Fish," she groaned. "Always seems to make me sick."

"Do you have any on you?" Zach hovered over her with storms raging in his eyes.

"Why the hell would I have a fish on me?"

"Don't play dumb. I'm not new to this with you or with anybody in your situation, for that matter. Where is it?"

The increased volume in his voice seared Oz's brain. She clutched her head, afraid of being consumed by another wave of nausea. "Do you think I'd be like this if I had any on me?" The tingling in her blood grew more maddening.

Zach took a step back and pointed a sharp finger at Riley, who stood wide eyed and clueless by the passenger door. "She doesn't get out of our sight. One of us needs to be with her always."

Oz watched Riley nod like she knew what she was doing. She wanted to smack her in the mouth. "I don't need a babysitter." She pushed her way back into the car. "Especially not her. She doesn't look like she could wipe her ass without someone's help."

"You'll be fine in a week," Zach said callously. "We need to get going. Are you done for now?"

"You're going to leave me like this?" Oz asked, horrified at the thought of at least six more days of hell.

"Your choice, not mine." He slammed the door.

Oz fumed in the backseat, although it was hard to stay mad with all the painful distractions overwhelming her system. *He doesn't know what it's like. He doesn't have a clue.* It wasn't her choice, not really. She had been months behind in payments—payments that were collected by a guy with a bat, not a guy in a suit with a cheap tie and an even worse pair of shoes. She'd had two days to get three grand together before ending up bloodied and fucked in a ditch when some guy offered her a good amount of money, enough to pay the bills and eat for a whole month.

On one condition…

Yeah, he'd wanted the usual opening between her legs, but he also wanted to stick a different needle in her, and he wanted her to help him sell. She'd be set so long as he could watch her do it once to know that she was all in. He'd even pay the back debt.

"She's right, though," she heard Zach say to Riley. "They'll be on us soon. I've been stupid to think we could make it all the way to Vegas unnoticed."

I've got to get away from here and find something. As Zach took over and the car accelerated at an aggressive pace, Oz clutched her head in her hands and tried to breathe away the overwhelming pain. Zach might as well hand her over to the authorities. As far as she was concerned, she was dead anyway.

———

Riley twisted Esther's ring around her finger as buildings popped up, signaling an approaching town. The unyielding desert finally gave up a few houses and even sparse greenery.

Heroin? Part of me is in the middle of a heroin crash?

She figured nothing would surprise or shock her anymore, but observing the convulsing image of herself retching and shaking in the backseat changed that notion. Riley was torn between feeling sorry for the pathetic girl and being angry. *It's my life too!*

Oz could accidentally kill herself anytime with an overdose or a bad drug, and Riley's life would be cut short as well. Her existence was a ticking time bomb, and Oz held the detonator—too carelessly at that. Apparently every breath was more random and precarious than she'd imagined.

Riley looked at Zach and sympathized with what he must be going through. Her heroin-addicted other soul seemed like an angel compared to his murderous one, but knowing what you were capable of still caused damage. *It's a good thing no one in my world knows about this. It would be chaos.*

The car jerked suddenly as Zach pulled into a junkyard parking lot and stopped under a peeling sign and a flickering street lamp. Shiny, broken humps of metal sparkled like rusted gems in the squared lot of the yard, and a coiling slinky of barbed wire rimmed the fence, sending the unspoken message to keep out.

He poked Oz. "I need you to pull yourself together for a second."

A low grumble answered.

Zach disappeared behind the car and returned with a pair of bolt cutters, a box of tools, and a small black duffel.

"Easy, Zach." Riley straightened in her seat. "What are you doing?"

"We'll never make it in this car." He rummaged through the bag and pulled out a flashlight. "I need our token criminal to wake up and put her skills to good use. Nobody will miss a car from a junkyard."

"Yeah, but don't you think they'll notice the cut lock?" Riley stepped from the car, feeling the need to talk sense into her new friend.

"Nah. Kids break into these places all the time. We should be fine. Let's go, Oz."

Oz moaned again and managed to slide out of the backseat. Her dark hair hung limply around an ashen face as she stood shaking in the darkness.

"Okay, Riley," Zach began. "Drive this car in there and park somewhere out of sight."

Riley stared dubiously at the once-sleek sports car now peppered with bullet holes. *Good luck with that.*

She hopped into the driver's seat and drove through the gate to a spot near the middle of the yard in between a rusted, sagging school bus and a T-boned single-cab truck. It felt wrong to abandon a nice car in such a broken-down area, although the battle wounds from earlier helped it blend in with the surrounding debris.

Riley quietly closed the car door and navigated back through corroded metal, aged tractors missing implements, dented and broken minivans, and the occasional bicycle that seemed to beg to be taken for one last ride. The whole place made her sad. It was like she'd come to the Island of Misfit Toys, but for old vehicles that had done the best they could yet still ended up discarded and left to die in the rain. She walked faster, reminding herself that these were inanimate objects without feelings.

Vrooooom. The sound of an engine up ahead to the right drew her attention.

She raced in the direction of the noise, leaping over a fallen bumper and tripping over a partially buried tire. Riley found her companions standing next to what was probably once a candy-apple-red Mustang, now more rust than red, and having misplaced a front bumper and two back windows somewhere along the way.

"You're joking, right?"

"Hop in." Zach laughed, now buttoning a faded shirt and wearing old Wranglers he must have pulled from the duffel. The officer and his sleek car had vanished somewhere in the night. Riley tried to convince herself there was nothing attractive about his rustic appearance, but somehow she kept picturing his muscled figure leaning against a truck on the cover of a romance novel.

"It's the only one we could find that would actually start." His voice snapped her back to reality.

"Is this car even street legal?" Her eyes left his handsome face for the pile of rubbish that was supposed to take her safely down the highway.

"Everyone is looking for a BMW, Riley. I don't think they'll be too concerned with a broken-down beater dragging along."

"If you say so." She jumped into the front seat. Oz had already curled up in the back, moaning and clutching her forehead.

"You did well," Zach told her. More grunts. "Just don't ever do it again."

"Mmmmmm."

Zach eased the heap of scrap metal out of the gate, and Riley hopped out to close it, noticing the stars still burning brightly in the peaceful evening. Looking back the way they had come, she felt farther from home than ever. She'd just stolen a car, something the old Riley would never dream of doing—something the old Riley would never have had a chance to do, because she would have been smart enough not to put herself in this kind of situation.

The way home lay at the end of an infinite night sky that stretched backward to inaccessible places full of inaccessible people. The road ahead was dark as well, although the lights from the next town created a warm, glowing haze above the shadowed ridge of the mountains that beckoned her forward. Light lay ahead, not behind. The quickest way back to the old Riley was to continue down the path that led her away from familiarity and safety.

Uh oh. Wailing cries and screaming blares came first, followed by red and blue lights on the horizon. An array of blinding flashes flew toward the idling car they had just stolen. The colors bounced off the rocks, creating grotesque shapes and shadows in the darkness. She ran and jumped into the front seat. "Go!"

"I'll never outrun them, Riley. There's no way they know we broke into this place. There were no alarms. Just stay calm and let them pass. I'd rather have them ahead of us anyway."

She tried to breathe deeply, but the approaching lights made her heart pound faster and throat grow smaller, as if the hands of all those chasing them pressed down on her windpipe. A half mile, a quarter mile. *At least they aren't slowing down.*

The first car whizzed past, and her blood froze into small arterial icicles. She ducked down, trying to make herself as small as possible. The imaginary hands clenched tighter. Car after car flew by with shrill wails that echoed through the busted windows. Lights distorted her companion's faces into warped red-and-blue masks of fear. Riley quivered in the front seat and held her hands over her ears, begging the screaming monster to stop, to crawl back into its cave and die.

"Did they send the whole state after us?" Panic threatened to take her under. "Do they even have any authority out here?"

Zach stared ahead, his shocked face illuminated by the dazzling display flying past. Finally it went dark, and the desert faded back into silence, but no one moved.

"Seventeen." He let out a pressured sigh. "I counted seventeen vehicles."

"Why am I so important to them?" Riley covered her face with her hands, not wanting to see anything else conjured up in this malevolent world.

Zach shook his head. "I think there's a lot more to this than we know."

"If we hadn't gotten off the road when we did…"

"I know." His voice rose barely over a whisper. "I know."

They sat in the hushed dark. Riley trembled, Zach turned to stone, and Oz mumbled and shuddered in the back.

"How much farther?" Riley finally asked.

"About two hours."

"Will we make it?"

She didn't like the answer his silence suggested.

Chapter Thirty

Zachary Stone was not a virgin to the concept of fear or disappointment. He'd been born into a world where, more often than not, someone wanted to hurt you and where most good deeds or friendly smiles came with a price. He had long ago resigned himself to the fact that people worth knowing were few and far between. Maybe that's why he'd never married, never really even looked for someone to spend his life with. He had friends, but his circle of trust was small. And given the number of times he'd been screwed over, he liked to keep it that way.

He figured that was why he spent his free time with his sister. She had no agenda and gave love unconditionally without wanting anything in return. But as much as he resisted the friendships of people around him, it wasn't because he had given up hope or just didn't care.

Oftentimes he'd spend long hours on his couch with a glass of whiskey, trying to figure out how to solve the world's problems. It was a daunting task, which was probably the reason it needed to be accompanied with a strong drink. So far all he had come up with was that if he could save one person, he'd made a difference. Hopefully there were others out there doing the same thing. Maybe if enough people did one good deed, there would actually be some change.

Oz was that person for him. Since the day he'd caught her under the bridge, something had tied them together. So far saving her had been an impossible task, with her always ending up at this party or that, with this guy or that, on this drug or that, steadily falling lower and lower into a pit he would soon be unable to reach.

And all the while his feelings grew and his connection strengthened, as if each time he pulled her up, he became a knight all over again, and someday she would lay down her masochistic weapons and see the brave man who actually cared. He glanced at the weak girl quivering in the backseat. At times like this, he felt bad, like it was his fault she hadn't found her way. He kept reminding himself that if it weren't for him, she'd probably be dead.

And now he'd met Riley, the other half of Oz. Maybe his role in all of this had been to keep Oz alive long enough to meet her other half. Maybe Riley could show Oz a life bigger than money and drugs.

Zach grew fonder of Riley—the girl he always knew Oz could be. Despite knowing about the split souls and separate worlds, the idea that the two girls in the car with him were one person still staggered his mind. *I doubt it will ever seem normal.*

But where Oz was hard and unyielding, Riley was kind and genuine. Even though her mind struggled with fear and unease, he knew he could trust her. If he could combine Riley's character with Oz's strength, he would have found the perfect woman.

Ahead Zach could make out a pointed spire looming above the surrounding mountains. The bedraggled car had somehow managed to chug along, and so far no one pursued. That would have been comforting if he didn't already know it would take a miracle to get in and out of Vegas unseen and alive. His only hope was for their enemies to assume the trio had already passed through town and were well on their way to Los Angeles. Either way, a fight was coming, and based on numbers, the outcome didn't look good.

Chapter Thirty-One

Desert plants dotted the dry landscape as red rocks rose up to meet brown hills and distant blue-tinted mountains. So far the drive into Vegas looked a lot like the postcards Riley had seen of the landscape around the Hoover Dam and Lake Powell. But the city Oz had described earlier did not match Riley's mental image of girls in tiny dresses and half-naked men in bowties. She could see the city in the distance, growing out of the arid wasteland. Tall, pointed buildings lay ahead, but Riley couldn't make out any detail from so far away.

"You all need to hunker down when we drive in." Zach pulled a baseball cap from the black duffel and tugged it low over his face. "We need it to look like I'm in this car by myself."

Riley squeezed into the small space between the dash and the front seat and shifted uncomfortably. She heard Oz roll haphazardly off the backseat onto the floorboards and let out a groan.

The minutes passed and Riley's numb legs began to scream for room to stretch. "What do you see up there?"

"Police. Everywhere. I'm going to park a little ways off from the bus station and walk over to get tickets. If I'm not back in forty-five minutes, you need to leave. Don't come looking for me. Just get out of here and get to Los Angeles."

"We can't do this without you!" Riley panicked at the thought of Zach leaving and having to rely on Oz alone for safety for the next three hundred miles. "Please come back."

He gave an encouraging nod. "If I don't, the man you need to find is Ezra Ahmad. At this point the cops may be watching his place if they think that's where we'll go. Always keep your head up and eyes open, and don't trust anyone."

Zach steered into a packed parking lot and shut off the engine. He pulled a small notepad from his pocket and scribbled directions on it.

"Here." He handed the paper to Riley. "This will get you to Ezra."

"Good luck." She watched as he shut the door and hurried out of sight. Wiggling from her cramped space, Riley peeked up to see out the windshield. *Holy shit.*

Zach hadn't lied. Red and blue lights flashed everywhere. Uniformed men and men in plain clothes who were on too much of a mission to just be passersby roved the streets.

But more shocking than the army of warm bodies out to get them were the monumental structures rising from the ground. Riley stared in awe at the ornate temples, churches, mosques, and cathedrals occupying spaces she had expected hotels and casinos to dominate. It appeared every religion in the world had set up shop in the deserts of Nevada and tried to outdo each other in grandeur.

She momentarily forgot about being hunted by the world at large. The city was beautiful, breathtaking—something that would fit better in Istanbul or Florence.

"Oz, you have to see this. It's amazing."

Oz heaved herself up and peered out the window. "Oh, great. Church." She flopped back down to the floor. "I already hate this place."

Riley couldn't take her eyes off the landscape. Moments of awe and happiness came few and far between and needed to be cherished. In the last few days, her world had grown exponentially—mostly for the worse. She couldn't let this one moment of splendor disappear too quickly.

CHAPTER THIRTY-TWO

Zach swore under his breath as he ducked into a small store-front doorway to avoid the gaggle of uniformed men marching toward him. The soldiers wore army green, their heads were shaved, and they had M-16s draped over their shoulders. *Please tell me there is someone else here the government is after.*

"Apparently this one's different, though," he heard one say as they passed. "Commander said she's to go straight to the president when we find her. There's a nice reward for the fella who brings her in."

Another soldier responded, and the group laughed, but they were too far away for Zach to hear. He'd understood enough, though. *It's not just Rutherford. The president wants them too.*

Zach scanned the road and headed for the bus station, trying to steady his pace to fit in with the rest of the crowd. Clergymen, nuns, tourists, religious fanatics, and protestors mingled in the street, hurried to work, and posed for pictures in front of the impressive structures. He recoiled again at the sight of uniformed officers hurrying down the avenue but let out a deep breath when he saw them headed to break up a fight. Zach thanked God for the division he'd brought among people today. It offered better cover than he'd hoped for.

As he examined his surroundings for signs of trouble, his eyes locked on the most disturbing sight he'd seen yet. Posters— big, small, and billboard size—plastered the street, asking for help locating a very dangerous individual illegally traveling with two Demies. The government had raised the reward to three million dollars. Zach stared at the distinct faces looking out from the posters. *They didn't even choose a good picture of me.* Anger mixed with fear coursed through his body. *And dangerous?*

He knew he lived in a backward world, but to think such evil and hate controlled so many was frightening. The three people in the picture didn't look dangerous at all, especially when you put them next to the hordes of vigilantes prowling the streets for innocent blood. *I know who the real enemy is.*

Zach strode forward with renewed purpose. *I have to get them to Ezra.*

He wanted more than anything to find Detective Rutherford and put a bullet through him. *That self-promoting devil can't be trusted to live with the rest of us.* The forceful desire to kill brought back the nightmarish images he'd been having of his other life. *This is different.*

But Zach knew the detective had a good side as well. Probably a family and people who cared for him. Somewhere the detective had another soul just like he did—a soul that would be ashamed of his vile other half.

"Damn it."

Knowing what he knew now only complicated things more. Zach was aware that everyone had two souls and that a better or worse version of each person existed. But until he'd met Riley and seen how stark the contrast was, and before hearing about the gruesome things he'd done, he hadn't realized just how wide the gap spanned between personalities. Somewhere out there the detective was probably a stand-up guy.

He looked down at his watch. *Twenty minutes. I need to hurry.*

Luckily, the bus station stood only a hundred yards ahead and appeared empty. Zach slowed his pace to appear relaxed as he approached the ticket counter. He tugged on his hat, hoping it would block out enough features to make him less recognizable. The clerk would have to be blind to have missed the wanted posters.

"Can I help you?" asked the middle-aged, overly made-up woman behind the counter.

"I need three tickets to Los Angeles." He lifted his head enough to flash a smile but still conceal his eyes. "Just want to take my family to see the capital."

Zach's heart tumbled into his stomach as the woman reached for a phone. "A hundred and twenty dollars." She never glanced up as she passed the tickets over the counter. "Bus leaves in an hour from the terminal to your left. Have a nice day."

Zach seized the tickets and grinned at the three passes to safety in his hand. *That was too easy.*

He stuck them in his pocket and turned to head back to the waiting car but found his way blocked by two large men whose faces registered somewhere in the depths of his brain.

"Excuse me." He kept his head down. They moved aside to reveal a smaller but no-less-menacing figure.

"Hello, Zach." Detective Rutherford stepped forward. "I thought I might find you here."

Chapter Thirty-Three

Oz clutched her stomach, begging the misery to stop. Zach had been gone for what felt like hours, and she was sick of hiding in the backseat and sick of feeling sick.

"I think we should leave," she said to Riley. "He's not coming back."

"It's only been thirty minutes," Riley responded.

The girl looked scared to death, and Oz wanted to laugh at her childlike demeanor. *We're so different.* "Well, I think I need to leave, then."

Riley peered at Oz through the front seats. "What do you mean?"

"I mean I'm back here dying, and no one gives a shit. You look like hell, I look like hell, and lying around in a piece-of-shit car isn't helping either of us."

"We told Zach we'd stay here."

"No, you told him that."

Terror creased Riley's face, and Oz could almost see the panic dribbling down her cheeks. "Fifteen minutes, Oz. I just want to stay alive."

Yeah, me too. That's why I have to get out of here. "Okay then, princess. Stay here. I'll see you later."

Oz opened the car door and crawled out. She felt terrible, but being out of the cramped space, warm sun penetrating her cold core, offered some relief. *Okay, now where would I be if I were smack in a place like this?*

She looked down the street to a large group assembled outside one of the big churches, holding protest signs and shouting. *That seems as good a place to start as any.*

"Oz, wait!" Riley stuck her head out the window. "We can't just go walking around. Someone will see us. Zach will be back soon. Just stay here and we'll be okay."

"I won't be okay." Oz motioned to her pale face and matted hair. "And *we're* not just walking around. I am."

"Oz, please!"

Turning her back on the girl, Oz walked out of the parking lot, ignoring the small part of her brain that urged her to stay. It felt good to be away from people who thought they were so much better than her. Just the way Riley looked at her, like she was subhuman, made Oz want to poke her eyes out. *Lucky you, they're my eyes too.*

She disappeared into the crowd, no longer in sight of the car. Men, women, and even children swarmed around, screaming for God, for Satan, for justice. Oz didn't care what they wanted, as long as someone had something she could inject into her veins.

———

A bright, cloudless sky hovered overhead, offering up a perfect day to imperfect circumstances. Riley hesitated in the car, weighing the consequences of her options. Zach would be back soon. She knew it. And if they weren't there, he would panic and come looking for them. Then they'd all be separated and lost. But if she let Oz go, they probably wouldn't find her before the authorities did. *Damn it, Oz.*

Riley grabbed the notepad, ripped out the directions, stuffed them into her pocket, and then left her own quick note: *"Went to find Oz. Meet you back here as soon as possible. Not my fault."*

She hurried from the car and rushed in the direction Oz had taken, keeping her eyes downcast and trying to avoid bumping into anyone. The edifices loomed high, staring down at her with gilded, knowing eyes, while people in various states of anger, fear, and ecstasy shot apathetic looks in her direction.

The crowd thickened, and she pushed her way through the throng, now so close to the mob that sweat and the stench of too many days in the sun without a shower assaulted her nostrils.

A tangibly dark energy hovered over the multitude she'd just entered, slashing the bright day with a swath of shadow. Women wept, clutching their children as if an invisible enemy might take them at any moment. Men kneeled in the streets, begging the indifferent sky to have mercy or save their starving families. Others simply stared hopelessly at the ground or moved glassy eyes over the people around them. A fight broke out ahead, and yelling, heated voices rose above the murmur of the horde.

"Hey, you made it, sister." Oz appeared from behind a group of singing nuns, shoving people out of her way and carelessly stepping over bent bodies. "Isn't this great? Although

I doubt this is where I'll find what I need. These people are nuts." Sweat streamed down her pale face, and wet strands of hair outlined her bloodshot eyes, but she seemed to be ignoring her discomfort for the moment.

"Yeah, well, I found you, so let's get back to the car." Riley didn't like the looks they received from the nearby people who had heard Oz's statement or who were rubbing parts of their bodies where she'd kicked or shoved them.

"You wanna see something funny?" Oz elbowed Riley in the side and smirked, clearly ignoring the growing dissent around them.

"No, Oz. I don't. I want to find Zach and get the hell out of here. It isn't safe for us to be out in the open like this."

Oz rolled her eyes and walked away, raising her tattooed arms high into the sky and shutting her eyes as if moved by the same powers that possessed the crowd around her. "Hey, everybody, look! It's Jesus!" Her eyes flew open and she pointed a shaking finger in Riley's direction. "He's here! He's finally here! And he's a woman, no less!"

A few people scowled and turned away, but many faces grew even darker, and the shadow expanded around them. Oz keeled over, laughing. Riley felt her anxiety intensify with each pair of loathing eyes that fell upon her.

"She said you can all go to hell and she'll meet you there!" Oz taunted.

"Stop!" Riley wanted to crawl into a dark hole and hide. The last thing she needed was a scene or to pass out from fear.

"Like I give a shit!" Oz growled. "These people are wack jobs. Look at them. They think the world is about to explode into fire and if they act insane, maybe they'll be saved from the chaos. It's bullshit and hilarious!"

Riley observed those closest to her. A man held a sign that read *Jesus Hates Fags*. A woman cradled her child, singing "Amazing Grace" and sobbing. A crowd of families begged for forgiveness and salvation, and a man screamed about hell, the end times, and everyone's impending doom.

She felt sorry for them and wanted to tell them that everything would be okay—that the end times were not about to destroy everything they held dear—that Jesus probably didn't hate anybody. But she understood fear, now more than ever, and the feelings brought on by the terrifying unknown.

She turned in a slow circle, the entirety of the mob watching her, and saw the marble columns that should have been a million sparkling LED lights and the pews inside the churches that should have been slot machines. Her eyes finally fell on Oz, her other half, the life she'd so narrowly escaped.

Oz had engaged in a heated argument with one of the sign-bearing men. Her dark hair, wild green eyes, and inked flesh made her look just like another raving lunatic in the throng.

"You pathetic, fearful son of a bitch," Oz shouted in his face. "Look at you. You make me sick. People like you make me despise religion and the phony God you worship. Take off your mask and be real!"

The crowd closed around her, and Riley lost sight of her companion. Threats bounced from mouth to mouth, and people left their prayers and sorrows to join in the fight against the heretic who'd found her way into their sacred place. *Oh, great. Just what we need.*

Part of her wanted to leave Oz to her own mess, to let the crowd wash over her and put the sad girl out of her misery, but she knew she couldn't survive this world, or any, without her. Riley pushed through the mob, trying to reach Oz.

"You can go to hell," the man shouted back at the purple-haired demon. "In fact, you will! I'm going to a place that is safe from people like you, a place where only good people are accepted. I suggest you beg for forgiveness. Even then, I'm sure it's too late for you."

Oz laughed and spat on the cobblestones at his feet. She crouched and turned like a cornered animal as the circle closed around her. "I wish I could be there to see you become worm shit. All of you."

She howled and threw up her arms, pointing at everyone and hissing swear words at them. Oz might be tough, but she was greatly outnumbered by a bunch of very angry and very passionate people. Riley swallowed and fought the urge to turn and run as her heart pummeled and an invisible weight crushed down on her chest.

"Stop!" She climbed onto the edge of a nearby stone fountain. Most of the group, including Oz, turned to look. Oz rolled her eyes, and Riley could see the recognition dawning on everyone's faces that she looked an awful lot like the nemesis in front of them, as well as like the face in the posters Riley had just noticed plastered up and down the street.

Glowering hate-filled eyes met hers, and her hands trembled. *Bad idea.* She swallowed again and sucked in a shallow breath. Public speaking was about as much fun for her as singing karaoke naked or living in a filthy, musty basement full of spiders.

"Listen to you all." Wobbly words spilled out as she scanned back and forth across the mob and tried to steady her voice. "Listen to the judgments being passed by each and every one of you when it is not your place to judge."

Her eyes rested on Oz's raised eyebrows and gaping mouth. Clearly Oz didn't think Riley had this in her.

"You are all so worried about the world ending and what will happen to you that you're forgetting to enjoy that it is still here for you to live in. Not just to exist but to really live. Go home. Be with your families. Be good people, but don't be afraid to live. You weren't given this life to spend in fear of some immortal tyrant. Don't turn the beauty of it into something it's not. I can't think of a bigger insult than to take no joy and no pride in it."

The crowd stirred but continued to listen. Some jeered but were hushed by others around them.

"And you." She directed her attention to Oz. "Who are you to tell these people that they are crazy and out of control? Look in a mirror! Fix yourself before you try and tell anyone else how to live."

She stood awkwardly on the fountain perch, looking down upon a mixture of emotions. Some people laughed, obviously thinking she was out of her mind; some looked annoyed by the interruption of their time; some continued to cry. But a few bore expressions of understanding, and they turned and made their way out of the crowd. Riley gave an embarrassed smile and climbed down on unsteady legs, searching for Oz. She didn't have to look far. Oz stomped over, looking furious.

"Well, if you're done being the goddamned pope, can we get out of here? The cops are everywhere now. Someone must have called them."

Riley's heart sank into her stomach. Oz grabbed her wrist, jerking her through the mass of people, bulldozing everyone in their path.

"What about Zach?" Riley shouted over the growing noise and excitement of the crowd. "We can't just leave him here!"

"No choice," Oz barked back. "You should have thought about him before you gave your sermon, preacher. This is about you and me now, and beyond that I couldn't give a shit."

"Where are we going?" Riley yanked her arm back. "And I didn't start that mess, you did! I was trying to save you from being burned at the stake, you witch! So you're welcome."

"We're hiding," Oz said, ignoring the comments. "No chance of catching a bus now. Since they know we're here, they'll be watching everything in and out of Vegas. We need to find a safe place to hide and regroup."

They ran through the crowd, the blind leading the blind. Oz's eyes darted from side to side, looking down streets and into buildings, but every church, synagogue, and mosque over-flowed with activity, and each side street moved with marching troops and policemen. Riley's mind drifted to Zach, and she couldn't help but wonder where he was and wish that he was with them now.

Oz muttered angrily, growing more and more frustrated as they tore down the streets. Suddenly she stopped, wild eyed, and turned. "How stupid can you be? If you could have just kept your 'always have to be so damn perfect' mouth shut, we would have been able to get out of here quietly."

"Me?" Riley bellowed back. "You've got to be kidding! I'm not sure if you noticed, but I saved your ass back there from a mob of very angry evangelicals. I think the scene you were causing drew much more attention than I did. And did I mention you ran away? If you had stayed put like Zach asked us to, I wouldn't have had to give my speech!"

"Yeah, well, everything is always my fault!" Oz retorted. "Glad you finally joined the club."

Riley glared and rolled her eyes. "I'm not playing your poor-pitiful-me game right now."

Screeching whistles brought them to their senses. More people closed in with clear intent written on their faces.

"Come on!" Riley took off through the mob, giving Oz the choice to follow. At this rate they weren't going to make it anywhere safe anyway, and she didn't really care what happened to Oz. To Riley's surprise, though, she followed.

The farther they ran, the thinner the crowd became, and she knew they had to find a place to hide—fast. Riley looked down a street to the right that seemed to lead to a residential area. If nothing else, they could hide in bushes until it got dark and pray the cops didn't sweep the area with dogs. She made the quick decision and darted right. Oz followed, and they sprinted down the road, neither looking back.

Freshly painted homes and well-manicured lawns flashed past, but none offered any real place to hide. All appeared occupied with someone who would gladly turn them in. The noise from the crowd had died down, but something more terrifying had replaced it—the dim roar of a helicopter. *Oh, come on. Give us a break!*

"Hurry up!"

Oz had fallen behind and slowed to a walk, gripping her side in pain. "I can't breathe! Chill out!"

"Oz, they've got helicopters." Riley pointed to the sky. "If they see us, we've got no chance."

Oz looked up, which seemed to be enough. She sped up at least, still holding her ribs and breathing so loudly Riley thought for sure someone would come out to see what was going on. Two houses ahead on the left, Riley spotted an open garage and a vacant driveway. *Please don't let anyone be home.* "In here!"

They darted into the garage, and Riley pushed the button to close the door. It seemed to take forever to reach the ground, and the slow rattle as it clanked down only helped remind her of the danger they were in. She panted, trying to catch her breath as the last beam of daylight disappeared and they plunged into darkness.

Oz vomited in some black corner and Riley sat motionless, as if that would help conceal them further. The room fell silent, each girl listening to the faint sound of the choppers disappear into the distance, hoping beyond hope that no one had seen them.

CHAPTER THIRTY-FOUR

Zach glared at the detective, furious at himself for walking into a trap. He knew it could end like this, but he had begun to feel hopeful that the trio might actually make it to their destination.

"You've been a busy man, haven't you?" The detective eyed Zach up and down. "I always thought better of you, though. Always thought you were one of the good guys." He paused, his face taking on a falsely pained look. "Such a shame to find out the true nature of someone's character."

"James, they've done nothing wrong. Please reconsider. This is bigger than the money."

"You're right, Zach, it is. If I bring these girls—and now you—in, the reward will be so much greater than money. They may even make me governor."

Zach took a step forward. "You're one to talk about character then, aren't you?"

Out of the corners of his eyes, he searched for an escape, but Rutherford blocked the path in front, and the two men he now remembered only seeing briefly before, flanking the detective while on patrol in Grand Junction, guarded the back. *His own personal bodyguards.* Reinforcements were probably on their way, and soon he'd be cuffed and even more outnumbered.

"You did this to yourself, Zachary," Rutherford scolded. "When you get home to no badge, no gun, no real vocation for your life, just remember you chose this." Suddenly his face changed, and he gripped his earpiece closer. Zach didn't like the large smile spreading across his face.

"Send up the choppers. I'll be there soon." He redirected his attention to Zach. "Looks like the game is over, son. Your girls were spotted heading north on Main. Maybe when I'm governor I'll pardon your crimes. You can come work for me, cleaning my shitter."

Rutherford rested a hand on his gun. "Take him to the jail, Isaac. I'll meet you there once I have the girls. Marco, you come with me." He patted Zach's cheek lightly and walked toward a waiting unmarked sedan. "Behave, Zachary. You've done enough already."

The protective doors slammed shut, and the vehicle disappeared around the parked bus that was supposed to shuttle Riley, Oz, and him to safety.

"Come on," the man called Isaac demanded, gripping Zach's arm with large, strong hands that he used to pat down Zach's body and remove the pistol that had been tucked into the back of his pants. His heart sank as Isaac directed him to another parked car down the street.

Zach studied his captor's surly-looking muscles made for a bull and hands that could crush a skull with one squeeze. In a fight, there was no doubt who would win. But he knew if he got in the car, he'd have no chance of escape. His only option was to get away immediately, and unfortunately, that meant fighting Isaac. Best-case scenario: he'd escape. Worst-case scenario: he'd be beaten to a bloody pulp. It would be no worse than what they would do once they had him in custody anyway.

"So what's in this for you?" Zach goaded. "Get yourself a nice job as the governor's pet when all this is over? Does he pat your head and tell you good boy, or do you respond better to treats?"

Isaac's dark eyes remained fixed on the waiting car. "Unlike you, I take my job seriously and with commitment."

"No. Unlike me, you don't use your brain to determine that you're being used for something that isn't right. You're James's puppet. He likes you because you're slow and don't like to think. I'm too smart for him. That's why I'm a threat. But you're perfect. Dumb as a box of rocks." Zach laughed and shook his head. "Dumb as…"

The fist met his face with as much force as he'd anticipated. He fought to hold onto consciousness as his head spun around and his jaw wrangled to stay in one piece. Rough concrete greeted the side of his face that had missed out on the blow as a finger snapped under the weight of his body. Searing pain shot up his side as Isaac's boot made contact with his ribs. He rolled onto his hands and knees, spitting blood on the gritty surface and staring down at the twisted, swelling sausage that was his finger.

"Get up and shut up," Isaac demanded.

Zach touched the tender surface of his cheek. Somehow he had to find his feet and outrun the brute. He doubted the odds of that happening, though, as his vision swayed and his ribs pleaded against movement. He probably wouldn't make it ten feet. But he had to try.

It all happened fast after that. Zach sprinted down the street, Isaac on his heels, shouting commands and obscenities. His body protested against the work it had to do when it should be working to repair itself. *Suck it up or die.*

He ran like his life depended on it, which it did. Adrenaline coursed through his veins and dripped off his body instead of sweat. On and on he pushed, the predator ever on his heels. A park appeared on his right, and he cut hard, hoping to find a hiding place among the wide hedges or wooded groves. Isaac's boots hammered the ground close behind.

Zach felt like a small deer hunted by a pack of wolves, the ever-growing fear rising over what fangs tearing into flesh would feel like. The worst-case scenario was not getting his ass kicked by this man or the detective. It was death. They wouldn't let him live, even if they did capture the girls. He'd known that all along but ignored it. But now the wolves closed in, and he pumped his arms harder, driven by the biological will to live that prevailed above all else. He thought about Riley being chased through the cornfield by his other half and could sympathize with her now. *I guess karma really is a bitch.*

Zach raced out the edge of the park and back onto the city streets into a part of town made up mostly of small, rundown storefronts, tired diners, and empty warehouses. The crowds occupying the holy district seemed oblivious that this even existed. Silence in the air gave him the confidence to glance back. His pursuer had fallen behind but had not given up the chase. Zach darted right, then left, then right again, zigzagging his way through the maze of small streets in this lonely part of the city. He would lose Isaac in here, find a place to hide, and wait for nightfall to figure out an escape. He thought about Riley and Oz. *I hope you guys are doing better than I am.* Sprinting through the maze, Zach prayed they wouldn't sic the helicopters on him too.

CHAPTER THIRTY-FIVE

The smell of sawdust, used oil, and stale grass clippings reminded Riley of her grandpa's workshop, where she used to sit and watch him create wonders out of a shapeless piece of wood or metal. He had magic hands, the hands of a wizard, to create such delicate detail out of nothing. She'd watch him for hours, overcome by peace and stillness she couldn't find elsewhere. He'd talk about fishing, sports, and the meaning of life, and she'd just listen, completely in awe as the wizard worked.

Riley took a deep breath and felt comforted by the heavy smell, as if her grandfather sat hidden somewhere in the dark, creating another masterpiece and talking her into tranquility. She heard Oz get up and shuffle around and was suddenly blinded by an illumination of light, revealing the messy garage devoid of the wizard.

"Why do you have to be so selfish?" Riley shook her head and fiddled with a screwdriver that lay on the floor. "You acting like this is my fault is insane."

"You wanna know why I left, princess? Yeah, maybe I needed a fix, but I also don't trust you. I don't trust you, and I don't trust him. You're probably taking me someplace to get rid of me and collect whatever's in it for you and then get the hell out."

"That doesn't even make sense." Riley stood and dusted the dried grass bits from her pants. "Why would I turn you in if they can hurt me through you? Did that ever cross your mind?"

Oz scowled, stalked over to the workbench, and sat down on the swivel seat. Dusty boxes and an old weed trimmer lay propped against a wall. The workbench was covered in tools, dust, and a partially built rocking chair with ornately detailed carvings. *Only the man is missing.*

"Maybe I'm not used to trusting people, okay?" Oz spun slowly on the chair and traced her finger across the dusty table, leaving a wavy line. "I don't know you. I don't know what you want. All I know is that there's a price for everything, and I wasn't sticking around long enough to be screwed over."

Riley kicked a crumpled beer can and watched it sputter across the ground and disappear under a rack of storage shelves. "You just want to cause problems. Ever since I met you, you've loved stirring the pot and ruining everything for everyone. You either love messing things up or you don't know how to be a normal person. I guess I just don't understand how it's so hard to tell what's right and what's wrong. If it hurts you or other people, it's probably wrong. If it's gonna help you do something with your life, it's probably right. That seems pretty straightforward to me."

"Yep. I'm the bad guy. I guess you got the good genes." Oz turned to face the wall.

"We've got the same genes." Riley's irritation mounted. "We come from the same set of parents. I guess I just got the better sense. Are you sure they called you Oz because you need a heart? I think what you need is a brain."

"Oh yeah?" Oz spun back around and raised an eyebrow. Her shoulders tensed. "What are they like? Our parents? Or your version of our parents."

"They're really great." Riley added extra silk to her voice. "In fact, they're the best. Dad's awesome. He's friendly and successful and cooks the most amazing food you've ever eaten. And mom is intense and the most caring woman in the world. I mean I've never met a more passionate person in my life. And Kiersten, well, she puts me to shame. She's beautiful and brilliant." Riley wanted to rub it in her face. Oz needed to be knocked off her high horse.

"That just sounds wonderful." Oz shot Riley a look of equal parts anger, hatred, and sadness. "A little different than mine, but no big deal." She paused, looking up at the ceiling, and laughed drily. "No, my version of life is a little bit different than yours, princess. Dad molested me as a kid, for one. Kiersten and I both. I probably can't count how many times he crawled in bed with us. He beat Mom too. Put her in the hospital. She'd try to stop him from hurting us, but she was a weak woman. He damn near killed her. He was a drunk bastard most of the time. We weren't worried about the quality of food we got as long as there was something to eat. There were lots of times I could feel my stomach eating itself, I was so hungry. It was during those times that Mom had to do whatever horrible shit to get money."

She paused, clearly making sure Riley missed nothing. Her face contorted in pain and disgust, Riley's in shock and horror. "I used to cry about it. I'd lie awake with tears streaming down my face, worried about Mom and who she was with and if they were gonna hurt her, and terrified at the same time that my own dad would come in and break me even more. So don't give me this bullshit that we are all born with the ability to make our own lives and have the same opportunities to be perfect. Yeah, I know drugs are bad and can hurt you, but there are pains out there so deep that you'll do anything to take the edge off."

Riley gaped as tears formed in her eyes. "I—I'm so sorry. I didn't realize."

"Yeah, well, I'd like to see you try to lead the same life you've led, graduating from college with your preppy boyfriends, when you'd spent eighteen years with your pants in Daddy's teeth and your mom and sister so messed up they don't have to feel the shame that comes along with what they do. Shit, I'd be proud of you too."

Riley hated it, wanted it all to go back inside Oz where it lived and festered. Her parents were good people. It wasn't real. It couldn't be.

"So go on thinking you're better than me," Oz spat. "Go on bragging about the life you had and treating me like I brought this upon myself. You say the world doesn't owe me anything? Shit, after seeing you, I say the world owes me everything. You want to talk about not fair? Well, here it is staring you in the fucking face."

Riley recoiled. "Oz, please. I didn't know."

Oz laughed and hopped off the bench, pacing the oil-stained floor and clenching her hands into tight fists. "No, I think you knew. It was just a lot easier to imagine me as a worthless piece of shit than to take a look in the mirror." She paused, doing a small turn on her heel to face Riley. "Well, take a good look now. Here I am, the epitome of what you are capable of. The shadow piece of you that lives in the corner of your mind that you fight back every time it tries to come out. And good for you. But the harder you fight it back, the harder it is for me. The nicer your daddy is to you, the harder mine hits."

Oz sank onto a cardboard box and glared at the garage door. "So am I broken? You bet I'm broken. I never had a chance."

Riley wanted to say something, anything, to Oz, but words wouldn't come. She hadn't stopped to think about her family's other halves. But if good-hearted Zach could be a serial killer, why couldn't Riley's father be a monster too, and her mother a pathetic druggie like Oz? Each new piece of this other world brought about horrible truths and painful questions. *Why? Why is it necessary to have a parallel world where a girl's suffering is linked to my happiness?*

"Oz, back in the crowd, I yelled at them and you for being so judgmental. I guess I haven't been the best about it myself, either. I'm sorry."

Oz blew air out of her lips, making the sound of an idling motor. "It's easy to expect certain things from someone when you've been able to lead a good life. Lots of people have a hard time seeing it from another's perspective."

Riley pulled her knees into her chest and leaned against the concrete wall. "Well, I'm sorry I've been one of them."

"That's why those church people make me so mad." The room reverberated with rattling metal as Oz launched a hammer into the garage door. Riley cringed at the noise but let her other half continue without a sarcastic remark or scolding. Now didn't seem like the time.

"They come at me like I'm some monster made in hell, and maybe I am. But it's easy for them to say when they grew up with their white picket fences and food on the table, thinking they worked really hard to get where they are today, when really they had parents who gave them everything they needed. I can hardly stand to hear one more self-righteous prick tell me they deserve what they have. I wish them one day in my life."

"Or they need to meet their other half." Riley's sigh contained a heartless chuckle. "You want to talk about a real eye opener."

"Or that."

The room fell silent again, and Riley felt nervous to even move or breathe. A part of her she didn't know existed had been raped, molested, abused, high on deadly drugs, and God knew what else. In some way those things had happened to her, no matter how far removed—even a world away. Her parents, such good people, had done awful things. She shook her head. They were still good people. Just like she was. She couldn't lose sight of that.

"I wish you could meet the parents I know," Riley said. "I wish you could experience the love they have in them."

"I wouldn't know what to do with it if I did. I do better by myself anyway." Oz stood and walked circles around the garage. "So what's our plan to get out of here? I feel like shit and sure as hell can't do any more running."

"I don't know." Riley pulled the crumpled wad of paper from her pocket. "I have the directions to Ezra's, but how we get all the way to LA is beyond me. I just wish we had someone on our side. We need help, Oz."

Oz stopped pacing. "Well, there is someone we could go to. Course, last time I went there he refused to help, and I kinda stole some of his shit. I don't think he's very fond of me, though. Probably loves you to death."

"Who, Oz?"

"Uncle Kevin," she said. "He has a really nice house on the edge of town. Kind of a far walk. I guess he won't turn us over, at least, but I'm not sure how happy he'll be to see me."

Uncle Kevin. The prodigal son. Of course he's not the same here. "I haven't seen him in years," Riley said. "He's different where I come from."

"Oh yeah? What's he like?"

"Um, well…I guess he's a lot like you."

"The irony." Oz laughed. "This should be interesting. We'll wait till dark, and I'll take you over there. Maybe when you tell him what he's really like, he'll be in a more forgiving mood."

a seat behind a mahogany desk and motioned the girls into chairs facing him. Their uncle continued to stare, a smile growing on his face.

"Brilliant," he said. "Now, I take it you girls didn't come all this way for a visit. Word on the street and, well, everywhere is that you are wanted fugitives. You I can understand." He motioned to Oz. "But Riley, if all accounts are correct, then you should be just shy of a saint."

She blushed under his amused stare. "Well, I don't know about that." It was strange being addressed by this version of her uncle in a house her real uncle would only see if he were robbing it. "We haven't done anything. They put me in jail, but we escaped and are trying to get to Los Angeles. We need help."

They launched into a full account of all that had happened since Riley ended up in the apple orchards a few days back, including the recent event of losing Zach and needing to get to LA to find a man named Ezra Ahmad. Kevin listened and nodded, perking up at certain parts and looking concerned at others. When the tale ended, he directed his attention to Riley.

"So what's it like?"

"What's what like?"

"The other world. The place you come from. The people, what are they like? And your cities?"

"For one, Washington, DC, is the capital in my world, not Los Angeles. Mostly our worlds are pretty similar, only opposite. For instance, where I come from, Las Vegas is filled with casinos instead of churches." She glanced sideways at Oz, trying to sort out her words. "And the people are similar too. I mean, we look identical, but we don't act the same."

"Brilliant." His eyes gleamed with mischief. "So what am I like?"

"Apparently, you're like me." Oz eagerly shared the news.

"You don't say?" Kevin looked as if he'd just discovered how a telephone works. "Am I that bad?"

Oz grunted.

"Well, you're very different than this." Riley gestured to the decadent room they sat in. "The last time I saw you was a few Christmases ago at Grandma's. Mom caught you and some girl in the bathroom doing drugs. You went crazy, threw something at her, and spent the night in jail. No one has heard from you since."

"Fascinating." Kevin clapped his hands together. "It's marvelous, really, if you think about it. I have a whole other part to me that I don't even know: an evil twin occupying my same space, representing me to the world."

He stood and paced back and forth behind his desk, rubbing his chin and occasionally bursting with a small laugh. This man was so different than the Kevin Riley knew. He was wealthy and successful, albeit a little eccentric. If only her mom could see him now, dressed in rich black slacks and a crushed-velvet smoking jacket while prancing around his own personal library. Without the sunken look of a drug addict or the lack of muscles from too much cocaine and not enough food, he actually looked a lot like her grandparents—even like her.

"You know, the last time I saw your mom, she asked for money, and I sent her away," he paused. "This is so big. We've always heard...but to see the two of you sitting here in front of me, actually existing—well, it's mind blowing."

Kevin ran frazzled hands through his shiny hair. "Look at you two. How does it feel being in each other's presence? Is it different? Do you feel more complete?"

"I feel sick," Oz said. "Since she's been here, I can't stop yarking."

Riley rolled her eyes, pondering the question. She didn't think she felt different, but her adrenaline had probably not stopped pumping long enough to really feel anything. "I'm still getting used to it all," she finally said.

"I'm sure it's a lot to take in." Kevin said. "Listen, you girls are exhausted and, let's be honest, could use a shower and some beauty sleep. You are welcome to stay here as long as you like."

He led them up a flight of stairs to a pair of rooms adjoined by a bathroom. "Please make yourselves comfortable. I'll send someone to town tomorrow to get new clothes. The police have already been here asking questions, and it wouldn't do to have you running around town for all to see—again. And, Oz"—he wagged a finger in her direction—"please leave everything where it is. I'm quite fond of my belongings. If I wasn't, I wouldn't have them. Well, good night."

Riley stared around the room at the canopied bed and delicately carved furniture. A nightgown had been laid out on the powder-blue comforter, and the bathroom was stocked with everything she needed to clean up. She jumped in the shower before Oz could and sighed as the grime of the last few days disappeared down the drain in a brown whirlpool. The warm water felt good on her aching body, and she gently scrubbed the dried blood from her skin. Deep bruises colored her ribs, and she was covered in scabs and healing cuts. Riley had almost forgotten about falling out of a second-story window. It seemed so long ago, like a dream.

Out of the shower, she pulled a comb through her hair, managing to remove the knots. The gash on her forehead where she had hit the dresser was healing, but it was still broken and leaking small droplets of pus and blood. Thankfully it hadn't been deep enough to need stitches, although she'd be lucky to get by without a scar. Riley pulled the nightgown over her weary shoulders and fell into the bed. *How long has it been since I've slept?*

The soft mattress cradled her body, and she pulled the comforter up around her face, wishing she could live in this cloud forever. Her mind fought to stay awake, to worry about Zach and what they would do next, but her exhausted body won over and finally shut down. *I'm so sorry, Zach.*

He would have to wait until morning.

CHAPTER THIRTY-SEVEN

A dull grayness drifted in an open window. Riley bolted upright, startled to see the clock read noon. Rubbing sleep from her eyes, she noticed various shopping bags piled by the door. In one she found a new pair of jeans, a clean top, and a light jacket. Another contained a fresh pair of sturdy boots. There was also a backpack with a water bottle, nonperishable food, a flashlight, some matches, and a box of red hair dye.

Riley changed into her new outfit, left the dye in the bathroom, and went downstairs to find everyone. Uncle Kevin sat reading a newspaper out on the back porch. Oz was nowhere in sight.

"Ah, good morning." He closed the paper as she stepped into the garden. "Did you sleep well?"

"It was amazing." Riley plopped into the deep cushion of a wicker chair and leaned back. "And thank you for the clothes. We were in pretty bad shape."

A woman brought out a tray with coffee, juice, eggs, sausage, and biscuits, and Riley dug in eagerly. Last night she'd been too tired to feel hungry, but today she was ravenous. She eyed the woman suspiciously, trying to gauge her reaction between bites of bread.

"You can trust Ana." Kevin met Riley's hesitant stare. "My staff is all loyal to me and my family. Ana would never turn you over."

The woman offered a slight bow, and left the room. Riley watched her leave, deciding to trust Kevin and just enjoy the food.

"I wish I could take you to Los Angeles myself," her uncle began. "But if I disappear, they will know where I've gone, and it may be easier to track you. I think it best if I drop you on the outskirts of town and come back here to throw anyone asking questions off your scent."

Riley continued stuffing biscuits and sausages into her mouth. Warm, flaky crumbles coated her tongue, and the meat oozed juices and creamy cheese that made it hard to breathe.

"They are watching the house," he continued. "I'm not sure how you all snuck in, but leaving is going to be tricky. I've got a car, one that will take you across whatever terrain you need it to, and I'm working on a map with the route I think best to take. At this point the main roads are off limits."

Riley swallowed a large sip of coffee, trying to clear her esophagus and her mind.

"Uncle Kevin, I can't thank you enough." She paused her feast. "I wish there was a way to repay you. I've been so scared here, and I just want to get home. The crazy thing is I now know you exist. It will be strange to miss people who live in places you can't reach."

He smiled and grabbed her hand. "My sweet niece, I wish you could stay and tell me everything about where you come from. I wish I could go with you and meet my sister, who is apparently a normal woman, and see the wreck of a man that is my other half."

Riley shook her head and stared at her plate. "How does one go on with their life once they know all of this? I mean, how can my life ever go back to the way it was? If I tell anyone, they'll put me in the madhouse. But if I keep it all to myself, I may end up there anyway."

Kevin chuckled and leaned back in his chair, his green eyes twinkling. "I think that is where the saying 'Ignorance is bliss' comes from. Just remember, people survive much more traumatic experiences than this and still go on living. You will find an outlet for your sanity. You will be okay, my dear."

Sometime in the night, the weather had become oddly chilly for the summer. Riley watched the water cascading into one of the pools in the backyard and pulled her jacket tighter. She hated the idea of leaving this fortress. Once they left, the hounds would be after them again, and there would be no walls to keep them safe.

"I've heard another rumor about your world, or really our worlds," he said. "I heard that if a person dies in one, the other half of them dies as well."

"I heard that too," Riley said.

Kevin stirred his coffee, staring thoughtfully at the pool. "Mom—your grandma—how is she?"

Riley gazed at Kevin. "Dead."

"When?"

"A few weeks ago."

"How?"

"Heart attack. That's what the doctors said."

"Gunshot," he corrected. "Here it was a gunshot."

Riley flashed back to her own vision of Esther's death, remembering the reverberating sound of the bullet that took her grandma's life. "Uncle Kevin, where did Grandma live?"

"She moved back to Germany after Dad died. I hadn't seen her in a few years. She was troubled."

They sat in silence, listening to the water crashing into the pools. Riley held her breath, sensing more of the puzzle falling into place. The sky darkened, and a cool breeze picked up, fluttering the long curtains by the back door and blowing a cloud of fallen rose petals onto the stoop below their chairs.

"They found her body…" he began.

"In a cabin with a dirt floor somewhere in Germany," Riley continued. "Yeah, I know."

Kevin gave her a bewildered look. "But how?"

"Uncle Kevin, I don't know how to explain what's happening—in fact, you're the first person I've told everything to since I've been here. I was there when Grandma was shot. I saw the men with the guns, and I saw Grandma pinned to the ground. The men even turned when I shrieked after they pulled the trigger. They knew I was there. But then I woke up like it had been a dream. I knew that it wasn't. It was too vivid, but what else could it be?"

She went on to describe her other visions, the encounter with the strange old man, and her grandma's and Gabe's ambiguous answers, like they knew something and didn't want to tell her. "She knew. The grandma from my world knew, but how? Did she know about this world? Or was there something more? Something bigger?"

Kevin shook his head. "You are having visions and bouncing between worlds. Some kind of powerful force is at work. I don't know how any of us could understand."

Riley looked down at her ring and removed it, placing it in Kevin's hand. "Have you seen this before?"

"No," he replied. "It's very pretty."

"Grandma wore this every day I can remember. She never took it off. And she left it to me. I know this sounds crazy, but somehow I think this ring is involved. And that tree there." She pointed to the twisting branches dotted with blue sapphires. "That tree is the one from my vision."

Kevin reached for her hands again, gently placing them in his own, and offered an encouraging look. "I hope this man in LA can help you. I'm beyond words. All I can do is try to get you there in one piece."

They spent the rest of the afternoon planning and packing supplies. Oz finally stumbled out of her room around three, looking slightly better but still in the painful grips of drug withdrawal. She stayed focused through most of the discussion, especially once Kevin began rationing pain pills and cigarettes.

The vehicle he promised could get them to Mars if need be. Riley loaded the souped-up Jeep full of food, water, gas cans, the backpacks, and any other little things Kevin kept bringing out and saying they might need. At six o'clock they rested and enjoyed a delicious meal of steak, potatoes, and roasted asparagus. Riley ate enough to last a week and still wanted more. She was sad to leave Kevin and his hospitality and scared to head back out into the unknown.

"Go get some rest," he told them after dinner. "I'll wake you all up around three to get out of here. I know it will be hard, but try to sleep. It may be a while before you get any good rest."

The girls said good night and headed upstairs. Oz pulled Riley into the bathroom. "Time to disguise." She held up the hair dye and grinned. Riley let Oz cut and dye her hair and was startled at her new appearance in the mirror. Red tresses framed by blunt bangs outlined her face, making her eyes pop and features appear sharper.

"What about you?" she asked Oz.

"Oh, please, I've been doing this for years. I don't need help."

Riley averted her eyes as Oz stripped naked. *Not like I haven't seen that before.*

"I don't know about you, but I could stay here forever." Oz mixed the dye and squirted it into her hair. "You sure you want to try and go home?"

"I have to," Riley said. "And aren't you a little curious to hear what Ezra has to say?"

"I guess." Oz removed her rubber gloves and tossed them into the trash. "It's kinda cool that you're you and I'm me and here we are."

Riley smiled. It was the closest thing to something nice Oz had said. Out of curiosity, Riley peeked at her companion's naked body, noticing not only the tattooed sleeve of flowers but also a black star on each wrist, a black widow spider in the small of her lower back, a piercing in her belly button, and the word *Spero* written in italics across her right shoulder.

"Pretty sexy, huh?" Oz asked, noticing her stare and winking. "You've got good potential. Don't feel bad about not being as skinny. Years of crack will do that to ya."

Riley blushed and turned away, now staring at the pile of clothes strewn across the floor. "What does it mean? *Spero?*"

Oz's eyes hardened, and she stopped moving. Her hand went gently to her back and touched the soft letters, fingering each one in turn as if she'd done it a hundred times and memorized their locations. "It means hope. I got it when I still had some."

Riley nodded and went to her bedroom. "Good night, Oz."

"Good night, princess." Oz closed the door behind her.

Riley crawled back into the bed she never wanted to leave and willed herself to sleep, but the anticipation of the following day kept her up until nearly midnight. She couldn't shake the fear that came with setting out across the deserts of the Southwest with Oz and a bunch of bad guys. And then there was Zach. *Where is he, and is he okay?* Before he left, he said if they got separated, he would meet them in Los Angeles. She hoped he would be waiting when they rolled into town.

———

"Riley, wake up." Oz's voice cut through a dream about Gabe that Riley didn't want to leave. Hands shook her, and the threat of water in the face pulled her the rest of the way out of dreamland.

"All right, I'm up!" Her eyes focused on her harasser and she jumped, hardly recognizing the familiar face. "Whoa."

Oz's hair was stripped of all color and cropped close to her head. She had styled the bleached mop in an edgy bob and looked more rock star than fugitive. "You like?"

"Well, you certainly won't be recognizable." Riley rolled out of bed, fingering her own brightly colored coif. "We look like Japanese cartoon characters."

The frightening thought of leaving this place fed her anxiety a huge helping of chaos. Dangers lurked on the outskirts of Kevin's home. Kindness and help had become as evasive as terror was prevalent, although Riley knew she'd been lucky so far.

She picked out one of the new outfits that looked perfect for traveling as well as running if things got bad. Kevin had a pot of coffee brewing downstairs and had laid out another delicious breakfast. Good food, good bed, good company—it would be hard to leave.

"Good morning, sunshines," Kevin greeted them. "Join me. I really will miss your company. And nice job on the hair. I wouldn't be able to pick you all out of a crowd."

They sat down, but no one seemed in the mood to talk except Kevin. Oz sipped her coffee and munched on a cinnamon roll while Riley stirred her oatmeal, lost in what the day would bring.

"Well, here we are on the last day I get to have you all, and you're about as much company as a pair of rocks." He shook his head in mock reproach. "We may as well get down to business."

Kevin pulled out a large map on which he had outlined the route they would take and began marking points along the way.

A young man dressed in black slacks and a sports coat walked into the room and nodded curtly at the girls. "The car is ready, Mr. Miller. I've seen that all the additions you asked for are in place."

"Great. Thank you, Chas." Kevin patted the man's arm. "Now here's a man I would trust with my life."

The young man tried to remain stoic and professional, but a pleased smile danced at the corner of his lips.

"I will drive the Jeep with you girls hidden in a storage compartment I had installed in the back until we get to the outskirts of town," Kevin began. "I made the space to hide and store expensive camera equipment for my photography excursions, but I think with a little flexibility, we can squeeze you girls into it. Good thing you're such good friends!

"There is a back road out of town that ties in with the main route to Los Angeles about a hundred miles past the city. I'm putting a lot of stock in the notion that it will not be heavily guarded—if at all."

Oz snorted but Kevin continued, ignoring her obvious disdain. "Chas will follow a few minutes after in another car to pick me up when I send you on your way. My guess is they will be watching all roads in and out of town, but the hidden compartment should throw anyone off." He paused. "Unless, of course, they want to search the vehicle—but no worries, loves!"

He took a long swig of coffee and swallowed hard. "You will follow this route and should get to Los Angeles safely. No one will think you took back roads through the desert. There's nothing out there but a bunch of coyotes waiting to eat your scorched remains."

"And why is this a good plan?" Oz asked.

Kevin laughed. "Because what they don't know is that you have a vehicle with enough gas, water, and supplies to survive two weeks of whatever hell you end up in. I'd advise not pushing it much beyond that. I've removed the car's GPS and any system they could use to track you. You'll be driving blind except for the map."

Riley followed the route with her eyes as he pointed out key features and things to look for.

"I went there as a kid." She pointed to a spot on the map. "The Mojave National Preserve."

"I'm not familiar with the term," Kevin mused. "National preserve?"

"You know, like a park. Pretty places owned by the government. The land can't really be developed, so people can go visit." She saw his blank expression and continued. "You know, places people go camping and hiking and things."

A deep smile revealed dimples at the corners of his cheeks, making his already friendly face even kinder. "Charming. Though I can't imagine why anyone would want to vacation in such a barren location. I really do wish we had more time to chat. What a fascinating place you come from that sets aside land for public enjoyment. It sounds like a beautiful concept. I ought to buy a national preserve and start the first one ever."

Riley appreciated his vigor but realized he didn't fully understand.

"I'm afraid the Mojave you will be traveling through is no park," Kevin warned. "You probably won't see a soul the entire time until you hit the outskirts of LA. From there I cannot help you. Only send blessings."

The girls nodded. Riley wondered if Oz felt scared too. Apprehension shadowed her face, but she couldn't read Oz enough to know if turmoil boiled inside as well. She remembered the man with the gun at the gas station and the evil detective's grin. They were on a dangerous mission. To not be afraid would be ignorant.

"Don't be scared," Kevin said, as if reading her mind. "We have done simply all we can to make this work. You must now use your heads, your intuition, and your hearts to survive the rest of this. I think between the two of you, you have everything needed to endure this. Remember to rely on each other. You girls are in a unique position. Think of how tough you can be if you play off each other's strengths. I'd say you'd be unstoppable."

Riley hadn't thought of that before. She'd only seen Oz as weak minded, jaded, and broken. But Oz must have a certain strength about her to have survived all she had been through—must have a drive to live that Riley could never even imagine.

Riley brought the common sense, the compassion, and the self-control needed to survive, but she was also anxious, scared, and deeply overwhelmed. No one could deny that Oz brought strength and an uncanny ability to survive to the table. A small sense of peace quelled Riley's inner storm.

"Well, there's no point delaying." Kevin tapped his fingers on the table next to his mug. "The sooner we get out of here, the better. Chas?"

The young man reentered the room as if he had been standing just out of sight waiting for the call. "I'm ready to go when you are, sir."

Kevin stood and hugged each girl. "Oz, I forgive you for what you've done in the past. You have a clean slate with me, and you should for yourself as well. This is your chance to start over. Embrace it, and do it well."

Oz nodded. A sickly color still highlighted her face, and deep pains shook her body, but it seemed like the rest and food had helped tremendously. Riley wondered if she'd heed his advice.

"Take care of each other. Riley, remember how important forgiveness and compassion are. She needs you and you need her. She can't change without you."

Riley nodded as well. "I wish you were my uncle. Oz is lucky to have you."

He took one last deep breath and clapped his hands together. "I am your uncle. And you will always know where to find me if you need anything."

Chapter Thirty-Eight

"**G**et your foot out of my face." Oz tried to shove Riley off. The hiding space in the Jeep was tight for one person. For two it was miserable.

"You think I have anywhere to go?" Riley's claustrophobia reached a new high. *Breathe. Just breathe.* With the small compartment already filled with two girls, she feared the addition of tension and anxiety might make the place explode.

The engine revved, and they bumped around in silence, remaining quiet through the discomfort. Riley thought this must be how people in the Holocaust or the Underground Railroad had felt. Only they weren't lucky enough to have modern-day supplies and gear. Even Oz, who always had something to complain about, said nothing.

Half an hour into the hushed ride, the car came to a sudden stop, and Riley rolled into Oz's side, causing the girl to grunt and give her a rough shove. Riley fought the urge to push back when she heard people approaching the car and Kevin's voice calling out to them. "Good morning, gentlemen. What can I do for you?"

Riley tensed, holding her breath for fear that even the quietest of exhalations would echo through the car. She felt Oz's body tighten as well.

"Strange time of morning to be going for a drive, Mr. Miller," a man's voice stated.

"Not at all," Kevin replied. "I'm trying to beat the sun to a lovely place in the desert where I like to photograph the great orb as she rises above the horizon. Nothing more beautiful than the promise of a stunning day, is there?"

"Listen, Kevin," the same voice spoke. "You're the girls' uncle, so you know I can't just let you leave town."

"You mean Riley Dale?" Disdain dripped from Kevin's voice. "The last time I saw that girl she stole three thousand dollars worth of stuff from my house. I say good riddance to her and good luck to you, boys. That one ought to be off the streets."

Silence. Riley wished she could peek out the windows. They might be able to escape from one man, but an entire group of soldiers or policemen could be tricky or impossible.

The stranger's voice broke the hush. "We're going to have to search your car at least. If you're just going out into the desert to take pictures, then we shouldn't find anything, should we?"

"I want to take photos and explore," Kevin said. "I plan to be out for a few weeks. I've got to get away from the city and get some fresh air every now and again. I'm even thinking about purchasing a national preserve, so I'd like to check out the area first, if you know what I mean. You can never be too careful with those sorts of things."

The man didn't seem to know or care what he meant. "We're going to need you to get out of the vehicle."

"I'm in an awfully big hurry," Kevin replied. "What if I give you boys a couple extra dollars and you let me get to my spot before the sun rises and I've missed a golden opportunity?"

"We've got direct orders that cannot be disobeyed. Get out of the car, Mr. Miller, or my men will remove you from it."

Riley's heart sank. They would be pulled from their hideout like prisoners. She felt Oz shaking beside her—from lack of drugs or from fear, Riley couldn't tell. Probably both.

"Now wait just a minute," she heard Kevin say as a door slammed. "You don't even have a gate blocking the road. If I had had the mind to, I could have driven through and gotten away from you boys. There are plenty of back roads you'd never find me on, and if I could just get around the edge of that bluff, I'd be good to go. If I could just make it a mile or so before someone came after me—"

It only took a moment for Riley to grasp his message. She flung open the trap door and leapt into the driver's seat. For a split second her eyes fell on Kevin in the rearview mirror. *I'm so sorry, Uncle.*

She slammed her foot down on the gas pedal, and the Jeep roared ahead, faster than she figured a normal Jeep could. Shots rang out as bullets peppered the ground near the tires. She swerved left and right, trying to throw off any shooters, her eyes glued to the place Uncle Kevin said she'd be safe.

The half moon cut through the darkness, and she could just make out the bluff they needed to reach. Oz crawled out of the chamber and began shuffling through the packs.

In half a mile they'd be hidden from sight and could turn off and hide. Riley glanced back and saw flashing lights in pursuit.

"Come on!" She urged the Jeep forward.

"Roll down the back window," Oz said.

"Why?"

"Just do it. I'm trying to help."

Riley rolled the window down and noticed the pursuit car gaining. It would be too close to shake. The Jeep curved around the bluff, and the web of roads leading off of the main highway stunned Riley. Most were dirt roads, leading God knew where. They certainly weren't marked on the map Kevin gave them. She picked one that looked like it headed in the right direction, and she swerved off the highway, kicking up a cloud of dust and causing Oz to cough. "Watch it!"

The Jeep careened down the road, Riley trying to maintain control as the vehicle bounded over washed-out dips and rocks. The wheel jerked back and forth between her hands, trying desperately to lose control and flip.

"He's almost here!" Oz shouted.

Riley looked back and saw the vehicle closing in. *How can they follow on this road?*

"I've got no place to go but forward, Oz."

"Just keep going," Oz shouted with a little too much glee in her voice. "I've got us covered."

Riley jumped two feet off her seat as shots suddenly rang out from within the car. "They hit us!"

"No, we're trying to hit them." Oz loaded another bullet into the chamber of a rifle.

"Where did that come from?" Riley's eyes grew wide, and for a moment her attention shifted from the road. The Jeep plowed over some large rocks, and the rumble brought her back to attention.

"I knew Kevin wouldn't leave us unprotected." Oz grinned. "I figured there'd be something."

An answering bullet hit the back of the car just below Oz, causing the Jeep to swerve. "Shit."

"You can't kill them, Oz!" Riley shouted in disbelief.

"Yeah, I guess you wouldn't want that on your conscience."

Oz fired off more shots, but Riley couldn't tell if she hit her mark. Her pulse ran wild as a shot tore the side mirror from the car, jerking the wheel even harder. She wanted to laugh. Just a few weeks earlier, or maybe a month, she'd been apprehensive to go to a party because there would be too many people. Now she glanced in the rearview and chuckled. *Now…*

The car had gained on them, its front bumper nearly level with the back of the Jeep.

"Kevin put some serious tires on this thing," Oz said. "The bullets are bouncing off."

"Well, shoot theirs out," Riley shouted. "At some point they'll cut us off."

"I'm trying to. It's a little difficult when I get shot at every time I lift my head."

Riley scanned the road. Through the darkness it seemed to go on endlessly to the horizon and then disappear into the mountains. Unless she left the road completely, there would be no way to shake their pursuers. Luckily, only one car had caught up with them. This meant little, though, since others were probably tracking them and only minutes behind.

Their own vehicle lurched again as shotgun pellets peppered the glass in the backseat window and little cracks spread out from the center, growing larger as they reached the edges. A small dip in the dirt was enough to send the fragile shards cascading into a shimmery waterfall.

"Any day now, Oz," Riley urged.

The car was almost even with them now. She risked a glance out the window and met the cold eyes of the passenger in the pursuit car. Her blood turned to ice. *So they were fleeing the devil himself?*

Suddenly the other car faltered as if it had hit a patch of ice and began to spin wildly out of control. Oz whooped from the backseat, yelling obscenities and throwing crude gestures at the flailing car.

"I got 'em!" she yelled. "Hit the back right tire." She spat out of the broken rear window and flipped them a painted middle finger. "Take that, you bastards!"

Even Riley let out a thrilled laugh. It seemed they had once again bested death.

"Good job, Oz!" She watched in the rearview mirror as the men stepped from the immobile vehicle. "That was Detective Rutherford. He *personally* came after us."

"No shit?" Oz asked. "I hope Kevin got away. I wouldn't want to deal with that man."

Riley swallowed hard, feeling guilty and empty about leaving Kevin to that fate. The detective would question him, torture him no doubt, and maybe even kill him. Any joy at having escaped the detective's clutches vanished because Kevin hadn't. Kevin had been willing to sacrifice his life for theirs. She choked back tears.

"I know." Oz hauled herself into the front seat and stared ahead at the infinite emptiness. "It sucks, what happened to him." She paused and let out a deep, slow breath. "No one's ever done something like that for me, ya know? And I definitely didn't deserve it from him."

Riley nodded. So far the two people who'd tried to help them had gotten into trouble: first Zach and now Kevin. *How many people will suffer on my account?* It made her sick, thinking about the fates of both men. Good people didn't seem to belong in this world. Good people didn't seem to belong in any world.

"How in the hell are we supposed to find LA in this mess?" Oz asked after a few miles of lonely desert sped past.

She had a point. Riley had no idea where they were. The car's internal compass said they were headed southwest, which was the direction they needed to go, but for all she knew, this road would dead-end at the edge of a giant cliff, and they would run out of supplies and food before the bad guys even found them.

"Do you think they'll send the helicopters again?" Oz asked.

Riley nodded hopelessly. They would send the helicopters, and spotting the only moving dot on the still ground would be too easy. She thought about what Kevin told her—to rely on each other, and that would make them unstoppable. Oz probably felt just as hopeless as she did, but they needed to pull it together if they had any hope of surviving.

"Keep your eyes on the sky." Riley gripped the steering wheel tighter and flipped off the car's headlights. Only the dimmers lit their dangerous path forward. "And listen hard. Maybe we'll hear them before they see us. And get the packs ready." She paused, hating to think it would come to that. "If they attack from the air, we will have to abandon the car. Put enough in the packs that we can survive on foot the rest of the way."

Oz's face scrunched into an incredulous glare. "We can't survive on foot the rest of the way. We'll never make it. I don't know if you've noticed, but I'm suffering from a severe case of the shakes and vomits. I can't go traipsing through the desert in this condition."

"We have a better chance on foot than we do in captivity." Riley dreaded the idea as she said it. "It's going to come down to how much we really want to live. It's going to come down to how hard we're willing to fight."

"Whatever you say, princess." Oz crawled into the back, rummaging through the mess of supplies. "How the hell am I supposed to fit all of this shit in here?"

Riley threw an exasperated hand into the air. "Food, water, jackets, some matches. The things people need to survive."

"What about this?" Oz held up a roll of silver duct tape.

"Why not?" Riley sighed. "We may need it."

It took nearly three hours for the helicopters to find them, which surprised Riley. She'd figured maybe an hour max. They probably couldn't see anything yet, but the faint buzz of the machine hummed audibly over the purr of the Jeep rumbling across the sand.

"Are the backpacks ready, Oz?"

"Yep. But how the hell are we supposed to get away from them?"

Riley looked hopelessly at the empty expanse of desert and the mountains, faint shadows in the distance that offered no safety. Dense clumps of yucca, creosote, and other strange desert plants Riley didn't recognize provided the only form of shelter for miles. She stopped the car, took a deep breath, and grabbed her pack from Oz.

"Let's go."

They ran as fast as they could, each step kicking up clouds of dust in desperate need of rain. Riley hated leaving the Jeep. Their chances of making it had just decreased significantly, but she ran on, wanting to put as much distance between herself and the vehicle as possible. Once the detective found it, it would be easy to track the boot prints through the sand. Riley prayed for wind or rain or anything to obscure their trail of breadcrumbs.

The sound of the helicopters hovered but had not grown louder. *Hopefully they're following some other road.* Oz panted heavily behind her, clutching her backpack straps and the rifle as if she'd lose them at any moment. After a few miles, Riley paused, eyeing a dense clump of yuccas they could squeeze into.

"Get in there," she commanded.

"In there?" Oz shook her head. "But it'll hurt."

"It's this or the prickly pear bush back there." Riley pointed at the spiny cactus to her right. "You decide."

Oz groaned and disappeared into the yucca. Riley followed, cramming into the small space next to her.

"Now what?" Oz asked.

"We'll wait here until it gets dark and then continue. We'll travel at night from now on. It's too open to be out in the daylight."

"We don't even know where we are. Ow!" Oz yelped as she leaned back into one of the sharp spines. "How are we supposed to walk out of this wasteland in the dark?"

"We'll watch where the sun sets." Riley scooted toward the entrance of their hideout. "And then use the stars. Now get some rest. I'll take first watch."

Oz handed the rifle to Riley and closed her eyes. Riley stared out into the sand, watching the heat rise like a shimmering curtain into the air as the sun crested the dark hills.

A small white spider crawled around in the mouth of one of the white flowers that bloomed in clusters all around them. Riley stared, hypnotized by the delicate creature that hid so well in his matching home.

She thought of her own home, how her parents would be panicked at this point, probably thinking she was dead after seeing the signs of struggle in her bedroom. She thought about Zach, wondering on one hand if he had been captured in her world and on the other if he had escaped in this one.

The sun hung high in the sky now, beginning its slow descent into the west. The sounds of the helicopters grew louder. They would find the Jeep soon. Riley glanced back at Oz, who had managed to fall asleep in the tight space. *Good for her.* It would be a long night.

Riley fought off sleep in the hot, dry air, her eyes growing heavier with each passing minute. She felt her head bob and would occasionally jolt up after accidentally dozing. As the hours wore on, she gave in to fatigue and decided a lookout wasn't needed. If someone discovered them, there would be no place to go, so she might as well get some rest.

Chapter Thirty-Nine

The earth below trembled as if the core of the planet had exploded, sending a fiery burst of energy to the surface where they slept. Boulders rained down across the desert sands, sending up puffs of dust that clouded out a hazy sun. Oz sat up, gasping—awakened from a restless dream where she and Riley had been caught leaving Vegas and her fingers were being painfully removed as a form of torture. She noticed Riley sound asleep with the rifle slumped over her body.

"Hey, wake up." Oz shook her companion. "Something's happening."

Riley stirred and rubbed sleep from her eyes. Her expression grew wide as she watched the yucca spines rattle and the rocks outside the opening bounce up and down against the dirt like bouncy balls on cement. And then it stopped. The pebbles lay still and the plants resumed their static stations.

"Does that happen here often?" Riley asked, still wide eyed and trembling.

"I don't know what the hell that was." Oz pressed her hands against the now-silent earth. "Do you think it's safe to go out?"

Riley glanced through the opening, noticing the creeping darkness to the east. She crawled from their hiding place, stretching, and looked in all directions for signs of life. The western sky lit up like a wildfire. Dark ground faded into purple mountains that seeped into a glowing mix of yellow, red, and orange flames streaking across the sky. Oz followed, and the two girls stared at the sunset in front of them.

"I think we're safe for now." Riley no longer heard the roar from the helicopters or the sounds of the earth exploding. "They must have gone in for the night."

"Do you think they found the Jeep?" Oz twisted her shoulders back and forth and bent over to stretch her spine.

"I'm certain they did." Riley eyed the dry dirt around her feet. "They probably know it will be easy to pick up a trail tomorrow in the daylight and that we don't have much of a chance."

"What do you think?"

Riley sighed. "I think we're about to walk all night until the sun rises. You ready?"

Oz shrugged and hoisted her backpack onto her shoulders. "No."

They hiked in silence, checking the stars for accuracy and trying not to stumble on cacti and loose chucks of rock. The cold desert night made Riley pull her jacket tighter around her body and wish she had a warm bed and heater, or at least a sleeping bag and open fire. They were still a good two hundred miles from Los Angeles. *How can we do this?*

Somehow Oz kept up. The occasional splash of vomit decorated the desert floor, but she seemed to be on the upward end of whatever she was dealing with. Riley kept glancing sideways, watching her silent partner struggle through the night. There were so many things she wanted to ask, so many questions she had about her other life.

"What do you do for fun?" she finally asked Oz as she handed her a granola bar and a fresh canteen of water.

Oz laughed and took a drink. "You really wanna know?"

Riley shrugged. "I mean besides the drugs and sleeping around. Like, surely you do some normal-people things."

"Hah. Well, you have to promise not to tell." Oz unzipped Riley's pack and returned the water bottle. "It'll ruin the reputation that I'm so proud of."

"Sure, whatever."

Oz leaned down and pulled a small yellow flower from a scraggly bush. "I like to garden. You know, plants and shit. And I'm really good at it. When I was a kid, I used to want to do it for money. Plant gardens for people." She paused and plucked each petal from the stem. "I just never got around to it, and no one really wanted to hire me, so I just do it for myself at home."

"I like it too." Riley smiled. "And our grandma liked it. I think that's who we got it from."

"I never really knew her." Oz tossed the rest of the flower to the ground and kept walking. "She moved back to Germany, and I didn't get to see her after that."

"She was an interesting lady." Riley felt for her ring. "She taught me everything about growing things."

"Who'd've thought we'd have something in common?" Oz laughed. "Besides good looks, I mean."

Riley peered up at the stars. The half moon provided enough light to see by but not enough to avoid all the obstacles on the ground. It would take weeks to reach their destination if something didn't change.

"You know, I wasn't always doing bad things," Oz said. "I've done some really good things, actually. Like one time I saw a lady drop her wallet in a parking lot, and I caught up with her and returned it. My friends thought I was an idiot. Dunno why I did it, but I did." She kicked a rock and watched it roll away under a bush. "Must've been sometime when you were bad and I couldn't help it."

"When I was thirteen, I stole a pair of sunglasses from the store," Riley said, blushing. "My friends dared me to, and honestly, I felt a rush doing it. I've never done something like that since, but I guess I wasn't always doing good things either."

They walked in silence, mile upon mile through dark nothingness. Each rock and shrub just like the previous, the horizon never growing closer.

"Pretty weird that you're here." Oz interrupted the silence. "It sucks 'cause now everyone has you to compare me to. They knew I was fucked up, but now they can be like 'Why can't you be more like her?'" She stopped walking. "I've spent my whole life disappointing one person or another, and I always knew you were out there—and I always hated you."

"I didn't know you were out there, but if I had, I would have hated you too."

Oz laughed and shook her head. "It's kinda funny if you think about it. They put two people in the world who are supposed to be one, and you'd think they'd be best friends, but instead they're enemies."

"You can't stand me, can you?" Riley asked.

"Not really." Oz looked away. "Personally, I'd rather be in this desert with anyone but you."

Riley threw her hands up, frustrated. "And just when I start to think you're actually human, you remind me that you're merely a poor replica of one. You know, you actually owe a lot to me. I didn't spend every day of my life trying to kill us like you did. If anyone should be angry, it's me. You've done nothing but trash me since the day you were born. Hell, I bet you found the morphine in the hospital before they even brought you home."

Oz let out a high-pitched laugh. "See, that's the problem with you. You act like you give a shit, but you really think I'm worthless, and I see through it. People always try to act like they care, but no one really does. Quit trying to act and let's just tell it like it is. I don't like you. You don't like me. Let's get to LA and send you home. Problem solved."

"No. It's not solved," Riley said, anger boiling up inside. "Because now I know you exist, and I'm going to spend the rest of my life wondering when you're going to overdose and kill us both, or get some horrific disease that kills me slowly. No, I can't forget you. You'll be my nightmare the rest of my life."

"It'll be my pleasure."

Riley had never met anyone who made her so mad. She played with the idea of leaving Oz to fend for herself or turning her over to the authorities. It was unfair that their fates were tied together. Riley wanted nothing more than to rid herself of the girl for good.

Hours passed without a word. The stars and constellations crept across the sky. Riley imagined coming out to this place with her family and camping. Such normal ideas rarely crossed her mind now. She thought about the animals she'd studied in class and how life for them was just about survival. Humans had the luxury of things like camping and hanging out with friends. Animals had to focus everything on eating or being eaten. *The lines are beginning to blur.*

"I'm tired," Oz whined as her feet dragged behind.

"Suck it up."

"I can just stop when I want to, you know?"

Riley ignored her and kept walking. She knew Oz would follow.

"Ouch!" Oz shrieked. "Damn it!"

"What?" Riley turned to see Oz on the ground, her right hand and arm retreating from a cactus patch. Riley fought the urge to laugh. *Serves you right.*

"Help me get these out," Oz bellowed. "I can't see!"

"Oz, you're fine." Riley pulled the flashlight from her back-pack and shone it on her companion's arm. Fine red cactus hairs coated her skin like an extra layer of fur, and Oz yelped at the sight.

"Get them off! Get them off!"

Riley dug through the backpacks, but the first aid kit had nothing that would help. She came across the roll of duct tape and pulled it out. "For all we know there are people following us right now, and if you don't keep your voice down, you'll have bigger problems than this." Riley ripped a large strip of tape off the roll and stuck it to Oz's arm. "No yelling, got it?"

Oz grimaced and looked away as Riley pulled the tape off. The small thorns clung to the adhesive. Oz whimpered but stayed still as Riley repeated the act until most of the thorns were removed.

"I still see some," Oz grumbled, pointing out individual hairs scattered over her arm.

"You'll live." Riley stood and looked for a place to take shelter. A faint glow rose in the east, promising a resumed search for the girls. Scanning the area, she noticed large rocks and boulders jutting up from the ground. It would be a great place to rest and pass the day, but also an obvious place to look for people hiding. *Hopefully they won't think we could have covered this much distance.* There was no way to know how far they had walked in the night, but Riley guessed somewhere around twenty miles.

"We'll rest here." Riley motioned to the rocks overhanging a dry creek bed.

They crawled in between two of the larger boulders and found a hidden space that was big enough to lie down in. They gulped water and ate a ration of the food, but Riley's stomach groaned painfully for more. She tried to ignore it.

"Watch for snakes." She lay down and pulled her jacket tighter around her body.

The boulders provided enough shade to keep in the cool and dark, and the soft sand of the creek bed was an improvement from the previous night. Riley's exhaustion welcomed sleep, even though the company was not welcome. She glanced at Oz, who lay curled up facing away from her, and she saw the black widow tattoo peeking up from her waistline. Part of Riley hoped the spider would somehow bite Oz while she slept. *But I'd die too. I can't even wish that upon you.* It was so unfair.

CHAPTER FORTY

Riley woke up shivering as a cool wind penetrated her thin jacket. *What is with this weather?* A chilly northern gust blasted her face as she crawled to the opening in the rocks. The sky had darkened with thunderheads that roiled with impatience to release their flood. *Uh oh.*

"Oz. Oz, wake up." She scooted back into the shelter. "We've got to move. It's about to pour, and this creek will flood."

"Well, I'm not going out in the rain, if that's what you're suggesting." Oz rolled over and glared. "I'll take my chances in here."

Riley threw a handful of sand at the wall in frustration and crawled out from the rocks. She scanned her surroundings but saw no place that would provide shelter. The other rocks were vertical pillars rising from the ground that might provide refuge from the wind but would offer no protection from the rain. Downstream, she noticed a small stand of cottonwoods blowing in the wind. She glanced back at the sky, a churning mass of blacks, grays, greens, and yellows. This wouldn't be a light shower. They were in for dangerous weather, and the cottonwoods would only attract the lightning that was sure to follow. *Damn it!*

"Lucky you, we have no other place but this." Riley crawled back in between the rocks. The temperature dropped rapidly, and she wished they had grabbed more clothes out of the Jeep before they left. "You'd better pray this creek doesn't start running."

"I don't pray." Oz turned to face the wall.

Riley rolled her eyes and rubbed her hands together, trying to stave off the impending chill. "I guess the good part of this is that the rain will erase all of our tracks and make it harder to find us."

She looked around their small cave at the flat, sandy creek bed and its incline up to the base of the rocks that formed a space like the underside of a bridge. *At least there's an area to retreat to.*

Boom. A huge clap of thunder shook the rock shelter and echoed off the surrounding boulders as sharp flashes struck the earth and lit up the mouth of their hideout.

"Holy shit!" Oz bolted upright. "How am I supposed to sleep with that?"

Within seconds it sounded like someone was standing over them with an open fire hose. Rain sprayed through the cracks, and the wind gusted harder, quickly soaking through their clothes. Lightning pelted the ground all around, and the rocks trembled at the noise of the thunder. Riley worried the stones might collapse.

"Let's move higher up the incline," she yelled. "It won't take long for this dry creek to flashflood."

Oz grabbed her backpack and the rifle and crawled up the slope. Riley followed and dug out a place to sit partway up. She peered through a crack in the rocks and surveyed the cottonwood stand as it jerked madly in the wind when the lightning flashed. Shivers escaped through her wet clothes as the wind bit into her skin. The temperature continued to drop as if it had forgotten that it was summer.

In no time the creek started to run. Riley watched helplessly as the water slowly rose, the rain refusing to cease in its intensity. Oz munched on a piece of beef jerky, scared eyes watching the creeping water. Both girls trembled with violent quakes. Riley opened her backpack to find something to keep them warm and removed a folded newspaper.

"Really?" she asked Oz. "You thought this was important when you loaded the backpacks?"

Oz snatched it out of her hands. "I thought we'd need it to start a fire."

Riley pulled another paper from her bag, wishing it were a blanket, or better yet, a tarp. "Come here, Oz. We'll never make it through the night if we don't use each other's body heat."

Oz gave a look of disgust but rolled over. Riley opened the newspapers and laid them across their bodies, hoping to keep some of the wind at bay.

Misery owned the night. The moisture soaked their clothes so deeply that no amount of thin newspaper could keep the chill northern wind off their damp bodies. The girls huddled together under the rocks, shivering. The combined heat from their bodies did little against the moist air ripping through the cracks in the rock shelter. It didn't take long for the newspaper to soak through, and they peeled it off their skin before it could make them even colder.

"We're not gonna make it." Oz stared at the rising creek below.

Riley bobbed her head in numb agreement. If the wet, biting cold didn't kill them, the flooding creek probably would. *But we have no place to go!*

This rock shelter provided the only cover for miles. Riley had seen nothing else. The desert offered little in the form of protection, and it was now too dark and treacherous to try and find a new sanctuary. The lightning struck all around them like darts on a dartboard, with their small cave forming the center ring. The thunder bellowed across the sky, drumming to the beat the lightning set for it.

They were trapped. The only option was to crawl farther up the bank and wedge against the stone base that held the rock up from the ground. But that extra space vanished each time they retreated. The rain continued falling, the wind continued howling, and the creek continued to rise. Riley stared at the place in the raging water where the entrance to their refuge had been.

"So what's plan B, sister?" Oz's bluing lips stretched into a helpless grin.

Riley felt her hand reach for her own mouth, wondering if she too were developing signs of hypothermia. Her fingers were too numb to feel her own flesh. *Well, there's my answer.*

"Oz, we can't die here," she replied with new resolve, reaching for her companion's hands. "We can't just be erased like this."

"So what do you suggest, then?" Oz pulled herself closer to Riley, tucking her legs into her chest. "You know I'm always up for not dying."

"Well, I can't guarantee the not-dying part," Riley began. "But we at least have a choice in the matter of our demise."

A clap of thunder shattered the air as a bolt of lightning illuminated the sky, igniting the cottonwood grove downstream in a blaze of fire. Riley glanced down at the creek that had now swelled to just two feet below them, raging and threatening to pull them under, trapping them in the cave to die.

"And you say people come stay out here for fun?" Oz scratched her head and chewed the corner of her mouth. "This has got to be the ass end of the world."

Riley laughed. "Yeah, it seems kind of crazy right about now. So what will it be—drowning or a lightning strike? I choose lightning. I think it will be over sooner."

Oz stared at the angry creek, illuminated by the constant flashes of blinding light. "And once we begin to run through this minefield, where do you suggest we go?"

Riley's teeth chattered through her frozen lips. "Los Angeles. And I think we'd better crawl. We don't want to be the tallest thing out there."

Oz snorted and stretched her legs down into the churning water. "You want to crawl to Los Angeles through dirt and cacti with an inland hurricane raging overhead?"

"I guess that's what I'm saying."

"You've got more balls than I gave you credit for." A smirk broke through the cold exterior of Oz's face.

"I just value my life." Fog accompanied Riley's breathy laugh, and for a moment she felt proud of the only compliment her other half had ever given.

Oz pulled her backpack on and shouldered the rifle. "Well, shit. Let's get on to Los Angeles." She slid into the rolling creek and glanced up at Riley. "Here goes!" She dove under the water and tried to locate the opening to the cave, but the icy liquid sucked the air from her lungs and made her already frozen body nearly immovable. *Swim. Get out of here or die.* She kicked her legs and moved forward, feeling for an opening against the slick rock. Nothing. She surfaced and took a deep breath. "I can't find it!"

Riley slid into the water next to her. "Try again."

Oz plunged under, her head swimming with numbness as the cold strangled her brain. She flailed her arms, searching, and finally found the opening. She tugged at Riley's pant leg and swam forward. Her head broke the surface, and she gasped for air as the swollen creek rushed her downstream and the sky above assaulted her with liquid ammo. She swam for the shore and got tangled in a mess of tree limbs and submerged tumbleweeds. *Where are you, Riley?*

The current kept trying to suck her under the pile of debris, to trap her like in the cave. The rifle tore from her arm as the current succeeded in pulling her under. Icy brown water filled her lungs, and her brain threatened to explode.

She kicked furiously, but the pull was too strong and she was still too weak. The water burned her insides, and she began to feel warm—a trickling sensation that encompassed her body. She welcomed the feeling after being so cold and so miserable. The last thing she remembered before blacking out was an irritating tugging sensation on her shoulders. She wanted it to go away. Everything was so peaceful except for the tugging.

———

Lightning struck less than thirty feet away, shaking the ground as Riley dragged Oz onto the bank, ripping the weeds from her legs and trying not to slip on the dicey ground. Her own mind hummed with white noise, but she fought it and pressed on Oz's chest, trying to get her to respond. *Come on. Come on.* On and on she compressed, feeling death knocking on her own fragile door as the rain sprayed her back and the lightning pierced all around. Finally Oz coughed and choked up the water, rolling onto her side and heaving.

"Oh, thank God." Riley fell back into the mud as drowning's death grip released its clutch from her brain.

Oz curled into a ball, still coughing, and strained to catch her breath. "My lungs."

"I know," Riley shouted over the storm. "My lungs too. But we have to get moving. It isn't safe by the creek."

Oz lifted her head and looked around. "It isn't safe anywhere."

Riley's lungs burned, and her body struggled to wiggle even a toe. "Oz, we have to move, if for no other reason than we will freeze if we stay still. I know you feel bad, and I can't guarantee things won't get worse, but we can't sit here."

Oz looked up helplessly and rolled onto her stomach, dragging herself away from the swollen creek. Frigid strands of hair fell like icicles around her forehead, and every part of her body was drenched with icy water. Each inch she crawled shot a pain worse than withdrawal through her body.

Riley inched forward next to her, having no idea where they would go. It was hard enough to tell up from down in the squall, let alone determine direction. She felt her teeth trying to chatter from her head and knew Oz's would be audible if the thunder didn't drown them out.

All her life she'd loved storms, but now she felt she would be scarred forever. Each earth-shattering boom caused her heart to skip a beat, wondering if the next strike would penetrate her own fragile organ. She saw the cacti as she crawled through them, but her body was too numb to feel the pain. She tried hard to stay positive and motivate Oz to keep moving, but inside a terminal voice kept repeating the word *death*, and soon the voice screamed louder than the storm.

Chapter Forty-One

Detective Rutherford smashed his knobby fist on the dashboard and let out a frustrated bellow that rumbled with the thunder. *God damn this weather.* Earlier they had found the girls' Jeep and had had an easy time following their dusty tracks to the group of yuccas where they had camped. Then the storm hit.

Now he sat stranded in the desert with two other Hummers full of his officers, waiting for the storm of the century to recede. Every minute that passed, he felt the tires sink lower into the rain-washed mud that piled up against the rubber and threatened to lock them in place. His fury built with each strike of lightning, his anger matched only by that of the raging storm.

The girls' uncle had been little help, refusing to speak to anyone or do anything but sing show tunes in his cell. Thus far he'd managed to scrape by with only a severe beating. A little blood, bruising, and a cracked skull were a blessing compared to what they would do to him if need be.

Rutherford lit a cigarette and exhaled smoke into the small cab. One officer in the back stifled a cough but clearly knew better than to challenge his superior. The detective wiped the fog off the windshield and stared out at the black tempest, hoping to catch a glimpse of the fleeing girls in the illuminated desert.

"Maybe this storm will kill them, sir," the young officer offered from the back.

"I don't want them dead," the detective seethed. "I want them alive, and I want my money. Someone else can kill them once that's done. Hell, I wouldn't mind being the one to do it in the end."

The cab filled with smoke, and the detective became an eerie figure shrouded in haze. His dark hair lay matted to his face, and his bloodshot eyes filled with crazed hate. His teeth clawed at the corner of his mouth, and the cigarette bounced up and down every time he spoke, making him look more like a cartoon villain than a high-profile detective.

"Hey, boss." The officer in the front seat pointed to the eastern sky. "Look over there."

The detective turned to peer out the side of the car and smiled at the soft glow sneaking out of the darkness. "Do you hear that, boys?"

"Hear what, sir?"

"Quiet. The rain is letting up. Sun's starting to creep out." He lit another cigarette, wiped the condensation off the front windshield, and held his radio up to his lips. "One forty to one twenty and one ninety."

"Go ahead."

"Get your guns ready, boys." The fresh cigarette bobbed as he talked. "Let's trap some Demies."

Chapter Forty-Two

Even after the rain stopped, Oz's shakes continued. The rising sun crept up from the east, but her bones had turned to ice during the night, and no amount of daylight could thaw them. Tears in her pants exposed bloody knees, and her elbows and underarms were scrubbed raw from dragging across rock and cacti. Thorns stuck out from all parts of her body, and her lungs still burned from the icy water. She rolled onto her back and let the morning sun make an effort to save her. *I wish I'd just died last night.* Oz glanced at Riley, who wiped dirt from open sores and picked thorns from her stomach.

"Thanks for saving me back there." Oz propped herself up on her elbows and glanced down at her ragged body. "Although at this point I kind of wish I'd just drowned."

"You're welcome." Riley didn't look up.

"Listen, I owe you one, okay? I don't forget shit like that."

"Sure." Riley still didn't look at her. "We need to get moving. They'll be following us again now that it's clear."

Oz felt annoyed by Riley's detached and apathetic tone. They had just survived a night in hell together, and Riley brushed it off like it was nothing. *I should be nicer to her.* But Oz didn't like opening up to people. It made her vulnerable, and she couldn't afford that. "Got any more of that duct tape?"

Riley unzipped her drenched backpack and tossed the tape to Oz.

"Listen, princess." Oz tried to avoid the bloody areas as she ripped strips of thorns from her arms. "I don't think we'll make LA like this. Another night like last, and I'm toast."

Riley shrugged and tore a piece of jerky with her teeth. Blood ran down the side of her arm, dripping onto the wet sand.

"You're hurt."

Riley looked at the wound and wrapped her fingers around it, trying to stop the bleeding. "I ran into a sharp rock last night. I barely felt it through the numbness, but I figured it did some damage if I felt it at all."

Oz ripped off the bottom of her shirt and handed it to Riley. "Use this."

Riley tied the fabric around her arm as a bandage and turned her face to the sun. "A few more hours of this, and I may actually survive."

"No kidding." Oz stretched her arms and legs out into the warming dirt. "I feel like a lizard."

Little beads of water sparkled in the sun and rolled from the smooth cactus leaves onto the saturated ground. A clear blue sky—a total transformation from the night before—promised to deliver a hot and stifling day. The ruby on Riley's ring caught the light and shone an even brighter red than the blood dripping from her elbow.

"We could sell that, you know?" Oz pointed to the heirloom. "It's the only thing we've got that's worth a damn now."

"No." Riley glanced down at the ring and twisted it on her finger. She didn't trust Oz with its secret or its power and wasn't about to tell her what she suspected. She changed the subject. "We look terrible."

Oz laughed. "Bleeding, wet rats. No one will recognize us now." She pulled her water bottle out of the backpack and swirled the last remaining bit around the bottom. "Would you believe after a night like that, I'm almost out of water? Idiot."

"Well, we were a little distracted. Hopefully we can hit a running creek and top off. You almost ready?"

"I guess as much as I will be. Let's get out of here before Rutherford can finish the job."

Riley stood up slowly, willing the chill from her bones and the pain from her open wounds. She turned back toward the east and stared wistfully at where they'd come from. How long had it been since she'd left home now? *A few days? Maybe a week?* It seemed like an eternity. She suddenly felt like a small child—hurt, lost, afraid, and in need of her mother. *I'd give anything to be home.* She touched her hand to her wet hair and twisted a strand with grimy, chipped fingernails. She wanted to cry, to sit down and wait for the detective.

Riley turned back to the vast emptiness stretching out before them and the path they must travel. *I can't go back now.* She took a step and then another. *I can't look back anymore. Looking back will just get us killed.*

"We'll walk until we find a place to hide," she said. "Then we rest until dark."

"Aye, aye, captain."

They stumbled through the desert, the cold wind from the night before replaced by a scorching stillness. Sweat ran down their faces like rain, with no breeze to dry it off or bring any amount of relief. The sands dried and the rocks faded back to their parched color. The landscape appeared unchanged by the tempest. If it weren't for the bedraggled figures trudging through the untouched wasteland, there would be no evidence that anything bizarre had occurred the night before.

After they'd been walking for a few hours, Oz squinted into the distance. "Is that a mirage? I think the heat is playing tricks on my brain."

Riley narrowed her eyes, seeing the image Oz indicated. *A road? A gas station?* Her heart quickened, and her feet flew into a brisk walk and then a full-out run.

"Hey, wait!" Oz shouted, but Riley was already in a dead sprint toward the welcome sight.

Fifty yards from the structure, Riley took cover behind a small stand of trees. She peered at the building, noticing a parking lot full of eighteen-wheelers and their drivers milling around. The smell of buttered popcorn, fried chicken, and hot dogs wafted out from the station, and Riley's stomach churned, aching for a hot meal and a clean restroom.

"Are you crazy?" Oz panted, skidding to a halt beside her. "We can't just go running into places that probably have our pictures posted all over them."

"You're one to talk. That's why I stopped here. I've got a plan."

"We gonna rob it?" A new energy leapt from Oz's voice.

"No." Riley dropped her pack to the ground and rolled her eyes at the nearest tree as if it too understood the absurdity of her companion's words. "We'll wait until dark and climb into the back of a truck. One of the ones heading to LA. We can ride the rest of the way."

"What if they're locked?"

"We'll find one that isn't."

"Maybe so, but I see some serious holes in your plan."

"Got a better one?"

Oz's eyes lit up as she sniffed the air. "Yep. Get some of that fried chicken and then wait until dark and crawl into the back of one of those trucks."

"We can't go in there. You said it yourself."

"*We* can't go in there, but I can. No one will recognize me with this hair and without you."

Riley sighed and shook her head, plopping down on the ground next to her pack. "Get some water while you're at it. If anything goes wrong and they get you, just try not to die, okay?"

"Deal." Oz dug through her backpack and pulled out the wad of cash Kevin had given her. "Don't wait up." She emerged from the bushes, combing her fingers through her hair and strutting up to the gas station. Riley watched her disappear around the front and leaned back against one of the trees. *Please let this go well.* In an instant she fell asleep.

"Wake up." Oz shook Riley by the shoulders. "I found a ride."

Sunlight spattered through holes in the leaves and branches, so Riley knew it was still daytime. Her back ached, and she struggled to sit up, but the smell of fresh food provided motivation.

"What?" Riley squinted at Oz, noticing that the mud and dried blood were missing from her skin, and she had fresh, combed hair. *And are those clean clothes?* "What happened to you? How long was I asleep?"

"They have showers in there. And washing machines. And food. Here." She shoved a box of fried chicken into Riley's hands and plopped down on the ground beside her. Riley threw open the lid and took a moment to inhale the delicious smell before stuffing a chicken leg into her mouth.

"Wait, you had time to wash and dry your clothes?"

"I was in there for a while. Met a guy who says he'll take us to Los Angeles."

"You told him about us?" Riley dropped the piece of chicken she was worrying and grabbed Oz's arm. "We're supposed to sneak into Los Angeles, not fall into a trap."

"Relax. We're fine. Guy's not saying anything to anyone. He thinks you're my sister." Oz snatched a piece of chicken from the box and ripped off a huge bite. "Man, it feels good to be clean."

"So some guy just volunteered to take us to LA?" Riley moved the box of food away from Oz to a place she couldn't reach. "Just like that?"

"Of course not. You're lucky you have me along to do all the dirty work."

Riley's face contorted in disgust, and she gagged on the bite in her mouth. "Oz, you didn't."

"Relax. You should be thanking me."

"Ew." Riley set the box down and stared at the dirt under her legs.

"Yeah, he was pretty bad," Oz acknowledged. "But at least we've got a ride. Life and death, right, sister?"

Riley shuddered. "Sure."

"He said he'd be ready to go in about an hour." Oz brushed blond hair from her face, grinning. "You should go clean up. You look like shit."

———

An hour later Riley and Oz perched in the cab of the eighteen-wheeler, clean, fed, and headed in the right direction. Their driver—Pete was how he introduced himself—seemed nice enough, but Riley couldn't help gagging every time she looked over and saw back hairs creeping from beneath his shirt or yellow teeth jutting from his face. *A beaver.* That's what he reminded her of. A large, hairy beaver. *Jesus, Oz.*

"What business you girls got in the capital?" Pete turned down the radio and spat a wad of tobacco into an empty soda bottle that Riley tried to avoid looking at. "It's a strange time for two young beauties like yourselves to be headin' to a place like that."

"Family." Oz rolled her eyes and gave an exasperated sigh. "I told you that, Pete. We've got a brother we haven't seen in a while, and he's sick. We're trying to get to him before…" She chocked back fake tears and buried her head in Pete's shoulder. He looked helplessly at Riley, who tried to fake her own distress in return.

"We were very close." Oz leaned into him with a sad, far-away expression.

"I'm real sorry." He patted Oz on the shoulder and gave her a stern look. "It's just the capital ain't a real safe place right now, what with the soldiers everywhere and the chaos."

"Soldiers?" Riley's heart raced. "Are they looking for someone?"

"Well, sure, they're always looking for someone." His hand flew into the air before crashing back down on the steering wheel. "But these boys are fighting to protect us from the A-rabs. Just yesterday they dropped two bombs on the city. People are hurt everywhere, with no water or nothin'."

Riley and Oz stared openmouthed at Pete.

"Bombs?" Oz shot Riley a worried glance.

He nodded. "You girls been livin' under a rock or somethin'? Whole world's gone to hell in the last few days. They're sayin' this may be it. Like World War III or somethin'."

The rumblings in the desert. Riley could see the rocks bouncing on the ground and the plants trembling under the force of an unseen producer. *It was a bomb...*

"Well, why the hell are you going there?" Oz folded her arms across her chest and glared at Pete.

"I got a truck full of medical supplies and food. These folks are our brothers and sisters dyin' in the streets." He shook his head angrily. "It's those damn Muslims. Worshippin' idols and hatin' America."

Oz's face squished up, and she shook her head. "Didn't President Cain attack them first? I mean, he bombed some mosque a few months back for no reason."

"He had every reason." Pete slammed his fist on the steering wheel again. "President Cain is protectin' our freedom from blasphemous infidels."

"Okay." Oz backed down and cast Riley a *this man is nuts* look. "So, assuming where we need to go isn't blown to shit, you can take us there?"

"Yes, ma'am. Already put the directions in my GPS."

They rode the rest of the way, listening to Pete's horrible renditions of country classics and watching the landscape and small towns fly past. Riley stared out the window, feeling that their eensy bit of luck had been short lived. She hoped Zach would be waiting for them at Ezra's house, if it had survived the bombing, but after the struggle they'd faced getting out of Las Vegas, his escape seemed impossible.

And if he did evade capture, what if he'd been blown to bits with Ezra? A tear slid down her cheek. *I'll never see my family again.* She'd have to spend the rest of her short and miserable life in hiding with a girl who hated her, being pursued by a man who seemed to hate her even more.

CHAPTER FORTY-THREE

Los Angeles was unrecognizable—not just because in this universe it was the nation's capital and not Hollywood, but also because the scene in front of them didn't belong in America. Riley clasped her hand over her mouth, stifling a gasp. Battles happened other places in the world, not on US soil. Horrific images like this were supposed to be removed by thousands of miles and a television screen, not to be viewed up close and in person.

"Ho-ly shit." Oz stared wide eyed at the chaos ahead.

Smoke and fire billowed from crumbling buildings. Glass shards littered the road among human bodies and busted cars. Bleeding, shocked faces staggered through the streets, searching for loved ones or staring blankly ahead. It reminded Riley of slides Dr. Reitz had posted in class—horrific scenes of death and destruction from the war. But the man limping and clutching the bleeding stub that used to be his arm was different than a picture. His pain, his grief, was immediate, was right now. Riley wanted to run to him, but they had to get to Ezra's. She had to get out of this terrible place.

"Jesus, Pete, you weren't kidding." Oz shook her head and let out a low whistle. "How the hell are you going to save these people?"

Pete's mouth gaped. "One at a time, with the good Lord's help. One at a time."

Oz leaned over to Riley and whispered in her ear. "At least they won't be looking for us here. Hopefully they think we got blown up."

Riley nodded slowly. White ash fell like snow, dusting everything and everyone in a soft powder. Every block they turned down looked as bad as or worse than the first. Whoever did this didn't just want to send a message. They wanted to annihilate an entire city.

"Well, this is as far as I can get ya." Pete pulled the truck to a stop behind a barricade of rubble. "Stay down this road about a half mile and take a right. If he's there, you'll find him."

"Thanks, Pete." Oz offered a forced smile and placed a hand on his leg before scooting for the door.

"No, thank *you*." He winked, slapping her rear as she got out of the truck.

Their boots left cloudy footprints in the fresh ash, and Riley covered her mouth for fear of breathing in more than just burned-up buildings.

"Now that's one of those ironic do-gooders," Oz said as she hopped over an empty stroller that had twisted into a metallic pretzel. "Man trades sex for a ride to LA, hates most of the damn world, but risks his life to come help people he doesn't have to. I don't get it."

They climbed over the wall of debris, carefully searching the ground for holes, nails, or body parts they might step on. Riley pleaded not to look down and find a pair of vacant eyes.

"I mean, you'd think people would be one way or the other, right?" Oz continued. "For instance, you either want to help everybody, love everybody, or you don't give a crap about any of it. Take me, for example. I know who I am, and I'm cool with it. I'm not gonna go around helping people, especially not in a hellhole like this. But I'm also going to equally dislike everyone—no discrimination. I think they're all crazy. People may not like me, but at least I'm consistent."

Riley tried to listen but was too horrified by their surroundings to pay much attention to anything except staying focused and not stepping on someone's face. Torn curtains flapped through broken windows, and sirens blared to a sickeningly absent audience. People and their lives littered the streets: teddy bears, photo albums, lamps, books—normal things that shouldn't be charred and abandoned.

She bent down and picked up a child's shoe no bigger than a doll's and stared at the blood droplets on the pale pink fabric. She forced back tears. It was too much—the bodies, the rubble, the blood, the shoe. *This was a child. Someone too innocent to understand the angry fights of men.* Riley felt the color drain from her face and sat down on a ragged piece of concrete, avoiding the broken rebar jutting out.

"I wonder if Pete still thinks God's on his side?" Oz plucked the shoe from Riley's hand and, to Riley's surprise, held it to her lips and kissed it. "I'm sorry, little friend. You didn't deserve this." She set the shoe down gently beside Riley. "Come on, we've got to keep going. I don't think it's safe to linger."

Riley stood, her numb legs wanting nothing more than to shrink into the destruction, to disappear from this horrible world forever. "I just can't believe what's happened here. All these people—I knew people in Los Angeles back home. I had friends here."

"You can't think about it right now." Oz grabbed onto her shoulders and met her eyes with intensity. "We can't fix this, and it's too much if you let it in. Get your shit together and let's find Ezra."

Riley glanced at the small shoe one last time and took a dusty step forward.

"Just think." Oz trudged off down the street. "This time tomorrow you'll probably be back home safe in your bed, thinking you just woke up from the craziest dream you've ever had."

"Is there a chance that's what this is?"

Oz snorted. "If that's what you need to tell yourself. I wouldn't mind waking up tomorrow with things back to normal. The shitty thing for me is you get to wake up and pretend if you want to. There's no other place but this hellhole for me."

"I can't pretend." Riley sucked in an ashy breath. "If I make it home, I'll be reminded that this place exists when I turn on the news and see that hundreds of thousands, maybe millions of people in California died from some freak accident. I'll think of the little girl and her shoe and remember what her blood looked like." She touched Oz's arm and looked into her eyes. "This nightmare is mine as well. I'm stuck here just like you."

They reached the turnoff point and stared down the street to their right. Broken buildings smoldered above the pavement besieged with wreckage.

"We're looking for a bookstore on the left-hand side. Ezra lives above it." Riley read from the small paper Zach had handed her in Vegas. "It's called Treasured Tomes."

She looked up at the sound of a hacking cough. An old man hurried up the street, bleeding from the head and carrying a bag loaded to the seams.

"Excuse me," Oz shouted. "We're looking for a bookstore on this street. Can you point us in the right direction?"

The man paused, looking confused. "What in the hell do you need a book for right now? Whole city's blown up and you're looking for a goddamned book?" His front teeth were missing, and Riley saw where the blood from his head originated. His left ear had been torn off, taking part of his scalp with it. She shuddered and looked away, but Oz seemed unfazed by the gore.

"Listen, I don't really care about your opinions on the matter." Oz tapped her foot impatiently. "But your directions would be great."

The man glowered and shifted his heavy load across his back. "Fourth pile of rubble on your left. Good luck finding anything you need there."

He headed up the road, and Riley stared at the indicated location. A roofless structure rose from the dust with a splintered sign that may once have said Treasured Tomes hanging idly from a nail above the blown-out windows. Nothing remained of Ezra's upstairs home. Bent and broken pieces of rebar provided the only evidence that the structure had ever existed.

"Oh, come on, give us a fucking break," Oz yelled at the mess.

Riley pushed open the cracked door and stared at the toppled shelves and dusty books lying in piles of ash. She picked up one of the old volumes and blew the soot from the cover— *A History of the Eve'n Wars. Volume I.*

Oz peered over her shoulder. "What are the Eve'n Wars?"

"No idea." Riley set the book back on the ground and sank to the floor. She glared at the ancient text and fought the tears and panic that threatened to overtake her. *I will never get home.* Her breaths quickened and her mind grew hazy. "Oz." Her voice shook. "Oz, I'm trapped here. I'm never going home." She stared at the destroyed buildings. "Mom, Dad, Kiersten, Abby, Gabe…"

"Relax." Oz paced across what remained of the room. "So maybe it won't happen today, but we'll figure something out."

"There's nothing left," Riley shouted. "There's no place else to go. We will spend the rest of our lives running from some unseen enemy and trying not to kill each other."

"Panicking isn't gonna help," Oz grumbled. "I'm stuck here as much as you. Just be happy you have a family to miss. I'd take fire and brimstone any day if it meant I was free from mine."

Tears slid down Riley's cheeks. "When I was a kid, I used to think how incredible it would have been to be one of the first people to explore America. I was so jealous of Lewis and Clark for getting to take off into a completely unknown place and just be free. I wanted so badly to have an opportunity like that."

She smiled up at Oz through her tears, shaking her head and gesturing to their surroundings. "I don't know if you've noticed, but I'm kind of a coward. I'm scared of everything and overwhelmed by life. The only time I ever feel calm and at peace is when I'm by myself in the wilderness. That's where my stillness is. But now I'm realizing even that's a sham."

Her hand flew to her mouth to stifle a sob. "Because here I am, the golden opportunity in my hand, and all I want is to turn around and go home. You see, what you don't think about as a kid is that being out on your own in a new world isn't glorious or easy or peaceful. I didn't think about the pain and hunger and death that those people faced, just the excitement. I romanticized the idea of adventure so much. It was safe wishing I would have that chance when I knew it was impossible."

Oz sat down on the corner of an overturned bookshelf and stared out at the road. "When I was a kid, I used to dream about being a princess. I was jealous of the girls in school who had money and parents who loved them. I wanted their shiny shoes and overstuffed lunch boxes. I wanted what they had. I saw a movie one time about a poor girl who found out her dad was really a rich man who loved her and saved her from her miserable life. I used to pretend that was me and that my real dad would come someday and save me. But the years went by, and I became hungrier and sadder, and I did things no princess would ever do." She kicked a rock and watched it tumble through the ash. "Do you think it's too late for me?"

"No." Riley wiped the tears from her face. "I don't think it's ever too late."

Oz hardened her expression before Riley could see her emotions. "Well, I think you're braver than you give yourself credit for. You may not be Lewis or Clark, whoever they are, but you damn sure got us through the desert as if you were." She stood and walked toward the back of the store. "So I may not be a princess, and you may not be a Boy Scout, but I think we're doing a helluva good job, whoever we are."

Riley sat in silence, staring vacantly across the street to the crumbling foundation on the other side. "Hey, Oz?"

"Yeah?"

"Back there you kissed that shoe. Why?"

Oz bit her bottom lip as she nodded slowly. "Just because I'm not a saint doesn't make me a monster."

Riley sighed and shook her head. "You're actually being nice to me now."

"You saved my life."

"If I let you die, it would have killed me too."

A moment passed before Oz spoke. "Yeah, but even if it wouldn't have, you still would have pulled me out."

"How do you know?" Riley's tear-streaked face grew taut as she eyed her other half.

"Because you're the opposite of me."

"So you would have let me drown?"

"Not sure." Oz walked back to the front of the store and kneeled down in front of Riley. "Listen, people don't do nice things for me. They just don't. Never have. You saved my life, regardless of why you did it. I don't forget when someone does something like that for me, okay?"

Riley watched as Oz stood and continued walking around the rubble. "What are you hoping to find?"

"Answers. There are tracks here. Footprints. And more than one set."

Riley stood and joined Oz at the back of the room, noticing the weaving pattern of shoe marks in the dust. "They all lead here." She pointed to a dusty place on the floor where all the tracks seemed to disappear into a small area of disturbed ash. Riley bent down and brushed the soot away from the old and knotted floor. A small hole appeared, just big enough for a human finger. "Oz, get over here."

Without thinking, Riley stuck her finger into the hole and yanked. A small square lifted up like a hinged lid from the floor, leading down into a lightless void. "What do you think?"

"I'm not going down there." Oz backed away. "It's dark. If anyone's down there, we would see a light or hear them shouting at us."

"I don't think we have a choice. We've come this far, and we have nowhere else to go."

Oz huffed. "Fine. Give me your flashlight."

Riley pulled the light from her backpack, relieved Oz had volunteered to go first.

"There's a ladder." Oz paused partway down and looked up. "If my legs get ripped off by some monster, I'm blaming you."

"Fair enough." Riley watched her disappear into the darkness and followed. The door closed down above her, sealing them into the black chamber.

The glow from the flashlight danced across the concrete walls as she followed Oz down the passage. The narrow tunnel grew thinner with each step. "What is this place?

"No idea. Some kind of tunnel under the city, maybe? Doesn't smell like a sewer, thank God."

A quarter mile in, they came to a dead end. Oz pushed against the cold wall, scanning the cracks and corners for something they might be missing. She kicked the partition in frustration and let out a bellow.

"Are you sure we didn't miss a side tunnel or something leading off?" Riley asked.

"No way. There was nothing."

Riley leaned against the wall, feeling exhausted. *Another dead end.* They kept falling into impossible situations. *But we keep getting out.* "Let's rest here. I can't go much farther or even try to come up with a plan until I get some sleep." She glanced around the dark, cool tunnel. "And this looks like as safe a place as any."

"Agreed." Oz dropped her gear to the floor and slid down the wall. "Should we worry about people coming down here? There were those footprints."

Riley thought for a minute. "At this point I don't really care." She sat down on the hard floor, and while it lacked comfort, it was cold and there wasn't a risk of a flash flood or psychotic killer to interrupt their rest. Oz lay down next to her, and within minutes sleep consumed both girls.

———

The dream came immediately. Riley ran down a dark hallway, fear coursing through her body, adrenaline pumping hard. Footsteps echoed off the walls, reverberating like the thunder from the storm, causing her to crouch low as she sprinted forward. *Where am I?*

She looked around for someplace to hide from whatever pursued, but the solid walls grew narrower and narrower as she ran, revealing nothing. The air hung heavy with moisture, and the smell of something awful burning assaulted her senses, bringing tears to her eyes and a tingling sensation to the back of her throat.

Up ahead she saw a faint glow, a fire flickering through the black. She had no desire to continue on to the blaze, but the rumbling footsteps continued pounding the ground behind her, making the choice impossible. A new sound rose in the disorder rumbling through the air—the high-pitched scream of a woman. Riley touched her throat, thinking it might be coming from her, but she felt nothing except the throbbing of her neck veins.

"Help!" Riley screamed, hoping the crying woman could save her. She was so close to the flames now, could almost feel the heat.

Something dark rose up out of the fire: the something that made the air toxic and putrid to breathe. The blackened body of a man hung from a post in the center of the fire, his scorched face frozen forever in a pained scream. Dripping blobs of flesh fell like hot wax from his dead body, hissing like bacon as they hit the flames. Riley screamed. Her hands flew to her face to cover her eyes. *Oh, God!*

"Riley!" a voice shrieked to her right.

She turned and saw in horror another figure attached to a post, positioned over an unlit fire. *This must be the woman who screamed.*

"What's happening here? Who did this to you?" *Wait, how do you know my name?* She looked up at the woman's face, and her blood turned cold. The dark, terrified eyes of her best friend stared down at her, pleading. "Oh my God, Abby. Who did this to you?"

"Riley, please get me out of here. They're going to kill me! Now that you're here, they have no use for me." Abby looked thin and shrunken, her eyes red from crying and her voice hoarse.

"Abby, what are you talking about?"

"Get me down, and I'll explain," she pleaded. "Hurry."

Riley climbed up the pile of logs at the base of her friend, her whole body shaking. She found the ropes binding Abby to the post. "Abby, I'm so sorry," she cried, trying to untie the knots. "If this has to do with me, then I'm so…"

Firm hands grabbed her from behind and yanked her off the pyre. She kicked and flailed at her assailant and heard Abby wail in terror. The footsteps stopped their relentless pursuit. The silent air broke only with the girl's screams.

"Abby!" She had one last glimpse of her friend before the hands dragged her through an opening in the wall. She clawed and hit her attacker in the darkness, but the hands held strong. "What do you want from me? Let her go. She has nothing to do with any of this. *Please*."

A small light appeared on the end of a thin candle with a single flame that outlined a man's visage. Dark eyes flecked with gold stared down at her from a sharp face with a thin, twisting beard—a face she'd seen in a dream once before.

"What happens next," a deep, heavily accented voice began, "depends on you. Welcome, Riley Dale. We need to talk."

Chapter Forty-Four

"Riley. Riley!" The arms shook her, more rapidly now. "Earth to crazy."

Riley lifted her lids, blinking. Oz sat over her, staring down. The fires vanished. The charred body, Abby, and the man called Emir lingered only in her mind.

"Jesus, Riley, you had a bad dream. You've been screaming for the last five minutes."

"Oz, they have Abby." She stood up and looked around, hoping they were really in the chamber with the burning man and Abby's unlit fire. Nothing. "They're going to kill her."

"Wait, what? Who has Abby? Who is Abby?"

"My best friend. I have no idea who has her. Some Middle Eastern man called Emir. I've seen him once before, in a different dream."

"Riley, no one has your best friend. It was a dream. You just said so."

"It's not just a dream, Oz. It's never just a dream anymore. Somewhere in this world, the people trying to find us have Abby. They want me, and they're willing to kill her to get what they want."

Oz stared but her face remained unreadable. "What do you want to do?"

Tears streamed down Riley's face. She felt crazy, like she was losing her mind again. *I spend more time crying and falling apart now than I do keeping my head up and staying alert.* "We have to find her."

"What did you see in there? Any clues as to where they're keeping her?"

Riley shook her head. "It was dark. Must have been underground or in a tunnel like this. It opened up into a bigger room." She told Oz about the fires and the burned man. "They pulled me into a separate room, told me they'd been waiting for me, and then I woke up."

Riley slid down the end wall and curled into a ball at the base. "Maybe if I go back to sleep, I can find her again."

Oz wished she knew what the hell to do next. Her cravings for heroin had subsided a lot, but she still felt a nagging from within. *I could really use a fix right now.* This whole experience had been exhausting. One minute she hated her other half, the next she felt sorry for her.

Something stirred in the corner of the wall, catching Oz's eye. She rotated her flashlight to the movement and stared at the gaping hole that spread across the concrete. The barrier disappeared, sliding into the side of the tunnel. Riley leapt up and stood by Oz, grabbing her hand and watching the opening grow.

A man appeared deeper down the tunnel, walking toward them with a lantern. *Was this Emir?* He came into the light, and Oz inhaled deeply. She felt Riley's squeeze on her hand intensify. It wasn't Emir. It was someone they both recognized.

For a moment Riley thought she must be dreaming again. Against many other odds, the city had been destroyed, leaving any chance of survival slim at best. But here he stood, the first good news she'd had in a long time. "Zach," her voice barely raised above a whisper. "How?" The welcoming face of their handsome companion brought relief after all she'd been through.

"Riley. Oz. I thought they'd captured you all for sure."

Riley ran to him and threw her arms around his neck. Seeing Zach, the man who had tried to kill her in another life, was the most hopeful sight she could imagine. *How twisted things are here.* She wanted to sob, tell him all they had been through and have him make it okay. In her mind he had the answers. He could fix all of this. She pulled away and felt her lips parting, genuinely smiling.

"Damn, it's good to see you two." Zach looked back and forth between Riley and Oz as if they couldn't possibly be real. "I can't believe this."

"Oh, come on." Oz kissed his cheek as she hugged him tightly. "You know I'm a survivor. This ain't nothing." She nodded in Riley's direction. "Besides, it was good bonding time for me and Twinkie over there. We're practically best friends now."

Riley smiled and rolled her eyes. Despite all odds they had made it—evaded capture, crossed the desert, and found friendly company amid a ruined city. It shouldn't have worked out, but here she stood, reunited with Zach, safe and actually beginning to like—*well, at least tolerate*—her other soul. She felt like dancing.

"Come on." Zach motioned them to follow him behind the wall. "I bet you're hungry, and Ezra is dying to meet the Demies."

"He's here? He's alive?" Riley picked up her pace, eager to meet the man who would send her home.

"This is his place," Zach said. "Ezra's one of those superstitious, paranoid, end-of-the-world kind of guys. He built this place in case of a zombie apocalypse. It's stocked with enough supplies to last for two years. Guy's eccentric but a genius. Good man to have on our side right now."

"And he is on our side?" Oz cocked an eyebrow.

"Yes. This is what he lives for—the mysterious and the magical. I went to a seminar he held a few years ago in Denver. He's spent his whole life studying the things that don't make sense. The things he believes are real, that society has turned their backs on."

Oz laughed and rolled her eyes. "Like Bigfoot?"

"Well, yeah." Zach shrugged. "But also the things we need to know about."

"Like why I'm here." Riley reached for his arm, unable to wait another second for the answers that had led her down this hellacious path.

Zach gave her an understanding smile. "I'll let him fill you in on it all. This stuff goes way deeper than I ever thought. And there are worse people to worry about than the government."

Riley shuddered, remembering her dream of the melting body—the shadow man who held Abby. *Hopefully Ezra knows where to find her.*

"We've got a bit of a walk until we hit the living area, and I'm dying to know how you two survived the outside world. And each other." Zach's joy cast a deeper glow around the tunnel than even the lantern. Riley's heart twisted, and for a moment his eyes and smile washed away all the horror seeping through her brain.

The path slanted downward and began zigzagging in a ramp-like fashion deeper into the ground. Oz told Zach everything that had happened from the time he left them in the car in Vegas until the moment he stumbled upon them in the tunnel. Riley chimed in every once in a while to correct things Oz had exaggerated, left out, or completely gotten wrong. Mostly, though, she stayed lost in her own mind.

Descending into the dark passageway reminded her of the dream place where they held Abby. It was a relief to find Zach, but even that was short lived once she remembered about her captive friend. *There are worse people to worry about than the government.* She shrugged the fear away. Ezra was their ally, Zach their friend. He would not lead them into a trap.

The incline began to level out, and Riley was relieved not to go deeper into the earth.

"She started screaming, I woke her up and then you appeared. Pretty crazy, huh?" Oz finished accounting their whirlwind trip and turned to Riley, noticing her silence. "You okay?"

"Huh? Oh, yeah. I'm good." Riley nodded to feign happiness, but her distraught exterior couldn't be concealed.

"You've been through a lot." Zach offered a consoling smile. "I'm surprised you're holding up as well as you are. Thank God we have this place to recuperate. You're safe now. Everything is going to be okay."

Riley wanted to hug him again. His arms had felt so protective around her. It was inappropriate to think like that, with all they'd been through and his feelings for Oz. Zach was a friend, nothing more. He could never be more. As soon as she went back to her world, he would be a killer again, far from this man and these feelings. *A world away.* It was just a stupid crush on a handsome older man because he kept saving her life.

"What about you, Houdini? Were you able to get on the bus and ease out of town?" Oz bumped into him playfully and gazed up with seductive green eyes.

Riley pushed the onslaught of jealous feelings aside, reminding herself of the killer and not the man.

Zach laughed. "Not quite, although I did have it a little easier than you did."

He launched into his story, beginning with the encounter with Detective Rutherford and his escape from Isaac. "I lay low until dark, hoping Isaac and the detective had given up their search for the night. I guess you two must have taken precedence over me, because I didn't see them again.

"Around midnight I had to make a decision and trust someone. I found a small church down one of the back roads and knocked on the door to the pastor's house adjacent to the chapel. I was greeted by an old man in fleece pajamas who listened intently to my story and agreed to help.

"I left that night and traversed the mountains by foot, intending to meet the old man on the other side the next day. It was cold, tiring work, but I reached our meeting spot, and sure enough, he showed up as expected and brought me to Los Angeles. They searched his car when he left Las Vegas but of course found nothing and let him go. I'd been here no more than a few hours when Ezra caught wind of the impending bombings and brought me down here. I prayed you two hadn't made it to the city yet. I've been sick to my stomach about it until the moment I saw you at the underground entrance." He motioned to the ceiling. "Security cameras."

Zach stopped in front of a large steel door with a wheel-like knob and a keypad for entrance. "Here we are."

He punched in a series of numbers, and a voice echoed out of a speaker above, bouncing off the walls back up into the darkness. "Is that you, Zach?"

"Yep. I've got the girls."

A latch clicked, and Zach turned the wheel, swinging the heavy door inward. Riley didn't know what she expected to see. Maybe a dark room with musty couches and an old television screen with static running across the front. But Ezra's underground hideout was not just a bunker in the earth—it was a state-of-the-art luxury home.

White paint covered the walls to brighten up the space, and artificial windows lined the interior, showcasing sunny scenes from the outside world. The main room had plush leather couches, a pool table, a minibar, and a large-screen television hanging from one of the bright walls. *This is nicer than most homes above ground.*

"Welcome. Welcome," a voice greeted from behind, and Riley spun around to see a tall, lanky Arab man striding in from one of the hallways. His dark eyes twinkled as he shook hands with Riley and Oz. "I am Ezra Ahmad, and I am so pleased to meet you. To have a pair of Demies in my own home—it's almost too much."

He ran his fingers through his hair and stared back and forth between the two girls. "Oh, I'm being so rude! Please have a seat and let me get you something to eat and drink."

Riley sank into the soft leather, wishing she'd never have to move again. Ezra brought large glasses of ice water and platters of sliced meats, hummus, and vegetables. She inhaled the food and drank water until she thought she might drown. With a full stomach and a soft couch, she wanted nothing more than to sleep. *And find Abby in a dream.*

Once the girls had had their fill, Ezra sat down in a chair across from them and continued to stare, his eyes dancing with excitement.

"I know you must be exhausted, but Zach has told me so much, and as I understand it, you know so little. I feel some answers are in order."

Fighting to keep her eyes open, Riley glanced at Oz, collapsed on the couch beside her. Ezra turned his gaze upon Riley, and his eyes grew large at the sight of Esther's ring. Riley folded her arms to hide the heirloom, uncomfortable with his reaction. Ezra quickly composed himself, but his eyes never lost the new fire that had been sparked. "So you made it to our world. Very few people manage to do that."

Riley sipped more water. His gaze made her uneasy, as if he were trying to read her mind or pry something out of her.

"There are the people who end up here by accident—a slip in a wormhole, most likely. And then there are the very few who can control it. The few who can bounce back and forth between worlds as they please. So few, in fact, that there is only ever one with that power in the world at a time. The Electa is what she is called."

"She?" Riley coughed as water from her drink filled her lungs.

"As I understand it, Zach told you about the split world," Ezra continued after she'd hacked the liquid from her body. "How each of us, or most of us, have another piece of ourselves somewhere else. Simply put, like all things in balance, there must be opposites. Black must have white, yin must have yang, a magnet must have a positive and negative end." He paused and glanced at Oz, who had managed to sit up and keep her eyes open. "And good must have evil. Now, good and evil are subjective things. Not all of us are as good as one another, which means not all of us have a completely wicked side."

Oz nudged Riley. "Not completely wicked."

Riley returned a smile, partially at the joke and partially at the positive feelings that kept growing about her other half.

"Your friend Zach here tells me that his other half likes to rape and kill women." Ezra paused and looked at Zach, who managed to maintain composure. "You girls are very lucky to have him. With a malicious side like his, your companion in this universe must be as pure of heart as is humanly possible. We live in a dangerous world. Keep him close."

Riley looked up at Zach. Her heart thudded as his gray eyes seemed to be assuring her that he would protect them and keep her safe. She looked away quickly and back at Ezra. *He likes Oz.*

"Before I go any further, I must ask you a question, Miss Dale." Ezra directed his statement at Riley. "Do you believe in God?"

The room fell silent as Riley pondered the question.

"Hell, no." Oz straightened up and hardened her face.

Ezra nodded at her and directed his attention back to Riley.

"I guess so." She blushed under the scrutiny of all three sets of eyes.

He smiled. "Well, either way, this story will seem like a tall tale, whether you believe or not." Ezra took a sip of tea from an ornate teacup, crossed his legs, and took a deep breath.

"In the original plan, balance was in each of us. It set us apart from everything else on the planet. The world was in a state of divine equilibrium. And then something happened. Or rather some*one* happened." He paused for another sip of tea.

"Now, the book has it a bit wrong. You see, while Adam and Eve were the first humans on earth, they were not the only people in the initial creation. Eden had other inhabitants as well: men and women whose job it was to populate the earth and sustain it as a healthy and beautiful home. Adam was their king and Eve their beloved queen.

"On that fateful day that the serpent tricked Eve into taking a bite of the forbidden fruit, much more was lost than Eden and its safety. The tree she picked from shriveled and died. Eve doomed her people to a life outside the walls, a life full of danger. But she also took away their divine equilibrium. You see, when Eve bit the fruit—when Eve committed the first act of defiance—her soul split, and with it the soul of humanity and the world. Good and evil became two separate entities, and more importantly, mankind became aware of such things as good and evil, power and control.

"Wickedness spread like disease as each new generation was born without divine balance. A planet that was meant to remain wholesome, pure, and beautiful became an arena for tainted, depraved things. Men killed each other, they killed the land, and they killed the animals. Death and violence came to a place that was not built to weather that kind of storm.

"Outside the gates of Eden, all of Eve's people deserted her except for Adam, the one person whose soul remained pure. You see, Adam did not lose his balance, so his love for Eve and the world was still uncorrupted.

"And God, who watched all of this unfold with a heavy heart, took pity on Adam and Eve and gave their family a second chance—a chance that has yet to be fulfilled."

Riley searched her brain for something that made sense. She had never really believed the stories in the Bible. In her mind they were tales made up to teach lessons—no different than Aesop's fables or the Brothers Grimm.

It wasn't the details of Ezra's story that overwhelmed her but the implication that the story was real. She wanted to laugh and tell him how ridiculous this all was, but here she sat, with her other soul, on a leather couch beneath a destroyed Los Angeles, tired, afraid, and confused about what was real anyway.

"So we came all the way across the desert to listen to Bible stories?" Oz tossed a couch pillow across the room. "This is it? Our answer? Some thousands-of-years-old hocus-pocus? This is supposed to help Riley get home?"

Ezra didn't flinch. "My dear." He leaned into Riley, his eyes serious. "Mankind was given a second chance that day. Eve's female descendants carry the bloodline with the power to restore the world. She was also given a ring. A ring depicting the Tree of Life and the Tree of Knowledge of Good and Evil that was destroyed. Eve's descendants are the Electa, the chosen women who will save the world. The last one died a few weeks ago. The new one now sits before me on this couch."

Riley stared at the ring on her hand, her eyes weaving through the branches of the two twisting trees. She looked over at Oz, who appeared to have just eaten something bitter, and up at Zach, who chewed his lip and watched her intently. "I'm sorry, what?"

"Esther was Eve's heir and wore that ring her whole life. She was unable to complete her mission. You have inherited that destiny."

Oz laughed, and Riley felt inclined to join her. They sat on the couch enjoying the joke while Ezra perched silent and Zach looked uncomfortable.

"I'm supposed to save the world? I'm supposed to fix everyone's soul because oh, hey, my great-grandma is Eve and she messed up?" Riley's hands waved in the air with palms facing upward, using her whole body to pose the question.

"It's a lot to take in," Ezra acknowledged. "But the simple answer is yes. You must heal the world. You must mend the souls."

Riley stared at the floor, wanting to throw the ring across the room with Oz's pillow. *This is what all the craziness has been about?* "Do you have any liquor?"

Ezra smiled. "I'll make you a drink. Who else wants one?"

Zach and Oz raised their hands.

"So if Riley is supposed to save the world, what the hell am I supposed to do?" Oz stomped her feet and huffed.

"Help her." Ezra rummaged through his cabinets and began removing a colorful array of bottles. "It will be impossible for her to do this without you."

"Is that why we're being chased?" Riley asked. "Because of the ring?"

Ezra's face darkened, and he spilled the vodka he was pouring. "The government chases all Demies because they know one of them is out there with the ability to take away their power. People don't want to lose their power. It is a life force of its own." He handed everyone a drink and returned to his seat in front of Riley. "I must warn you, there are others that will begin pursuing you as well, if they haven't already. It is not just the government who values power. Your journey is neither easy nor safe."

"Is that why Esther was killed? Someone finally found her?"

"I don't know the answer to that, but if your visions are true, then it would be safe to say yes."

Riley's brow furrowed. "My visions? How do you…?"

"Zach filled me in. I had not heard that the Electa had such a power."

Riley took a grateful sip of the fruity cocktail and let the alcohol warm her insides. *Impossible. All of it.* Ezra had to be a lunatic. *I'll have to find my own way out of here.*

"Question." Oz raised her hand above her disapproving face. "Even if we were to believe all this, which I don't, why is Riley the Electa or whatever and not me? It seems a little unfair that my soul gets split off into the shitty world, and she gets the perfect life and then becomes a world hero overnight."

Ezra chuckled. "Don't waste your energy envying her. By the time this is all over, you'll be thankful that it's not you."

Oz rolled her eyes and downed her drink. "Got another?"

Ezra motioned to the bar, and she hurried over to inspect his stash. Zach sat down in her vacant seat and rested a reassuring arm across Riley's shoulders. She pressed into his side.

"Why me?" she asked Ezra. "Why not my mom or Kiersten? And if I am this chosen one, as you say, what am I supposed to do now?"

Ezra sighed and looked at the ground. "I'm afraid I don't have an answer to those questions yet."

"So that's it? I spend my life trying to avoid being killed, in hopes that I stumble across a way to fix this?"

"Not exactly," he began. "You're not going to like this, but there's a man who has dedicated his life to protecting and training the Demies that end up over here. His father did this before him, and he has grown up surrounded by people from your world. He knew your grandmother, and he will help get you trained."

"Trained?" Riley tilted forward, eyebrows raised. "To do what?"

"To stay alive."

Riley leaned into Zach, not caring if it was inappropriate. *Great, more running. More hiding. More secrets.* He tightened his grip around her shoulders and pulled her closer.

"Where does this man live?" she asked.

"A very safe place, if we can get there. His ranch is in northern Mexico. About a fifteen-hour drive from here. But we'll cross the border much sooner than that. Mexico is a safer place than the United States."

"And will you come?" Riley asked Ezra, glancing sideways at Zach.

"Yes," they both answered.

"I'm in this too deep to leave now." Zach shook his head and let out a hollow laugh. "I'll do my damnedest to keep you and Oz safe."

Ezra rested a hand on hers. "I know the way. And I know what hunts us."

Riley felt strength from their touches. Or maybe it was just the vodka. "And this man, you say he can help us?"

"Jorge Vela has a heart of gold. If anyone in this world can give you answers, it will be him."

Oz wandered back to the couch with two drinks in hand and slid in between Riley and Zach, moving Zach's arm around her shoulders and offering a smug smile to Riley. Zach grinned and let his hand rest on her shoulder. A look of triumph crossed his face.

Riley sighed despite her feelings. *Good for him.* For a moment Gabe's face appeared in her head, and her heart tightened. She knew how it felt to like someone who didn't see you in the same light. *I miss you, Gabe.*

Plans were made to leave Los Angeles early the next morning. Ezra led the girls down one of the side hallways and set each of them up in their own room.

"This place has six bedrooms, a living area, kitchen, office, dining room, exercise facility, and my personal library. It's pretty incredible, is it not?" Ezra showed Riley her own modernly decorated bedroom. "Please make yourself comfortable. Zach told me to be expecting you, so I've had the closet stocked with clothes that should fit you and a suitcase to pack them in for tomorrow."

Riley sucked in a breath of air and fought the urge to cry. People kept coming out of the woodwork to help. When everything seemed hopeless, someone appeared to give them enough of a spark to keep going. "Ezra, I can't tell you how much I appreciate all of this. I—I..."

"Please, Riley, it's my pleasure to work with the Electa. It is the least I can do for the woman who will restore humanity. Good night, Soul Mender."

"Good night." She watched the figure disappear down the hallway. *The woman who will restore humanity.* She laughed aloud. *Scared, timid Grandma was the woman who would restore humanity, and now it's scared, timid me.* She threw herself onto the bed and fingered the intricately sewn spirals on the comforter. *Tomorrow I head to Mexico. So much for going home.* The thought saddened her. All this time she'd thought they were coming to Los Angeles so she could find a way home. Now it seemed like Los Angeles meant never getting there. Probably not even living through the next year.

She twisted the ring in circles around her finger. *You and me, huh? We're going to save the world. Ridiculous.* She went to the closet and found a pair of sweatpants to slip into. She packed up her suitcase and got everything ready to leave in the morning. As tired as she'd been for days, the idea of sleep was almost as amusing as her being the Electa. She crept out of her room, heading for the living area. There had been a TV, and she didn't think Ezra would mind her staying up.

The screen was already lit up when she entered the room. Quiet voices of newscasters filtered through the speakers, and Zach's brown hair stuck up from the back of the couch.

"Mind if I join you?" She slid into the seat next to him.

"Couldn't sleep either?" He smiled and patted her knee.

Riley sucked in a breath of air but quickly regained composure. "Not a chance. It's crazy, you know? All of it."

"It is. But I believe him. And I believe in you."

She felt her cheeks burn and looked at the ground. "Well, I guess we'll find out, right?"

He scooted closer and pulled her into his side. "Relax. You're in no danger tonight. Enjoy it while it lasts."

Her pulse raced as she rested her head on his shoulder. She wanted so badly to kiss him, to get lost in him until she had to take off into the dangerous world again. *This can't happen. It's not real.* "So what's going on here?" She asked him about the news. *That's safe.* "What the hell happened to Los Angeles?"

"The United States bombed Iraq's embassy in Tehran a few months back. President Cain ordered it. Then about three weeks ago, two major buildings in Baghdad blew up. They couldn't tie it to America, but El-Hashem figured it out. Los Angeles is retaliation for what we did to his country."

"Wait, what?" Riley pulled away in disbelief.

"We've been terrorizing Iraq for years now, and they've finally had enough. We're going to kill each other over differing beliefs." His hands rested on the back of his head, and he placed an ankle on his knee.

Riley pondered his relaxed demeanor. "But you're saying the United States started this?"

"President Cain is a known Muslim hater. Here, listen." He turned up the volume. The president was addressing the nation from behind a podium surrounded by flags and crosses.

"Citizens of America. Three days ago the heart of our country was ripped out by a group of men who have been blinded to the true ways of our Lord. This attack will not go unanswered. We will not stop until every vicious idol worshiper has had the opportunity to stand before God and be judged for his or her crimes. I will fight for you, be a martyr for you if need be. Rest easy in the knowledge that God is on our side. Our fight now is against the Muslim world. Our retribution will be divine."

Silence followed the sound of loud applause as Zach muted the TV. "What do you think?"

"Holy shit."

"That's scary stuff right there." Zach nodded. "There's a fine line between devout and mad, and our president has tripped over it."

"It's the exact opposite where I come from. I actually really like President Cain. I have a lot of faith in him. We've been attacked by the Middle East and have answered, but we've never done something horrific like this in the name of God."

She'd voted for the man last time. He'd been level headed and so hopeful—a real representative for people in need and America as a whole. The man on the TV was not that man at all.

"Remember, everyone has an opposite half. Welcome to the other side of the mirror." He waved his hand and gave a seated bow, offering a ludicrous grin.

"It's terrifying."

"It's why you are so important. My guess is we need to figure out how you can fix all of this before we kill ourselves."

"No pressure." She laughed an empty laugh.

His face grew serious, and he turned to gaze into her eyes. "I'll help you until I can't."

"Why?" She met his stare. "Why would you help someone you barely know?"

His eyes drifted for a moment to a secret place. "I know you better than you think. I've spent the better part of seven years keeping your other half alive. I know you because I know her. I don't know how to explain it, but I feel like this is why I did it, why I became so invested. It may be your destiny to save the world, but it's mine to save you."

Riley took a deep breath and leaned in. *Oh, God.* "Zach, we can't do this. There's no possible way for it to work."

He leaned in closer, grinning. "I'm not hitting on you, I promise. You know how I feel about Oz. It's just really weird knowing that you're part of her. Those are hard feelings and concepts to sort through."

She shook her head, sinking into the couch, deflated. *Damn. But he is Oz's, and she needs him. I've gotten everything, and she's had nothing. I won't take him from her.*

Zach looked at the muted television without really watching it. "I've spent my life caring for Oz. And now I meet you. Talk about twisted circumstances. Come on." He stood and offered his hand. "Let me walk you to your room. We'd better try to get some sleep. Tomorrow could be a long day."

She took his hand and stood, her legs unsteady from the moment that had just passed between them. He gave her a hug outside of her room and turned toward his. "Good night, Riley."

"Good night, Zach." She closed her door and crawled into bed. *I definitely can't sleep now.*

But the next moment, Ezra shook her from a deep slumber.

"Get up, get up. We have to leave now. They've found us and have made it through the concrete wall. Your detective friend will be here in less than ten minutes!"

CHAPTER FORTY-FIVE

Ezra hurried through his underground home, grabbing supplies and cleaning out files. His computers, his books—everything contained information he could not let them have. Snatching a flash drive, he pulled all he could off the hard drives and began deleting his life's work.

Ezra kept moving. *It doesn't matter anymore. She's here. This will all be over soon.*

He ran to the lab in the back of his tunneled home, threw open the incinerator, and heaved heavy manuals and ancient handwritten texts into the fire. He couldn't think about it. Burning this kind of history was criminal. *But so is letting it slip into the wrong hands.* Finished, he walked through his home, his masterpiece, taking in the fine detail and ingenuity that crafted each room and hallway. It too would have to go.

"This way." Ezra motioned his guests to a separate hallway in the back of the room.

He led them to the end of the passage and pushed a series of buttons on a keypad, and the heavy concrete door slid open: the secret entrance to his secret world.

"Go." He sealed the opening to his home and leaned against the door for a moment, breathing deeply.

In seconds, his whole life would be destroyed. Everything his ancestors had collected and worked on would be gone. *But*

I have it in my mind. He wiped the sweat from his forehead and hurried up the dark passage after his companions. He thought about his father, a Muslim man who'd married a Jewish woman. A man who'd spent his whole life, lost his mind even, in search of Eve's descendant. He died when Ezra was seventeen, leaving the young man to pick up where he'd left off.

Ezra had done just that, spent the last seventeen years traveling the world, learning all he could about the Electa. Spending sleepless hours poring through old volumes in the Middle East and then Europe—volumes with lineages that finally led him to the United States and a woman named Esther Miller.

The Electa had finally come to America.

And then Esther died, leaving a new chosen one. And here she stood on the precipice of fulfilling her destiny. And here Ezra perched, about to fulfill his own destiny that had run parallel to hers since the beginning.

He pulled a pen-like object from his pocket and held it out in front of him. A small red button glowed in the darkness. "Heaven help us," he whispered as he pressed down.

———

Whoa. Riley grabbed Oz's arm to steady herself as the floor and walls rumbled and shifted. "What's happening?"

The earth around them seemed to bend and move as a deafening roar exploded from the darkness below.

"Move quickly," Ezra urged, catching up to the group. "I had to destroy the house. There's too much for them to see."

"You mean you blew it up?" Oz spun around, nearly knocking Riley off her feet. "That whole place is gone?"

"Yes," he said with a sigh. "I'm afraid I'm now homeless with the rest of you."

They picked up the pace to a jog, weaving back and forth up the path until they reached another coded entryway. Ezra punched in the combination. They burst out into a parking garage that had somehow missed being taken out in the bombing.

"Ah, good. I was worried." Ezra led them to a white SUV with heavily tinted windows and large, rugged tires. "Hop in."

Zach loaded their luggage, and Ezra started the engine. Riley glanced around the inside of Ezra's tank, awed by the gadgets and instruments that buzzed to life when the car started.

"I've been waiting to use this for a long time. Bulletproof glass, untraceable navigation, puncture-proof tires. Even a high-grade defense system. This baby is sweet." His eyes glowed with excitement as he pointed out each unique feature of the car. "Now here's hoping we can make it into Mexico without much trouble."

That'll be the day. Riley stared out the window as Ezra eased the vehicle from the parking garage and out onto the war-torn streets of Los Angeles. She'd almost forgotten how bad it was up above after being safe in Ezra's underground home.

Daylight had not yet vanquished the dark night. The only lights came from sparking wires, burning structures, a few unscathed buildings, and a bright, untouched moon. An eerie stillness hovered over the city, like it held its breath for something—was trying to hide from someone. *I feel ya, LA.* They drove through the streets, detouring when a road was blocked, surveying the city in silence.

"I hadn't seen this yet." Zach's head turned slowly back and forth, taking in the destruction. "We were already underground when it happened. All this in the name of God?"

"That's what I can't stand about religion." Oz spat, punching the side door and glowering at the scene outside. "Everyone's walking around like they own the place and anyone else is an idiot. The Muslims think the Christians got it wrong. Christians think the Muslims are crazy. We fight thinking God's on our side, cheering us on. And when we win because we have bigger guns and better resources, we think it's because we're the chosen ones, not just because we have the money. Shit, I bet God's up there right now saying, 'Fuck all y'all.' I know I am."

Riley waited for the lightning that would strike the vehicle down, but it never came.

"It is sad," Ezra agreed as he swerved to avoid a fallen telephone pole. "I grew up Muslim, and this is not how I was raised to please God. Death is not something he delights in. The Quran tells us that anyone who kills an innocent person, it is as if he has killed all of humanity."

Riley thought about the shoe they'd found with the child's blood on it. A child killed because Jackson Cain bombed some buildings halfway across the world due to differing beliefs. A child killed because Adil El-Hashem did the same thing in Riley's world.

"It's weird," she began, still staring out at the crumbled streets. "Back home when wars happened and my only connection to them was pictures on a TV, all I had to do to escape the reality was turn off the screen. But to see it here, up close, makes it so much more real. It makes the horror of it impossible to escape."

They drove past a wrecked car that had smashed into the railing on the side of the highway and stared at the arm, shoulders, and head that hung limply out the window. A bloody crack on the left rear pane told them that more than one had perished in the accident.

"It's a chilling thing when you find out there are two sides to everything." Ezra's voice was confident, but his face couldn't mask his horror. "When both sides are good and both sides are evil, it makes it very tricky to decide what is right and what is wrong."

"Well, they're all wrong," Oz scoffed. "Every one of 'em is backward."

Riley ran her fingers across the ring, trying to take in what Ezra had said the night before. *The Soul Mender. The Electa. I'm supposed to save the world?* She looked out the window and saw with surprise an exact replica of the White House, complete with matching Capitol building and what had been the Washington Monument. *Los Angeles Monument, I guess.*

Smoke drifted up from the shattered dome of the Capitol, and the partial spire of the broken monument reached helplessly for the sky. *I can't save this. I can't go up against the power that did this.* "Ezra, I'm not the one. I can't do this. I'll give you the ring. You can give it to someone who can."

Ezra met her eyes in the rearview mirror. "It doesn't work like that, Riley. It has to be you now. You or no one."

"Unless I die?"

He pursed his lips. "Is that an attractive option for you?"

"It seems inevitable, don't you think?"

Zach turned to give her an encouraging smile. "Not a chance. You've got us, and we're going to help you every step of the way."

Riley shook her head and stared at her feet. "I don't want this. I don't have it in me."

Ezra smiled to himself and looked toward Oz. "No, you are correct. Alone you don't have it in you. But lucky for us, we have your complete package. Between you and Oz, you have everything you need to succeed."

Oz gave a triumphant look, slapping the side of Zach's arm. "Bet you never thought I'd save the world, huh?"

"I never once doubted your ability to do great things." He laughed, rolling his eyes. "But at least now when I've got your back, it's not for something stupid."

"Hey. I'm a world hero. You can't talk to me like that." Oz's face softened as her cheeks turned a slight shade of pink.

Riley wished she shared their lightheartedness. *Does Oz think this will be easy?* They were headed to Mexico to meet another man who could supposedly help. *He'll probably just send us to China to meet someone else.* Her mind wandered back to Abby, and her heart tightened. Her friend was trapped somewhere, and here she sat, headed off in the wrong direction.

"Wait." She leaned forward over the console. "My friend. Someone has her prisoner. Someone who is looking for me. We have to help her."

"Where is she?" Ezra swerved to miss a large pothole but hit the corner, sending everyone bouncing off the seat.

Riley felt absurd even saying it. "I had another vision. They took Abby to get to me. They burned another man, and they were going to do the same to her. I was grabbed but woke up before they could do anything else."

"Grabbed by whom?" Zach asked.

"Emir," Riley whispered, searching her brain for anything that might help. "He was in my vision before with another man. They have accents. Middle Eastern. And he said they'd been waiting for me."

Ezra yanked the wheel to correct as the car veered to the shoulder. The SUV swung out into what would have been oncoming traffic under normal circumstances.

"Easy." Zach gave their driver a concerned look. "You okay?"

Ezra took a few deep breaths. "Yes, I'm fine." But his hands rattled against the steering wheel.

"Ezra, what do you know?" Riley demanded. A small sense of hope that he could find Abby grabbed hold of her heart.

"Burning people at the stake is not a common form of killing these days. This place where your friend is, what did it look like?"

Riley thought back to the dark passage leading into the open chamber. "I was chased through a tunnel but never saw who pursued me. And then it opened up into a large hall, almost like a cavern, and that's where they had Abby tied to a stake over an unlit fire. The man next to her was already burned. I was trying to help Abby escape when they pulled me from the pile and dragged me into another room. I couldn't see anything very well."

Ezra's face grew pale, his knuckles threatening to burst through the stretched flesh that held tightly to the wheel. "That didn't take long."

"What didn't take long?" Riley didn't like the way he said it.

"It didn't take long for them to find you, learn about you, and begin the task of killing you."

Riley shuddered, remembering the strong hands. "Who are they?"

Ezra sighed. "It is not just the government who hunts us now, Riley. Some want you dead because you threaten the balance of power. Those men are dangerous, but they value their lives. Power is worth nothing if they are not around to wield it." Ezra paused, trying to choose his next words carefully. "But there is something even stronger than power that men will fight for, kill for. Men like that are willing to die. And a man willing to die for something is far more dangerous than a man with power."

Not another living soul drove on the road, and even the skies hung empty. It wasn't cold outside, but Riley shivered anyway, feeling a chill deepening within.

"Weren't we just trying to convince Riley that she can do this?" Oz rolled her eyes and sighed. "I mean, I know I'm a badass and all, but the shit you're saying makes me want to back out too."

"She needs to know the truth," Ezra said. "All of it."

Riley leaned forward in her seat, both terrified and fascinated. More pieces of the puzzle fell into place. "Who are these men, Ezra?"

He took a deep breath. "They are the Jondi-Al-Haqq. The Soldiers of Truth. And they will level cities, kill innocent people, do whatever it takes to keep you from succeeding. You see, these men value knowledge above all else, and your destiny threatens to take that away. For thousands of years they have hunted your family, and for thousands of years they have been successful."

Riley wanted to laugh, more out of absurdity than hilarity. A twenty-two-year-old woman, destined to save the world, hunted by the government and a clandestine sect of assassins who wanted her dead. And she had no knowledge of how to do any of it, least of all survive. "How do I threaten their knowledge? I can't wipe their minds clear."

"There are theories." Ezra relaxed his grip on the steering wheel. "But I want to speak with Jorge first. Between the two of us, you will have your answers."

———

Oz pulled her jacket hood over her head and leaned against the window. *And these people think I'm wacked.* Her whole life had been spent trying to stay alive, like some animal, doing whatever was needed to eat, sleep, and breathe. It hadn't been an easy road, and it certainly hadn't been pretty.

Her mind wandered to an all-too-familiar scene from her life. She had just turned eighteen and gotten a job dancing at a local joint called the Gold Club. She hated the men twice her age who came in and drooled over her while scratching at themselves. Hated even more the men who came in nervous, blindly feeling the emptiness on their left hand where a wedding band should have been. They called her Glitter, and she hated the name most of all.

Many nights she went above and beyond her normal job duties. It paid the bills, kept a decent supply of smack on hand, and kept her fed. But it was empty. Most of her life had been empty.

She glanced sideways at Riley and watched her other half stare hopelessly out the window. At first the girl next to her had been a pain, an irritating reminder of how shitty her life had been. But now she was an opportunity to feel something other than emptiness. Ezra had said some crazy things, and none of it really made sense. But the piece she gleaned from everything else and held onto was that she was important, she was needed. And not by some disgusting middle-aged man with a wife. *I am significant for the first time.*

CHAPTER FORTY-SIX

They hit the interstate, relieved it had escaped damage from the bombs. The crumbled city flew by as Ezra punched the gas, heading southeast toward Mexico. Beyond the edge of the city, no record existed of the mass destruction and unburied dead they'd left behind. Just open skies, empty desert, and a great expanse of unknown.

"It looks like we'll make it out of the city well before the troops land. I was worried about that." Ezra scratched the back of his neck and glanced in the rearview mirror.

"What troops?" Oz sat up, stretching her arms into the air.

Riley raised her eyes from the floor, eager for another slice of information.

"Iraqi troops," Ezra stated. "Rumor was that the initial bombings would be followed by a ground invasion to take the city."

Riley choked on her own gasp. "You mean Iraq plans to invade this country? Like come in and take over?"

"That's their plan. They see Cain as a threat who needs to be eliminated."

She laughed. "You're kidding."

"Why is that so ridiculous?" Ezra met her eyes in the rear-view mirror.

She cocked an eyebrow win return. "Because this is America."

"Even the strongest rocks crumble if you get a large enough stick of dynamite." Ezra wagged his finger in the air and nodded to himself.

Riley leaned back into the seat, shocked. *Does this mean the United States is invading Iraq as we speak? Did we drop bombs too? If only everyone knew how messed up this all is.*

"I'm so sick of the damn desert," Oz muttered, pulling her hood lower onto her face. "I still have nightmares from the first time we had to go through here."

As if in response, the remaining buildings blended with the dirt and then disappeared completely into sand and rock.

———

More cacti, small shrubs, and dirt zoomed past. Zach hadn't slept well since leaving Grand Junction, and an uneasy feeling loomed about the journey ahead. He trusted Ezra and believed in this man Jorge, but the realization of how deep they were in this thing solidified in his mind.

This wouldn't be a two-week ordeal that would finish up easily and take him home before the month was over. He had pledged himself to protecting Riley and Oz, and based on what he had heard, that pledge was probably his death sentence.

Zach thought about his sister back in Colorado. She depended so heavily on him, and he'd probably never see her again. *I'm sorry, Samantha. I'm so sorry.*

And then there was Oz. He had to do this.

He closed his eyes, willing himself to sleep. Oz's green eyes and smiling face beamed in his thoughts.

———

Ezra's mind whirred. *I have the Electa. I have the Electa, and the Jondi-Al-Haqq know who she is. Do they know she is with me?*

Zach slept in the seat next to him, softly snoring. He glanced in the rearview mirror and saw that Oz too was asleep. Riley stared blankly out the window. Behind her, a motion in the mirror caught his eye. A lone rider on a motorcycle trailed them, closing the gap between vehicles. *It's nobody. It's your hyperactive mind.*

The rider was a black blur, his body completely covered in dark leather, obscuring his features. The distance between them shrunk. Ezra sped up, looking for a place to pull off the road. *This is just a man like us, trying to escape Los Angeles.*

The rider revved the bike's engine. Ezra slowed the SUV, hoping he would pass, but he decreased his speed as well. *Shit.* "Guys." His voice shook. "I think we're being followed."

Zach and Oz pulled themselves from sleep, and Riley turned to glance through the darkened window at the rider behind them.

"Is he bad?" she asked.

"I don't know." Ezra shook his head and peered again at their pursuer. "Why else would he be following us?"

Zach straightened in his seat. "Wouldn't there be more than one? Everyone who has chased us has brought an army along."

"He could be Jondi," Ezra muttered, his face paling. "But I think even they would send more than one rider in case something went wrong."

"Should we pull over?" Riley asked. She'd rather know if the rider was friendly or not than spend the next few hours in hyperactive panic. "We have guns. And better numbers."

Ezra released a deep sigh. "That won't matter if he is indeed a Soldier of Truth."

Oz stretched and yawned. "Yeah, I vote for not stopping. Maybe we can turn off the main road and drive someplace that the bike can't follow."

Riley eyed the lone rider and shivered, remembering the hands that had grabbed her in the dark, the hands that aimed to kill her friend. She hated always having to look over her shoulder. "Is there any way we can get the upper hand on this guy?"

Ezra glanced back at the biker. "I think we have a chance to escape him if we do go off road, but I think it would be unwise for us to try to engage him."

"I agree," Zach said. "Our goal is to keep you all safe." He touched the screen on Ezra's GPS and studied the map. "It looks like there's a dirt road in about two miles. Take it, Ezra."

Ezra accelerated, but the motorcycle kept pace. Riley's heart pounded. Her adrenaline raced.

The dusty road appeared up ahead, winding its way south from the main highway like a large brown snake. "Under your seats you will find guns and ammo. Now would be a good time to pull those out," Ezra said.

Zach reached down and removed a .45-caliber pistol and loaded the chamber. Oz followed suit.

Riley pulled the gun out from under her seat and stared at the cool metal barrel. She watched Oz eagerly loading her magazine and Zach looking more confident now that he had a means of protection. After fumbling with the bullets, Riley gave up. Guns had never been an interest. She placed the weapon back under the seat and took a deep breath. *Leave the killing to the others.*

Ezra jerked the wheel to the right and punched the gas, careening the SUV down the bumpy road and blasting sand into the air behind. "If nothing else, our foe will find it difficult to breathe."

Riley clutched the handhold above her and turned around, but all she could see was dust, a thick, heavy fog of brown dirt swirling in the air.

"He won't give up that easily." Zach craned to peer through the haze. "What do you all see back there?"

"Nothing," Oz said. "Just dust." She turned back to face the front, catching a flash of black in the corner of her eye. "Oh, shit." The black rider pulled up alongside the SUV, seemingly immune to the dirt and lack of visibility. He turned to look at her, visible eyes the only thing letting her know he was human. "Zach, look out! He's coming up on your right!"

Ezra swerved, but the rider anticipated and moved with them. Zach pointed the gun at the window, letting the rider know they meant business, but he kept pace, unfazed by the weapon. Suddenly his gloved hand rose, motioning Ezra to pull over.

"He wants you to stop." Zach relayed the unspoken message without lowering his gun.

"Of course he does," Ezra replied. In response he jerked the wheel to the left, leaving the dirt road. The SUV lurched over a bump and landed hard on a creosote bush. Ezra fishtailed out, forcing the vehicle up and over a pile of rocks, grinning like a child at Christmas. "Good tires."

"Well, that should have done it!" Oz whooped. "Badass driving, Ezra. Well done."

Ezra smiled, still careening the party off road. After a half hour with no sign of pursuit, he stopped. "Bathroom break."

Riley stumbled from the SUV, dizzy and nauseous from the whirlwind car ride. It felt good to be on solid ground. She walked away from the vehicle and over a short ledge into a ravine with some privacy.

"Pretty crazy, isn't it?" Oz asked, squatting behind a bush next to her. "You and me are going to save the world."

"Yeah. It's pretty insane."

Oz walked into sight and laughed. Her hands rose up by her shoulders and she proceeded to move in a way Riley could only fathom must be a victory dance. "I never in a million years would have thought it. Me, descended from Eve to save the world. I still don't believe that shit, but I like to say it."

Riley took deep breaths of the calm, dry air. It was still too much for her.

"And this Jorge Vela guy," Oz continued. "He's supposed to train us. We'll be like special ops by the time this is all done." She shoved Riley's shoulder. "Come on, this is exciting."

Riley stood, brushing dirt from her pants, and scanned the horizon for any signs of trouble. "Oz, we just got chased by the millionth person this week who wants us dead. I'm sorry, but exciting isn't how I'd describe it."

"Yeah, and we escaped. We escaped for the millionth time. You wanna know why? Because *we're heroes*."

Riley pulled herself from the dry creek bed and walked back to the SUV, Oz on her heels. When they reached the car, she didn't see anyone. "Zach?" she called. "Ezra?"

"Over here," Ezra responded from the other side of the car. Riley noticed a change in his voice. *Strained? Shaky?* "Ezra, are you okay?"

No answer. She hurried around the car and froze in her tracks. Ezra and Zach were on their knees facing her, hands tied behind their backs. The black rider stood behind them, a pistol pointed at each head, his gloved fingers already on the triggers.

She took a step forward. "What do you want? Please, don't hurt them."

"Stay where you are, Riley," he commanded, jabbing the pistols harder into her friends' heads. "Don't move."

CHAPTER FORTY-SEVEN

Jackson Cain stood behind his impromptu desk hidden deep within the Sierra Nevada Mountains, staring up at a large crucifix that hung above him while he worked. The magnificent piece of heavy oak had stood sentinel over his desk since he was elected to his first mayoral job in Las Vegas. It weighed well over four hundred pounds, but he had demanded they bring it along to safety.

Secret Service got wind of the bombs minutes before they were set to explode, and his team did a fantastic job getting him to the bunker. *My team and you, Lord.* His blood ran thick with anger at the infidels who did this to his country. This was not just an attack on America. It was an attack on God.

There was a soft knock, and his chief of staff, Martin Headley, peered in through the crack. "There's someone here to see you, Mr. President."

Jackson slowly took his eyes from the cross. "Martin, come in here, please."

Martin Headley walked nervously into the room.

"Take a seat."

He did as instructed.

"I know you'll be honest with me, Martin," President Cain began. "I've heard whispers that there are those who disagree with my actions." He paused, giving his staff member a hard look. "What do you know of this?"

Martin shifted uncomfortably in his seat. Jackson Cain demanded yes-men and destroyed those who went against him. "Well, sir, I've heard that the opposition, and some members of your cabinet, blame you for the attack." He paused, trying to ease his nerves with a deep breath. "They say you provoked El-Hashem and brought this upon our country. A few are calling for your impeachment."

Jackson Cain stood still as a statue, his hard features unflinching. "And what do you think?"

"I think you did the right thing." He didn't meet the president's eye.

"This is a Christian nation founded on Christian values, Martin. Anyone who would have me act in a manner other than that is against us and against the moral core of this country. I want names. I will try these men for treason. And then they will be tried again by the real judge." A stern finger motioned to the cross.

Martin peered up at it and looked away, hating it. The cross gave him the creeps, but it seemed to give Jackson Cain some sort of strange power. Three more people could have fit in the chopper if the president had left the cross behind. Instead he chose the monstrous slab of oak and left two interns and a reporter to face annihilation.

Martin wanted out, didn't want to be part of the president's madness, but he also wanted to live. He was trapped, and he blamed the stupid cross. "Yes, sir." He stood to leave.

"And one more thing," President Cain said.

"Yes, sir?"

"Where are the Dale girls, and why are they not already sitting in front of me?"

Martin took a deep breath and glanced toward the door. *Who am I kidding?* President Cain would find some way to get rid of him no matter what he did. He should have stayed in Los Angeles and taken his chances. "They've managed to escape again. It seems Mr. Ahmad has allied with them and helped them disappear."

Jackson Cain sat down at his desk, folded his hands together, and rested his chin on them. "Find them, Martin. I'm counting on you."

"Yes, sir. Can I send him in?"

"By all means. I hope he has better news than you."

Martin hurried from the room. "He'll see you now," he said to the sullen, dark-haired man who pushed past into the president's office. His scruffy face boasted a five-o'clock shadow many days past, and his angry eyes were sunken with exhaustion.

"Ah, Detective." President Cain smiled and motioned to the chair Martin had recently vacated. "I've had a day of most taxing and aggravating news. Please tell me you didn't come here to heap more of it upon me."

James Rutherford wiped a strand of oily hair from his face. "We've located the girls, Mr. President, and we know where they're headed."

"Good, good." Jackson Cain nodded approvingly.

"But there's something else." The detective leaned back in his chair, biting his lip.

"If you've located the girls and know where they're headed, then I don't see what the problem is, James."

Rutherford leaned forward in his chair, exhausted. It had been a hellacious few days, and they weren't getting easier. And the president wasn't going to like what he had to say. "Someone else found them first."

"So take him out."

Detective Rutherford wanted to roll his eyes. President Cain was a weak man hiding behind his Bible and cross in a private bunker where the world couldn't touch him. The country needed a stronger leader. They needed someone like Rutherford.

"With all due respect," the detective seethed. "One does not simply walk up to a Custos and blow his brains out."

Jackson Cain's face became a sickly shade of green. "They were found by a Custos?"

The detective nodded.

President Cain let out a deep shout, shoving the contents of his desktop to the floor. "I don't care if you and every one of your men dies, Rutherford. You bring me those girls and kill that man. I want his head sent back to me in a box."

Rutherford looked up at the ominous cross and gave the president a slimy smile. "That seems a little counterproductive to your mission, doesn't it? You think your man upstairs will be happy about that?"

"Get out!" the president shrieked. "I don't want to hear from you until you've had some actual success."

The detective rose from his chair and walked to the door, pausing in the entryway. "If I fail, they'll come for you. They'll come for you, or they'll come for him. They always do."

"Get out!"

The president's trashcan bounced off the door as Detective Rutherford slammed it shut.

Chapter Forty-Eight

"Stop!" Riley threw her hands into the air. "Please. What do you want?"

A hot wind blew, but otherwise the desert lay silent. Dust caked the armed rider's leather, making it appear as if he'd risen straight from the earth to sneak up on the group.

"What did you do with her?" he demanded. His steady hand still held a gun to Zach's head.

"With who?" Riley's voice shook as tears cascaded down her cheeks.

"With your other half."

Riley fought her eyes from wandering to the spot where Oz crouched. *He wants her?* "I don't know what you're talking about. It's just us."

"Oh yeah? And before you walked up here, these two said it was just them. Give me Riley, and I won't hurt them." He shoved a gun deep into Ezra's back.

"I am Riley," she cried. "Please."

A blond tuft rose from the cactus bush behind the rider. Riley stifled a gasp as Oz leapt out, pistol aimed at his head. "Drop the gun."

The rider froze but did nothing. For a moment even the wind seemed to hold its breath. Riley felt her brain demanding oxygen but was too afraid to inhale.

In a fluid motion the rider turned, twisting the gun from Oz's arm and bringing her to the ground with a painful moan next to Zach. He kicked her gun off into the dirt, then hesitated. His voice took on a confused tone. "Riley?"

Shaking and angry, Oz stood, glared at the rider, and joined her other half by the SUV. "What the hell do you want with me?"

The man scanned both girls before his eyes came to rest on the tattooed sleeve on Oz's arm.

"Have these men hurt you?" He addressed Riley this time, but both girls answered.

"No," they said.

Holstering his guns, the rider undid the black bandana from his face and pulled the black cap from his head. Golden curls spilled out, untouched by the dust, and familiar amber eyes met Riley's.

"Jesus, Gabe!" Riley's hands flew up as a momentary smile crossed her face. "What are you doing here?"

Relief swept over his face, and he rushed to her side, wrapping her in his arms. "I've been looking for you since you left. My God, Riley, they thought you were dead. They thought the son of a bitch killed you. There was blood all over your floor. I came as soon as I could."

Riley pushed away, staring up at him in fear. "No. My Gabe is good. So you can't be. Get away from us. Who sent you?"

Gabe backed off, hands in the air. "I'm not bad, Riley. And no one sent me. I tracked you here myself."

"Impossible."

"Is it?" A smile danced across his lips.

Riley scowled, overwhelmed by the thought that Gabe, the person she felt safest with, stood next to her, and by the notion that this had to be his bad side and she was being tricked.

"I found my way here, and I've tracked you through Vegas and into Los Angeles. I followed the men chasing you to the underground facility and barely escaped being blown up. I've come to help."

Riley turned to look at the rest of her companions, who all appeared shocked and confused as well—all except Ezra, who wore an expression like he'd just discovered fire.

"Gabriel?" he asked, eyes wide.

Gabe whirled around, having forgotten the two men he'd just held at gunpoint. "Sorry about that, guys. I've been chasing a lot of bad people. You'll have to forgive me."

Zach glared, rubbing the place in his neck where Gabe had jabbed the pistol. "How do we know we can trust you?"

"Because I've been doing this a lot longer than you have."

By this point Ezra was beside himself. He stood, shaking from head to toe, and extended his hand to Gabe. "Ezra Ahmad," he stammered. "It's a pleasure. I can't believe you're here. I mean, the girls—fascinating, amazing. But here I am now in the presence of the Electa *and* her Custos." He beamed, grinning from ear to ear. "Please know that I have dedicated my life to the same purpose. I am at your service." He gave an awkward bow.

"The pleasure is mine, Ezra. Anyone who has helped Riley is a friend to me as well. I've heard of you before. Your assistance in this quest will be invaluable."

Ezra beamed and gave an encouraging nod to Riley, who still stood unsure and closed off. "This man is a friend," he assured her. "I know it goes against what you've learned so far, but I left this part out because he was not around, and I didn't know what might have happened."

"How did he get here?"

Ezra glanced at Gabe, who nodded in approval. Both men understood Riley's trust lay in Ezra at the moment. "Gabe is special," he began. Riley looked at her friend, who smiled confidently. "Like you, he was born with a task, and he can travel between worlds."

Riley's eyes narrowed. "You called him my Custos. What does that mean?"

"Well, here's where it gets interesting. Every woman who becomes the Electa, or who will be the Electa if something should happen to her predecessor, is assigned a Custos: a protector of sorts, to see that she comes to no harm and to help her carry out her task. The Custos is picked from a select group of individuals who have no split soul. They are the purest of the pure. There is only one Gabriel Hart. He was assigned to you at birth, and he will be a part of your life until you die."

Riley's face darkened. "You hung out with me because you had to? All those years we spent together were just a task for you?" She shoved him, knowing it served no purpose.

"I thought this might get confusing," Ezra said, walking away to stand by the car.

"Riley, it wasn't like that. I could have protected you and kept my distance. But I got involved. I went against all the rules. You'd probably still be safe if you hadn't pushed me away."

"Don't turn this around on me!" Riley shouted. "Maybe if I had known you were only there to keep an eye on me, I wouldn't have misunderstood your intentions."

His tired face grew sad. "Look, Riley, I don't think this is the time or place. I owe you an explanation. I get it. But we've got to get you out of here. Both of you." He looked at Oz for the first time and nodded politely.

"Yeah, and why didn't I get one of you?" Oz asked, huffing. "I would have loved you hanging around me all the time. Protect me all you want."

Gabe laughed, his yellow eyes glittering like gold. "I checked on you often, Oz, but you appeared to be in good hands." He looked at Zach. "Thank you."

Zach gave an expressionless nod. Even though Riley seemed to know the guy, and Ezra looked like he practically worshipped him, Zach couldn't help feeling slighted. "We need to get going. We shouldn't be too far from Mexico."

Ezra nodded in agreement. "If we get across the border, our government can't touch us. The Mexican government will be glad to leave us alone out of respect for Jorge."

Riley shook her head. Mexico—the place in her world that was fraught with violence, drug trafficking, and the sex trade— was a safe place where people would protect her from her own government.

"You're taking her to Vela's?" Gabe asked. "Smart choice. You know the ins and outs of this pretty well, don't you?"

Ezra grinned. "I too have dedicated my life to it."

Gabe pulled an extra helmet from his bike and handed it to Riley. "Zach is right. We need to get out of here. You'll come with me."

"She'll be safer in the car." Zach folded his arms and blocked Riley's path to the bike. "Where they don't have an open shot at her."

"I can go faster on this and get into places you can't. We'll ride ahead. That way you can run interference if anyone comes from behind. We'll signal if anything approaches from the front."

Ezra agreed, and Zach returned to the car, glaring.

"See you guys on the other side." Gabe pulled on his own helmet and straddled the bike.

Red waves billowed behind like a flag as hot air whipped through Riley's dyed hair. It felt good to be in the open breeze. Ezra's home had been nice but constraining. She welcomed the freedom of the wind combing through her curls and blasting her face.

Riley buried her head into Gabe's shoulders and held on tightly. She chanced a glance back, seeing a speck in the distance that must be the SUV. Gabe drove as if his life depended on it, and Riley hoped they'd reach this safe place in Mexico before someone else caught up with them. The bike sped along, and she relaxed to the whirring sound of the motor. *I can't believe he's here. And my protector?*

Anger and irritation fluttered across her brain. *I was tricked.* She tried to push the thoughts aside. Right now wasn't the time to sort out Gabe's true intentions or hers. The whole mess had been so unbelievable, but if there was one person she could trust, she knew it was Gabe. If he said it was true, then it must be. *I'm the Electa. I can save the world.*

She squeezed tighter and felt Gabe lean in reassuringly. Real or not, it was still a lot to digest. She wished for bravery like Oz's. *To be brave and bold and daring. Why can't I be those things?*

———

Oz stretched out across the backseat, stuffing her jacket under her head and shutting her eyes. Just when she'd begun to forget how unfair her life had been compared to Riley's, some attractive guy showed up and claimed he'd dedicated his life to protecting her. *Seriously?* She pulled out her water bottle and took a long drink. *Damn that girl.*

"So we trust this guy?" she asked Ezra, propping herself up on her elbows.

"The Custos are as pure and trustworthy as anyone can be. There's a rumor, though no one really knows for sure, that they are sent here directly from the Big Man himself—that these are the same men who have been around for thousands of years, protecting humans and carrying out whatever tasks are given them."

"You're saying that guy's an angel?" Oz laughed. "Come on, Ezra, at some point the shit's gotta stop."

"Rumor is all I said. They may not be divine, but whatever they are, even the Jondi do not like going up against them. Angel or rogue special forces—it doesn't matter. That man is someone we want on our side."

Oz wanted him on her side for sure. And her front. And the back. If Riley didn't want Gabe, she would gladly take him off her hands. Oz thought about the golden-haired, golden-eyed, golden-skinned man, and her blood raced. He sure looked the part of an angel, but she wanted nothing more than to bring out the devil in him. They were all headed to Vela's, and from the sound of it, they would be there for a while to train and prepare for the mission ahead. There would be plenty of time to get friendly with this Custos.

"I hope this Jorge guy can help us out. I'm ready to fight back. I want to do something other than run and hide." *And I want Gabe...*

"Jorge Vela is our best chance. If he can't help us, hopefully the Custos can," Ezra said.

Oz lay back down and closed her eyes. *Goddamn, I need a cigarette.*

Zach stared out the front window, watching the small dot up ahead speed farther and farther away. *Get a grip, Zach. You have a job to do.* His pride had been hurt when Gabe appeared and held him at gunpoint on his knees. He knew his emotions were silly, but it still made him cringe to know that Riley and Oz were separated and their safety wasn't just in his hands anymore.

They'd been driving for a few hours now, the never-ending desert still flying past. *We have to be close.* He pushed buttons on Ezra's GPS screen and zoomed out. *Thirty minutes and we're safe.* Leaning back into the seat, he shut his eyes. Riley's face swam into vision, and he pushed it aside. It was replaced by Detective Rutherford's. *Where is he now?*

Zach knew his job was gone. When he finished with all of this, he'd be a fugitive and have to live his life under the radar in a place no one would look for him. Or he wouldn't even get to live that long if he was captured in the other world and put in prison. Rapists didn't last long in jail, and even if he did, the death penalty would follow, and in his world he'd randomly be hit by a bus or something.

He thought about his house and his sister—all the things and people waiting for him, wondering when he'd be back. He pushed these thoughts away as well and opened his eyes. Sleep was a dangerous place to go right now.

"So what's your fascination with the split souls and parallel worlds?" he asked Ezra. "I mean, it's incredible, but what makes someone give up a normal life to focus solely on this?"

Ezra smiled. "I inherited it. My father, and his before him, have been tracking the Electa, trying to figure out who she is and everything we can do to help her. I guess you could say I was born into it, and this *is* my normal life."

"Have you figured out how she travels between the worlds?"

Ezra sighed. "Sadly, no. The Electa and the Custos are the only ones who have the power to control it, though how they do it is beyond my knowledge. Anyone else who ends up here is merely an accident."

Zach thought about his other half and prayed he had been caught, even if it meant the end for him. He had hoped Ezra might know how to swap worlds, because if he could get over there, he would end the whole thing himself. He couldn't imagine that at any moment his other self could be sliding a knife across someone's throat and getting off by disfiguring a young girl. His countersoul had to be the worst one out there. "Have you found out anything about your other half?"

Ezra gave a nervous laugh and looked away. "No, I haven't. Never met him."

Zach shrugged, gazing out the window. "It's probably better that way. I wish I didn't know. And you're a good person, so you'd probably have some devil like I do."

Ezra gave another strange laugh and changed the subject. "Tell me, Zach. Are you really willing to die to protect these girls?"

Zach thought about killing his other half and his willingness to sacrifice his life for innocent people he didn't even know to stop his monster. Riley and Oz were so much more to him than that. "I wouldn't still be here if I wasn't."

"Good." Ezra leaned in closer and dropped his voice to a whisper. "Because we probably aren't going to make it out of this alive."

Chapter Forty-Nine

The border-check station appeared empty save a lone guard staring out at the dusty day. Across the line in America, an even lonelier check station stood sentinel. Juan Herdez couldn't remember a time when the small, crumbling building was manned. It seemed to him the Americans couldn't care less about who came in and out of their country. The idea was absurd to Juan. If their borders went unchecked, Mexico wouldn't be able to grow enough food to feed its own children, let alone every American beggar who stumbled over the line.

Sinking back into his chair, Juan clicked on the television. He was at a sleepy station, a place no one ever crossed. There was nothing worth crossing for within a hundred miles of him. He didn't even know why they still had him watch the area. Sure, he had a gun, but had he ever used it? Not since the academy many years before. He didn't even know if he remembered how. He had friends who worked checkpoints farther down the border who got into gunfights all the time. But not Juan Herdez. He earned his paycheck watching television and the occasional tumbleweed blow by.

The sound of a car door slamming jarred his eyes from the screen and his mind from its doldrums. *Quién?*

He stood and peered out the window at the armed men jumping out of two black SUVs. *Aye dios mio.* Juan ran to the door, locked it, and grabbed the radio. "Ayúdame! Ayúdame! Es Juan—" Before he could finish the transmission, the door blew back off its hinges, and another shot blasted the radio into pieces. Juan leapt back, trembling as he bumped into his desk.

"Hola," a dark-haired man said through the smoke with a very American accent. "We need your help with something, Pancho. You speak English?"

Juan stared at the men and their guns, not wanting to face the same fate as his door and radio. "Sí, señor. I speak English okay." He felt his legs quivering and hoped they wouldn't give way.

"Bien." The man directed more men into the small building while shouting commands. "We've got some really bad people coming through here, and we'd like to help you catch them before they enter your country." He flashed Juan a yellowed smile. "Lucky for you we showed up when we did. All you need to do is stand there looking pretty and listen to what I'm about to tell you." He pointed at Juan and then back to himself, nodding. "Amigos."

Juan didn't like the look of the gringo. Amigos didn't point guns at each other. The American had evil eyes and teeth, stained from too much cigarette smoke. His *abuela* told him as a child that only people who had the devil within them could live though inhaling that much smoke and fire. He shuddered and crossed himself. He didn't like to think that he was responsible for letting the devil into Mexico. His only hope was that someone had heard his cry for help before the radio was destroyed.

"What's your name?" the white man asked.

"Juan. Juan Herdez," he stammered.

"Well, it's nice to meet you, Juan." The devil pulled out a packet of cigarettes from his pocket, offering to share.

"No, gracias."

"I'm Detective James Rutherford, Mr. Herdez. And if you come through with this, I'll see that the US government rewards you and your family mightily."

So El Diablo has a name. Juan smiled as best he could and refocused on calming his wavering limbs. *The only reward I will get from him is a bullet in the back.*

CHAPTER FIFTY

We must be getting close. Hours passed as they flew down the highway like birds fleeing a winter storm. Riley's panic increased as the scenery became more barren with each passing mile. As if in response to her anxiety, Gabe squeezed her arms tighter to his body. *Her Custos, protecting her as always.* She leaned in closer.

She wanted to talk to him, to ask him even one of the million questions racing through her brain, but the wind flying past would just carry her voice away like a grain of sand in a dust storm. A few times her eyes had shut and sleep threatened to take over, but she fought hard every time, terrified of falling from her protected seat.

Her eyes grew heavy with the weight of the world. It was impossible to fight any longer. As if in response to her decision, the bike slowed and Gabe pulled off to the shoulder.

"You okay back there?"

"So long as I don't fall asleep and fall off the back of this thing."

He laughed, the idling bike rumbling with him. "We're close. The crossing point is only about five miles ahead. I promise, once we get to Jorge's, you can sleep for days if you need to. You'll be well fed, showered, and rested. It will be like nothing ever happened."

Riley grunted. "I could be the most pampered person on the planet, and it still wouldn't change the fact that people want me dead. And once we leave the protective bubble of Jorge's ranch, I'll be hunted again like an animal."

"Not like an animal, Riley. Like an Electa. Your purpose for living is much greater than mere survival."

She took a deep breath and sighed. Even temporarily, the safety of Mr. Vela's ranch was a blessing. Closing her eyes, she willed the others to hurry, and her mind wandered to Abby. *My sweet friend, where are you?* Her stomach twisted and knotted, her breath tangling in her throat. *Please be strong. I promise I'll find you. I won't let them hurt you.* If only Abby could read her mind.

Ezra brought the SUV up next to Gabe and rolled his window down. "Everything okay?"

"No problems," Gabe said. "I just wanted to make sure you all were safe. The checkpoint isn't far. We ought to stay close."

Ezra nodded. "Lead the way."

Gabe revved the engine and took off, keeping a steady pace with the car behind him. "It'll be over soon, Riley," he shouted. She burrowed into his back in answer.

The checkpoint was small, with nothing around but a few scraggly cacti and a rundown pickup truck. Oz noticed that the building on the American side was empty and abandoned. Paint peeled from the molding around the shattered windows, and wind and rain had clearly worked their power on the crumbling adobe bricks. She felt sorry for the lonely building and turned her attention to its sister on the other side.

The Mexican station was small as well and crafted from a similar mud brick. Cracks down the sides cried out for repair, but the building still looked like it would hold up in a storm. She glanced around nervously but saw nothing out of place. Still, being in the middle of nowhere with these ghost buildings made her uneasy.

Ahead Gabe and Riley had already pulled up next to a sliding glass door. A short, pole-thin man who looked to be in his early thirties, with dark hair and copper skin, stepped from the building. Oz stared at the man's dark eyes, noticing the strain. She watched his hand rise in a greeting and saw that more than formality drove the movement. "Something's wrong."

"What do you mean?" Ezra asked.

"That man is terrified. He's so nervous he's about to puke. I've seen that look a hundred times on people the first time they get caught slinging drugs. That man is scared to death."

Zach reached into the glove compartment and pulled out his gun. "She's right. Someone got here before us." Thrusting open the door, he jumped out of the SUV, racing to Riley and Gabe. "Something's wrong. We've got to get out of here."

Gabe revved the engine.

"Wait!" the border guard called, but his voice stuck and gurgled in his throat. A sharp blade sparkled in the sunlight as it retracted back through his neck. The sentry fell to his knees, clutching at his throat as blood poured out like wine from a barrel, revealing a heavily armed figure behind him. Kicking the dying guard out of his way, the figure stepped into the dust as two dark Suburbans wheeled in, blocking the road ahead and behind. Armed men jumped from each vehicle and fanned out in a circle around the group.

"Son of a bitch." Zach held his gun pointed at the detective's chest as the other wiped the dead man's blood from his knife onto his pants.

"Good to see you too, former Officer Stone. I must say, I never took you for a traitor to this country."

"And I didn't know you were a cold-blooded killer, Detective. I think we're all surprised by recent events."

Rutherford smiled, fingering the pistol at his side. Zach glanced behind at the SUV carrying Ezra and Oz but saw no motion. Gabe sat on the bike a few feet away, still as stone, with Riley holding on tightly. *So this is it.* "You can't touch us, Detective. We're on Mexican soil now, and you have no authority here."

The detective roared with laughter, but everything else remained hushed. Even the wind held its breath. "Do you think I give a shit where I am? Tell me, Zach. Who's going to uphold the law out here? I'll tell you what. I'll make you a hell of a deal. The only time this deal will be on the table. If you turn it down, all bets are off, and I'll leave your dead corpse here to be ripped apart by ants and coyotes, and I'll tell your sweet sister that you betrayed your country and are nothing more than a low-life, traitorous son of a bitch."

A hawk soared overhead, calling out a warning to the sun. Zach squinted up at it, keenly aware of every rifle trained on him. "I'm listening."

"Give me the girls," the detective said, hand still on the butt of his gun like an outlaw from ages past. "Both of them. You do that, and we'll let you three boys live." He glanced at the bike. Zach noticed his confident demeanor falter ever so slightly. "I promise I won't hurt them."

Zach nodded as if considering the deal. "That's an interesting proposal, Detective. But here's the thing. I don't trust you. I don't trust that you won't kill me, and I don't trust that you won't kill them."

"Zach, Zach." The detective clicked his tongue. "I really didn't want it to come to this."

Zach steadied his hand on the gun and took a deep breath. "I did, Detective."

Rutherford's gun roared as Zach dropped to the ground, rolling and kicking up dust to avoid being shot. The motorcycle screamed into gear, and he crouched as Gabe flung more sand into the air before heading off across the desert.

Zach crawled to the SUV, firing blindly in the direction of Rutherford's men. As Oz yanked him into the vehicle, a slug tore through the flesh of his leg. Grimacing, Zach heaved himself the rest of the way in and slammed the door.

"Where are they?" Oz yelled. "Find them, Ezra!"

Bullets rained down on the car, but Ezra had done his work well. They bounced off like rubber balls, and the passengers went unharmed.

"Punch it, damn it!" Oz yelled again, and Ezra slammed on the gas. The vehicle jerked forward into the clearing dust. They felt a thud as the tires crunched over one of Rutherford's dead men, and then they were clear. The car bounced back and forth across the desert, Ezra trying to gain control of the vehicle as he searched for the road.

"Where the hell are they?" he yelled.

Zach groaned in the back and ripped a piece of his shirt to bandage his bleeding leg. "I can't wait to kill that guy. If it's the last thing I do, I'm going to kill that man."

Oz helped him bind the wound, then rested a cool hand on his cheek before jumping into the front seat with Ezra. "We need to get him to a doctor."

"Jorge Vela has a doctor on his ranch. If we can get him there, he should be okay."

"What about Riley and Gabe? They're still out there!"

"If anyone can get her to safety, it's her Custos. I can't help them anymore. My duty now is to protect you."

"Damn it!" Oz kicked the glove compartment and crossed her arms. Fuming and staring out the window, she felt like a failure until she noticed a moving object—dust, off to the west. Dust and a flying blur of black and red. "Ezra, there they are. I see them!"

"Good. We will tie in with them at the road."

Oz leaned back, relaxing. "You okay back there?" Zach's labored breathing disturbed her.

"No, but I'll survive. It's just a flesh wound."

Oz peered out at her other half flying dangerously through the desert. *What in the hell happened to us?* Like a hawk, she watched the black fish in the dirty brown sea. Everybody appeared unharmed except Zach.

Crack! Oz jumped in her seat as the loud noise echoed through the car, and the vehicle threatened to roll. She spun around to look behind and saw cracks in the glass at the back of the vehicle spreading out like a road map of the country. Long, thin lines trembled with each bump, clinging precariously together and threatening to shatter into a million pieces. "I thought you said this thing couldn't break!"

"Oops. They must have brought out the big guns."

Oz looked out the window and watched as the other vehicle gained on the motorcycle. Dust kicked up all around the bike as gunfire threatened to take it and its passengers out. "Ezra, please, we have to help them!"

Ezra had to keep Oz safe, but if he lost Riley—and the ring—then the cause was lost anyway.

"Ahhh!" he yelled, turning the wheel sharply and careening toward the bike. Another shot hit the car, shattering what was left of the back windshield and spraying small shards of glass all over the interior.

Oz wiped the blood that dripped down her face from a hundred small lacerations. *Nothing can happen to Riley. Not because I really care, of course. But if something happens to her, I'll die too. I have to save her.* Oz fought the notion that she cared. *I owe her one anyway.*

The SUV sailed through the air, bouncing over small ravines and taking out a blooming ocotillo. Ezra's body had fared no better than hers. He hadn't taken the time to wipe his face, and one whole side looked as if someone had dumped bright red paint on it.

"Please let them be okay." Oz stared as dirt danced to the beat of a thousand bullets peppering the ground around the bike. And then one found its mark. The bullet ravaged the back tire, slinging the bike into a wild spin and sending it somersaulting over the crest of a hill into a dry creek bed. Oz watched in horror as two bodies flew through the air with the bike, disappearing into the ravine below.

Chapter Fifty-One

Air crashed from Riley's lungs like it had the night she'd escaped through her window. She lay in the sand, the heavy weight of the bike crushing her right leg. She tried to sit up, but the bike was too heavy and she was too broken. "Gabe!" she screamed. "Gabe!"

She heard coughing and felt weight lifted off her body. "It's okay, Riley. I'm here."

"Gabe, are you hurt?"

"Nah. I'll be okay." He grunted and shoved the bike away. "Can you walk?"

"I think my leg is messed up."

He bent down to help her crawl onto his back and began running down the creek bed.

"I'm scared."

"I know, Riley. But it's going to be okay."

"What if they catch us?"

He paused and looked at her from the corner of his eye. "They need you too badly to kill you."

Riley held onto him tightly. Oz was the brave one, not her. She was a middle-class girl from a comfortable home who didn't have to deal with stuff like this.

As they turned the corner in the rocky ravine, a black SUV blocked their way.

"Put the Demi down or we kill her instantly," a harsh voice commanded.

Gabe looked up, eyeing the skyline that was rimmed by men and guns. He closed his eyes as if deep in thought, then slowly lowered Riley to the ground with a look of angry frustration stretched across his face.

"Now back away or we shoot you both."

Gabe backed away and was immediately seized by three heavily armed, uneasy-looking men.

Seconds later a heavy boot pressed onto Riley's chest. Her mind flew back to the scene where she'd watched her grandmother—or, to be more exact, her grandmother's other half—murdered.

"Well, well, well," Rutherford said. "If you'd only stayed in your cell, we wouldn't have wasted all this time just to end up with the same result." He lifted his foot and stepped down on her injured leg. Riley let out a piercing scream. "Tie her up."

Two men rushed forward, holding her legs and binding her wrists behind her back. Gabe's face was unreadable, an angry stone carving.

Riley focused on his last words. *They need you too badly to kill you.* She found the eyes of her captor and met them fiercely. *If Oz can be brave, then so can I.* She glared up at the detective, hating him more every second.

The detective lit a cigarette and inhaled deeply, blowing the sour smoke into her face. "Good protector you've got there." He stared as Gabe was dragged behind the line of vehicles. Laughing, he leaned in to spit on her face and kick dirt into her eyes. "That's for all the shit you've put me through. I'm going to see to it that when they're through with you, you're given to me." He bent down and licked her ear, biting down and drawing blood from her tender flesh.

"Ahhhhhh!" she screamed, shaking her body and biting at the air. The men snickered—wicked men with wicked eyes and wicked thoughts. The detective shoved a wad of dirty cloth into her mouth, and she fought the urge to vomit.

"Keep her quiet," he commanded. "And take her to the car. Kill the Custos and get back up on the rim and watch for her friends. They're still out there somewhere—if Isaac hasn't disposed of them already."

Two guards lifted her to her feet, thrusting a gun at her neck and commanding that she walk. Riley stood motionless, her leg buckling under the pressure. *They're going to kill Gabe?* Heavy hands shoved her, and she fell forward into the dirt.

"Get up." A rifle jabbed into her back, and she stiffened with pain. *I can't do this.*

Struggling to her feet, Riley began hopping on one leg toward the vehicle. The men laughed even louder. Defeated, she bowed her head. *As if I had it in me to save the world. How stupid can I be?*

Honk! Honk! Honk! Riley looked toward the sound coming from just over the rim of the ravine. "Shoot!" the detective yelled, and gunfire assaulted the vehicle as it careened into the riverbed. Ezra swerved back and forth, dodging bullets. Riley's guards turned away, engaged in the firefight.

She stood still, staring at the scene and wanting to collapse. But she could see Ezra's determined face and Oz's angry snarl through the front windshield of the oncoming vehicle. *They willingly came to save me—to die for me.*

Riley took a deep breath. Courage could be found in that kind of sacrifice. Putting weight on her bad leg, she stifled a cry. *One foot in front of the other.*

And then she ran. A hobble of a run, but still a run. Hot air blew past her face as she fumbled through cactus thorns and over sharp, jagged rocks, each step sending jolts of fire through her shattered body.

"Stop!"

Riley knew she would never outrun him, but she didn't look back. The scent of tar and smoke on his clothes was overpowering, and the hatred radiating from him tasted almost as intense. Fighting through the pain, she limped faster.

Up ahead the ravine ended abruptly in a pour over. Riley kept running, shut her eyes, and took a deep breath. *I wish this had never happened. I wish I was back in Grand Junction, in my world.*

A scream came from way down inside as she careened over the edge, bracing for the pain. But all that followed was darkness.

Chapter Fifty-Two

Finally a dream that felt like a dream. What a relief to enjoy the magic of sleep without worrying about death or pain or unwanted knowledge. Riley floated in the clouds. She didn't feel hunger or fear, and the wounds on her body had healed. Even the scars were fading.

She laughed, spreading her arms as she soared through the bright emptiness. Her laughs lately had been driven by hopelessness and anger, but this was real. She knew Abby was somewhere in the sky too. And her mom and dad, Kiersten, Gabe, Zach, and Oz.

Faltering, she began to lose altitude. *Zach and Oz couldn't be here. They were somewhere in Mexico, probably captured by Detective Rutherford. And Gabe—Gabe had probably been killed.* She plummeted now, the bright sky and soft clouds giving way to a dark emptiness. Down and down she fell.

Her landing came softer than expected, but the solace of the sky disappeared with the impact of the ground. Riley was keenly aware of her twisted leg and the pain searing up from her calf. On her arm, the large gash ripped open by the rock a few days before still oozed ever so slightly, and every cut that had faded into a soft scar up above was bright and red and ugly again. And she was afraid. More than anything, she was afraid.

And then Riley became aware of the dirt between her fingers. Not the coarse sand of the desert, but the cool, moist soil she'd spent so many years working through her fingers while planting seeds. She opened her eyes and was blinded by the darkness. *It was just daytime.* Groping around, her fingers found hard earthen edges. *A hole?* She hauled herself out, grimacing in pain, and sat on the edge, eyes adjusting to the new surroundings.

A sliver of moon peeked from behind the clouds, and she was able to make out shapes in the distance. *It can't be.*

She struggled to her feet and peered into the distance. There it sat—a looming shadow on the horizon. The mesa. *Please don't let this be a mirage.* With her leg dragging behind, Riley limped over the furrowed field toward her house. The closer she got, the more anxious she became.

A lamp illuminated the family room. Ducking under the yellow police tape surrounding the yard, Riley peeked in. A pale woman with bloodshot eyes and unkempt hair stared blankly at nothing, clutching one of Riley's old teddy bears. *Mom.*

Riley's face contorted in agony, more from the pain of her thoughts than that of her injuries. She desperately wanted to race into her mother's arms and tell her everything was okay now. *Except it's not. My friends are still out there.*

Riley pressed her hand against the glass and then let it slide down. *Home will have to wait.*

Staring at her house and its promising comforts, Riley knew she would find no peace there—no stillness. *The Jondi will search for me even here. No matter what world I'm in, I am still the Electa. As much as I want to, I can't pretend that none of this ever happened.*

With one last aching glance at her home, she turned north and made her way to the house on the other edge of the field. The home welcomed her with friendly lights ablaze in every window, and a smiling porch wrapped around the front. She knocked on the turquoise door, and a familiar but shocked face opened it. The man was much older than Gabe, but he glowed with the aura of a protector, and his strength and power were still obvious to anyone who knew what she was looking for.

"Michael Flynn." Riley's green eyes bore into the old farmer's amber ones. "I'm sorry I ran from you. You were my grandmother's Custos, and I should have trusted you." She clutched her leg and looked up at him. "I don't know where else to go. You protected Esther for many years, and now I need you to protect me."

About the Author

R. S. Dabney lives in the Big Bend region of Texas with her husband, three dogs, and a cat. When she isn't lost in another dimension with her characters and stories, she enjoys mountain biking, exploring the desert, and eating way too much Mexican food.

The Soul Mender is book one in *The Soul Mender Trilogy* and is R. S. Dabney's first novel.

Made in the USA
San Bernardino, CA
20 November 2016